About the Author

Kevin McManus is an acclaimed Irish author and poet known for his gripping historical fiction and crime novels, who has earned a loyal readership and critical praise. He draws deep inspiration from Ireland's rich cultural heritage. His work often explores themes of resilience, justice and the human spirit. With a talent for weaving intricate plots and creating memorable characters. His award-winning writing has appeared in several international journals. His poem, *Lost Souls* was adapted into a film and won the Chicago Short Film Festival. McManus has a master's degree in history and has taught Irish history for thirty years.

Echoes of Freedom

Kevin McManus

Echoes of Freedom

Pegasus

Dedication

To my wife, Mary.

Acknowledgements

Thank you to all of the team at Pegasus Publishing.

Song of the Splintered Shillelagh

’Twas the night before battle and, gathered in groups,
The soldiers lay close at their quarters,
A-thinking, no doubt, of their loved ones at home
Of mothers, wives, sweethearts and daughters.
With a pipe in his mouth sat a handsome young blade,
And a song he was singing so gaily,
His name was Pat Murphy of Meagher’s Brigade
And he sang of the land of Shillelagh.
Said Pat to his comrades, it looks quare to see.
Brothers fighting in such a strange manner;
But I’ll fight ’til I die, If I never get killed
For America’s bright starry banner.
Far away in the west rode a dashing young blade
And the song he was singing so gaily,
’Twas honest Pat Murphy of the Irish Brigade
And the song of the splintered shillelagh.
Well, morning soon broke and poor Paddy awoke
He found rebels to give satisfaction
And the drummer was beating the Devil’s sad tune.
They were calling the troops into action.
Far away in the west rode a dashing young blade.
And the song he was singing so gaily,
’Twas honest Pat Murphy of the Irish Brigade
And the song of the splintered shillelagh.

Then the Irish Brigade into battle was seen,
Their blood for the cause shedding freely
With their bayonet charges they rushed on the foe
With a shout for the land of shillelagh.
Far away in the west rode a dashing young blade
And the song he was singing so gaily,
'Twas honest Pat Murphy of the Irish Brigade
And the song of the splintered shillelagh.
The day after battle, the dead lay in heaps
And Paddy lay bleeding and gory,
With a hole in his breast where some enemy's ball
Had ended his passion for glory,
No more in the camps will his letters be read
Nor his voice be heard singing so gaily
For he died far away from the friends that he loved
And far from the land of shillelagh.
Then, surely, Columbia can never forget,
While valour and fame hold communion,
How nobly the brave Irish Volunteers fought,
In defence of the flag of our Union:
And, if ever Old Ireland for freedom should strike,
We'll offer a helping hand quite freely:
And the Stars and the Stripes shall be seen alongside,
Of the Flag of the Land of Shillaly!

*Traditional Irish-American folk song, writer unknown

Chapter 1: The Battle of Sayler's Creek
April 6th 1865, Virginia, USA

The weather over Sayler's Creek hung heavy with the weight of history, bearing witness to a pivotal moment in the annals of conflict. The sky was a canvas painted in sombre hues, the grey clouds stretching across the horizon like a shroud over the battlefield. The air was charged with a palpable tension that mingled with the scent of damp earth and gunpowder.

As the sun struggled to pierce through the veil of clouds, casting long shadows upon the earth, the sounds of war echoed through the valley. Cannon fire reverberated like thunder, shaking the very ground, while the staccato rhythm of musket fire filled the air with its deadly cadence.

Amidst this chaos, amidst the clash of steel and the cries of the wounded, nature remained indifferent, a silent witness to the folly of man. The wind whispered through the trees, carrying with it the echoes of lives lost and dreams shattered. Rain began to fall, a gentle drizzle at first, then steadily increasing in intensity, as if the heavens themselves wept for the fallen.

The weather beheld the brutality of war, its tempestuous embrace mirroring the tumult that raged within the hearts of men. As the day wore on, and the clouds finally parted to reveal the pale light of evening, the landscape was forever marked by the scars of conflict, a testament to the enduring legacy of that fateful day.

Tom Ryan crouched behind a crumbling stone wall, his heart pounding in the chest of his large, muscular frame like a war drum. The battlefield stretched before him. Bullets whizzed past, tearing through the earth and the ranks of men with equal ferocity. Tom's hands trembled as he clutched his rifle, his knuckles white with tension. Sweat trickled down his brow, from his thick mane of brown matted hair mingling with the grime and blood that coated his face and his scruffy beard. He had seen too much death to last a lifetime, too much suffering, but still, the battle raged on, consuming everything in its path like a ravenous beast; it was relentless and unforgiving.

In the distance, he could hear the shouts of his comrades, their voices a chorus of defiance. But the sound was drowned out by the thunderous roar of battle, the cacophony of destruction that seemed to envelop him like a suffocating shroud. A sudden explosion rocked the ground beneath him, sending shards of debris flying through the air. Instinctively, Tom ducked for cover, his heart pounding in his ears as the world seemed to blur around him. For a moment, he was lost in the chaos, the line between life and death blurred beyond recognition.

But then, as suddenly as it had begun, the bombardment ceased, leaving behind an eerie silence broken only by the moans of the wounded and dying. Tom took a deep breath, his lungs burning with the taste of smoke and ash. He glanced around, taking stock of his surroundings, and felt a surge of relief as he realised he was still alive. But as he looked out across the battlefield, his heart sank. Amidst the haunting cries of the wounded, he witnessed the vile vision of the dead.

The blood-soaked earth was littered with bodies, both friend and foe, their lifeless forms sprawled amidst the wreckage like discarded puppets. Hundreds of corpses, some crushed by artillery, waggons and cavalry. Their entrails scattered about presenting a macabre sight. Many were Union soldiers like himself, others were Confederate. The silent witnesses to humanity's darkest hour. Bodies left on a battlefield like a tragic tableau.

Here, beneath the unforgiving sky, the aftermath of violence incarnate. The once vibrant fields now serve as a graveyard for the fallen, their lifeless forms scattered like forgotten pawns in a merciless game of death. Faces frozen in agony, limbs contorted in unnatural poses, they bear the scars of battle's brutal embrace.

Flies swarmed in a macabre dance around the corpses, their incessant buzzing a grim requiem for the fallen. Each body told a story of lives cut short and dreams extinguished in the relentless tide of war. Here lay the shattered innocence of a nation torn asunder by division and strife. Each body, a testament to the futility of war, a stark reminder of the cost of conflict in human lives.

Tom closed his eyes, trying to push back the horrors that threatened to overwhelm him. With a heavy heart, he rose to his feet, his muscles aching with exhaustion. He knew that the battle was far from over, that more blood would be spilled before the day was done. But as he looked out across the battlefield, he couldn't help but wonder:

how much longer could this madness continue? And would he survive to see the end of it?

Adrenaline coursing through his veins, as he rushed forward through the chaos and smoke of the battlefield. His eyes wide with fear and determination as he charged, his uniform torn open and stained with dirt and blood.

All around him, men were fighting and dying. The thunderous boom of cannons and the sporadic crack of rifles echoed across the field. He could see the flash of bayonets and hear the cries of the wounded, their pain drowned out by the fury of battle. The battlefield was a chaotic scene of flying debris, flashes of gunfire, craters in the ground, and soldiers running in all directions. The air was thick with black smoke, obscuring the view and causing everything to have a hazy and distorted, nightmarish quality. The battlefield was a blur of movement and colour, explosions created an ominous grey haze that blanketed the area. Tom can barely make out the shapes of his fellow soldiers running alongside him. The acrid scent of gunpowder and smoke filled Tom's nostrils, stinging his eyes and making it hard to breathe. The metallic tang of blood lingered in the air, mixed with the earthy smell of opened earth, sweat and charred flesh. The stench of death made his stomach churn.

He could also taste the dust in the air, making everything feel gritty and dry, making him cough and sputter. Tom's ears rang with the cacophony of war, making it hard to hear his own thoughts. The ground beneath Tom's feet was uneven and slippery, covered in mud and debris. His clothes were damp with sweat and blood, and he could feel his heart pounding in his chest with each step he took. As Tom pushed through the chaos, the rough terrain of the battlefield jostled Tom, the unevenness of the ground making it difficult to keep his balance. Rocks and debris slamming against his boots as he ran. Pounding against the hard ground, sending shockwaves through his feet with each step.

He could feel the heat of the flames licking at his skin, the sweat from his palms making his weapons slippery. Even in the midst of chaos, each step forward felt like a calculated dance through the bedlam of the battlefield.

Through the madness, he caught a glimpse of Dan Sheehan, fighting fiercely beside a young private. His friend turned and flashed him a wild grin. Dan stood tall and resolute, though his figure was weathered by the rigours of war. His face, etched with lines of determination and weariness, bore witness to the countless trials he had endured. Despite the exhaustion that weighed heavy upon him, there was a fierce intensity in his eyes, a fiery spark that refused to be extinguished. Maybe his eyes were alight with the madness of war.

His stature was lean but solid, honed by years of marching and fighting. Clad in the familiar, though worn and tattered, blue uniform of the Union army, he wore it with a sense of pride and duty that emanated from his very being. Dan's hair, once dark and unruly, was now streaked with strands of grey, evidence of the passage of time and the toll of war. The strains of battle had aged him prematurely, and he looked ten years older than his twenty-eight years. Yet, despite the ravages of battle, there was a strength in his bearing, a resilience that spoke of his indomitable spirit.

In that fleeting moment of camaraderie, as he flashed a wild grin at his friend, there was a glimpse of the youthful vigour that had propelled them into the fray so many years ago. It was a reminder of the bonds forged in the crucible of combat, bonds that transcended the horrors of war and endured against all odds.

They had been through hell and back, standing shoulder to shoulder against insurmountable odds. Fighting side by side in the New York 69th Regiment, part of the Irish Brigade. They had survived four long and bloody years from Manassas, in July 1861, the first dismal battle of Bull Run, to today, which hopefully would be the last stand of the Confederates, Tom prayed.

A cannonball landed nearby, kicking up dirt and debris. Tom ducked, throwing himself to the ground and rolling behind a large boulder. He leaned against the rock, panting for breath, and wiped the sweat and grime from his brow. His muscles burned and his limbs felt leaden, but he couldn't stop now – not when they were so close.

Dan dropped down beside him; rifle clutched in shaking hands. "Ready for another go?"

Tom looked at his friend and managed a tired smile. "After you."

Tom peered over the boulder and surveyed the battlefield, searching for any weakness in the Confederate line. His keen eyes spotted a gap in their flank, likely caused by the artillery fire from earlier.

"There, on the left flank," he said, pointing it out to

Dan. "If we can get a squad over there, we might be able to turn their position."

Dan nodded. "I'll go let Captain Williams know. Wait here." He clapped Tom on the shoulder, then darted off through the smoke.

Tom hunkered down behind the boulder again, rifle clutched tightly as he waited. The sounds of battle raged around him, an unending cacophony of gunfire, shouting, and death. A bullet ricocheted off the boulder, showering him with stone fragments. He flinched as a sharp pain lanced through his cheek; he brought a hand up and it came away bloody. Gritting his teeth against the sting, Tom peered around the boulder again to keep watch on the Confederate line.

Minutes ticked by with agonising slowness. Where was Dan? Unease coiled in the pit of his stomach at the thought of his friend wounded or worse. Then he spotted a familiar figure darting back toward him, followed by a squad of soldiers and Captain Williams who struggled to keep up.

Dan skidded to a stop at his side, slightly winded. "Captain's sending a squad around the flank. We're to provide cover fire." He glanced at Tom's cheek and frowned. "You're hit."

"'Tis but a scratch," Tom said with a lopsided grin. "Nothing to worry about."

Dan shook his head, a hint of fond exasperation on his face. "You could be half dead and still claim 'twas nothing to worry about."

Before Tom could reply, the captain shouted a

command and they turned as one, levelling their rifles at the Confederate line.

After providing covering fire for ten minutes, Captain Williams called for a halt. Tom studied the forward ground. He noticed a dip in the terrain that would provide cover for advancing troops. If they could distract the Rebs with a frontal assault, a squad advancing around the side might be able to flank them.

He tapped Williams on the arm and pointed out the dip. "Captain, if we charge straight at them, it could draw their fire long enough for a squad to circle around. Then we hit them from both sides."

Williams pondered for a moment and then answered, "Right, let's do it."

Dan nodded, eyes glinting with determination. "Let's give those Johnny Rebs a surprise."

They readied their rifles and waited for the captain's signal. At the blast of a whistle, they leapt up and charged forward, unleashing a battle cry. Rifle fire greeted them, bullets whizzing through the air and kicking up dirt around their feet. Tom gripped his rifle tightly and stood, steeling himself for the fight ahead. Together, they rushed into the fray, in the face of fear.

Tom fired off a few shots of his own, trying to keep the Rebs' heads down as their squad flanked around. His heart pounded wildly, a mix of anxiety and adrenaline. They were exposed out here, easy targets – but if they could distract the enemy for just a few minutes more…

There was a surge of blue-clad figures on the Confederate right, rifles crackling. The Reb line wavered in confusion, torn between the threats on two sides. Now was their chance.

"Charge!" Captain Williams bellowed.

They rushed forward with a roar. The Confederate line shattered, soldiers throwing down their weapons and fleeing in disarray. A cheer went up from the Union ranks. They'd done it – driven the enemy back and claimed more ground.

Breathless, Tom grasped Dan's shoulder. "We showed those greybacks, *eh*?"

Dan grinned. "We sure did. Now, how's that scratch of yours?"

Tom waved a dismissive hand, though his cheek still stung something fierce. "It's fine."

"You are a stubborn Irish bastard, Tom." Dan smiled.

"Like yourself, Dan," Tom said as he patted his friend on the back.

The squad rested for a few minutes, taking a breath, however, the battle was far from over.

"Right, men, we have them on the run, let's move forward, we have the wind at our backs now, but be careful men, they will fight like cornered rats from here on," Captain William ordered.

William's words were true, the worst of the fighting was yet to come. The confederates threw all they had at the advancing Yankees. All hell was unleashed upon them, death rained down from the sky as their Napoleon canons hammered the Bluecoats with 12 pounders. Tom and his squad were sent running for cover and their advancing line was broken. They darted in all directions to find safety.

Tom coughed and crawled on his belly through the fog of smoke and debris, ears ringing from the blast. His limbs felt leaden, body bruised and battered, but he forced himself up off his hands and knees. His Spencer rifle clutched in blistered hands. His whole body ached; vision blurred from exhaustion.

A sharp cry rang out nearby. "Tom."

Tom turned toward the sound. It was Dan's voice.

He staggered across the churned earth, oblivious to the fighting still raging around him. All that mattered was reaching Dan.

There lay his friend, clutching a bloody thigh. Dan's face was pale as chalk, eyes glazed with pain.

Tom dropped to his knees. "Oh God. Here, let me—"

"It's bad, Tom." Dan's voice was tight, breath coming fast. "The bone's shattered."

Bile and horror warred in Tom's throat as he glimpsed the ruin of Dan's leg, the severity of Dan's injuries. Black blood was also pouring from his stomach. He had to get him to the surgeons, now, before—

Another blast shook the ground, artillery fire creeping ever closer. They were out in the open here, exposed. He fumbled for his kerchief and tied it around the wound on Dan's leg, hands shaking. "We'll get you to the surgeons. They'll fix you up, you'll see."

Dan clutched at his arm. "Tom. Listen. I won't make it off this field. You know that as well as me."

"No, don't talk like that!" But one look at the blood-soaked cloth told him the truth. Dan was right.

"Go on without me," Dan said. "find our boys. Finish

this fight."

Tom squeezed his eyes shut. How could he leave Dan here, alone and broken on this godforsaken field? They'd been through everything together. He couldn't lose his brother, not like this.

A weak hand gripped his own. "You'll make it out of this war. Have a good life, Tom, for the both of us."

The whistle of incoming artillery shook him. He had to move, get to cover. A blast threw him to the ground, the world erupting into fire and bedlam. Tom picked himself up again and then leaned over Dan's body. He slid an arm under Dan's shoulders, ignoring his friend's cry of pain. "We have to move. Can you stand?"

"I'll try," Dan said as his friend lifted him.

Dan gritted his teeth and nodded. Tom hauled him upright, throwing Dan's arm over his shoulder to support his weight. Dan roared in pain as he tried to hobble along. Tom realised they would never get to cover at the rate they were moving.

"Sorry, Dan, this is going to hurt, there is no other way," Tom said.

As bullets continued to rain down around them, Tom felt clarity cut through the fear that clouded his mind. He knew that if he hesitated now, they would both be lost. With grim determination, he hoisted Dan onto his shoulder, using every ounce of strength he could muster.

Another roar of agony from Dan.

Step by step, they staggered through the haze, dodging behind trees and boulders whenever possible. Tom's muscles screamed in protest under Dan's bulk, his own injuries throbbing with every movement.

But he wouldn't stop. He couldn't. Dan's life depended on it. So, he pushed on through the smoke and flying debris, gripping Dan tighter as another blast nearly knocked them from their feet. They just had to make it to the Union lines. They were so close. Tom swallowed hard, summoning the last of his strength. "Almost there," he said, more to himself than Dan. They would make it. They had to.

Tom tasted blood in his mouth, each breath burning in his lungs. His vision swam as he struggled forward, Dan's weight threatening to drag them both down with every step. But he wouldn't give up. He couldn't.

Another blast erupted behind them, the shockwave sending them tumbling to the ground. Tom cried out as they hit the earth hard, agony lancing through his body. For a moment he could only lie there, gasping for air as debris rained down around them. Beside him, Dan had gone still and silent.

Tom's heart clenched. "Dan?" He shook his friend's shoulder with a trembling hand. "Dan, wake up!"

No response.

Panic rose in Tom's chest, swelling until he thought it might crush him. He fumbled for a pulse, barely daring to breathe until he felt the faint, irregular beat against his fingers.

Dan was alive. Barely.

Tom gritted his teeth against the pain and heaved himself upright, pulling Dan into his arms once more. Step by step, he dragged them onward, his vision tunnelling.

The Union lines were just ahead, a haven of safety in the turmoil. With the last of his strength, Tom surged forward and stumbled through. "Medic!" He rasped, barely able to remain standing. "Please, help him…"

Another blast, the earth trembled.

And then the world went dark.

Tom opened his eyes to find Dan gazing up at the smoke-stained sky. The light had already left his friend's eyes. Tom bent his head, shoulders shaking. They'd weathered so much together, only to be torn apart now. He was alone.

Chapter 2: Sawbone Station
April 9th

Tom Ryan stirred from the depths of unconsciousness, his senses slowly returning to him like shards of broken glass piecing together a fractured reality. His eyes fluttered open, his vision blurred as he tried to focus on the canvas roof above him. He let out a breath and sank back against the thin mattress. Alive – he was alive. For a moment, he was disoriented, unsure of where he was or how he had ended up here. As awareness seeped back into his battered body, he realised with a jolt that he lay upon a cot. A pulsating pain radiated from his right leg, every heartbeat magnifying the agony. Tom's brow furrowed in confusion as disjointed memories began to surface, like pieces of a broken mosaic coalescing into a semblance of coherence. He remembered the thunderous roar of cannons, the staccato rhythm of musket fire, the visceral terror that had gripped his heart as he fought for his life upon the blood-soaked fields of battle.

The field hospital tent was dimly lit by flickering lanterns hanging from the tent poles, providing a soft and sickly yellow glow as they cast eerie shadows on the canvas walls adding to the air of despair that hung heavy in the air. The flickering light gave the illusion of movement, as if the shadows were dancing to the moans and cries of the wounded. The space was cluttered with rows of cots, each one occupied by a wounded soldier with blood-stained bandages covering their injuries. Medical tools and supplies were scattered haphazardly about the tent, reflecting the hurried and chaotic nature of their usage, while the caustic smell of antiseptic hung heavy in the air. Despite the dimness, it was clear that this was a cathedral of chaos and suffering. The air was heavy with the scent of antiseptic and blood, and the quiet moans and occasional cries of pain created a chorus of pain, an atmosphere of sombre desperation. Despite the medical care being provided, the tent still held a sense of grimness and mortality. He was in what was referred to by many as the Sawbone Station, a place where you would be lucky to leave with all your four limbs intact.

A figure materialised beside him as Tom's eyes adjusted to the muted lighting. It was a nurse clad in a long, black, cotton dress. A functional garment to hide bloodstains acquired during their duties. Her hair was tied up in a bun and a white bonnet was placed upon it. Her face was a mask of compassion, her eyes pools of empathy in the midst of turmoil. With gentle hands, she tended to his wounds, her touch a fleeting balm against the searing ache that gnawed at his flesh.

"You're awake," she said as she leaned over him, her face half in shadow. "We were starting to worry you wouldn't come around."

"Wh-where am I?" Tom croaked; his voice hoarse from disuse.

"Easy, Mr Ryan," the nurse said gently, placing a

soothing hand on his shoulder. "You're in a field hospital in Virginia. You've been unconscious for some time."

He licked his cracked lips. "How long…"

"Three days." She pressed a cool cloth to his forehead. "You've been feverish. But the doctor says you'll recover, thanks to the mercy of God."

"Three days?" Tom repeated, his mind reeling. He winced as he struggled to sit up, gritting his teeth against the pain, only to be stopped by the nurse's firm grip.

"My leg…"

"I'm afraid there was shrapnel. Your right leg was hit by shrapnel during an artillery blast. We had to remove some fragments, but the wound is clean now." She explained. "You'll have a scar, but it's all right, soldier," she murmured, her voice a soothing melody. "You're going to be just fine; you'll walk again in a few weeks. And the good news is that the war is over."

"Over?" Tom muttered, his thoughts drifting back to the chaos at Sayler's Creek, the screams of wounded men and the deafening roar of gunfire. His heart clenched as he thought of Dan. "What about Dan Sheehan? Where is he? "Dan… Where's Dan Sheehan? Was he…"

The nurse hesitated, averted her eyes, her soft voice filled with sympathy. "I'm so sorry. Your friend didn't survive. He died on the battlefield."

The words struck like a blow, knocking the breath from his lungs and leaving him gasping for air. Dan, his brother-in-arms for four long years, gone. He squeezed his eyes shut but couldn't stop the tears that seeped out. A cold wave of grief washed over Tom, drowning him in a sea of anguish and despair. The memory of Dan's laughter, their shared dreams and struggles, all snuffed out in an instant on that godforsaken battlefield. "No," he whispered, his voice cracking, "…not Dan." They had endured so much together; they had promised to see this through to the end. And now, that end had come, sudden and unforgiving.

The nurse laid a gentle hand on his arm. "I know how close you were. I'm truly sorry for your loss."

He opened his mouth, but no words came out. How could he begin to express the emptiness opening inside him or the debt he owed to the man who had stood by his side until the last? Dan had given him courage when he had none left, had lifted him up from despair time and again with his unquenchable humour and optimism. It was a stark reminder of the fragility of life in the midst of war's relentless onslaught.

Tom turned his face to the wall, shoulders shaking. He had always known the price of war, but never had it struck so close or asked so dear a payment. The battle was over, the Union preserved. But in this tent, on this narrow cot, the true cost of victory had come home at last. It was like a thunderbolt from the heavens, which shattered whatever semblance of hope remained within him.

"Mr Ryan," the nurse said softly, "I know this must be incredibly difficult for you, but you need to focus on your own recovery now."

"Recovery?" Tom spat bitterly, his anger flaring.

"Because he would want you to live, Mr Ryan," she replied with quiet conviction. "Dan wouldn't have wanted you to give up."

Tom stared at her for a long moment, chewing on her words. He took a deep, shuddering breath and forced himself to nod.

*****

A week later, Tom was transferred to a hospital in New York, where he continued his physical and emotional recovery. As Tom's gaze wandered over the New York City skyline that filtered through the hospital window, he couldn't help but feel trapped within the confines of the small room. For a man who had faced adversity head-on for most of his life, the prospect of being bound to a bed was suffocating. He tortured himself as he replayed the events of Sayler's Creek over and over in his mind, each memory sharpened by pain and regret.

They flooded his mind, a torrent of images and emotions that threatened to overwhelm him. He tried to focus on other pictures from his past. As the days passed in the quiet solitude of the hospital ward, Tom found himself haunted by memories of times gone by. He recalled the days of his youth in the Five Points, where poverty and hardship had been constant companions, and yet, amidst the squalor and decay, there had been moments of fleeting happiness, moments that now seemed like distant echoes in the vast expanse of time.

He remembered Dromdaire, the village nestled amidst the verdant hills of County Kerry in Ireland, where he had spent his childhood in the shadow of the famine's cruel embrace. He was just a boy of eleven in black 47, leaving behind his home with his family – his father, John, his mother, Maureen, his sisters, Mary and Frances, and his older brother, Michael, as embarked on a journey fraught with hope and despair, a journey to escape the grip of starvation.

The voyage across the Atlantic was gruelling, marked by hunger, sickness and the relentless rough sea. But the cruellest blow came when they lost Michael to cholera's merciless grip aboard the coffin ship. The loss weighed heavy on them all, a shadow that lingered over their dreams of a new beginning in America. Ellis Island welcomed them with cold efficiency, teeming with humanity's desperate throng, a gateway to the promise of a better life. Yet, the reality of their circumstances soon became apparent. They found themselves in the teeming chaos of the Five Points, where survival was a daily struggle, and dreams were tempered by harsh realities. His father secured work on the docks, a meagre existence that sustained them but offered little more. His mother and the girls found employment as domestic servants, their days filled with toil and sacrifice.

As the years passed, Tom grew from a boy into a young man, shouldering burdens far beyond his years. At fourteen, he joined his father, learning the ways of labour in the harsh embrace of the cold New York docks. But tragedy struck once more, relentless in its cruelty. John, his father was taken from them, crushed beneath the weight of a falling crate, leaving Tom to bear the mantle of provider for his family. With no time for mourning, he sought extra work wherever he could find it, his hands calloused but his spirit unbowed.

On a construction site amid the clamour of hammers and the scent of sawdust, Tom found his place in the world. He toiled alongside men twice his age, it was there that he met and befriended Dan, another young man who had left Ireland behind. He worked alongside Dan until they both enlisted in the 69th regiment in 1861 at the start of the war. His mind flashed back to the fateful day working on the construction site.

The sun glared down mercilessly on Tom and Dan, a relentless judge of the men toiling beneath its gaze. Tom's shirt stuck to his broad back, sweat clinging his brow like stubborn beads of seawater. The beams they hoisted overhead seemed to grow heavier with each passing moment, their muscles straining against the oppressive weight of both the timber and their own exhaustion.

"Jesus, Tom." Dan grunted, wiping his forehead with the back of his hand. "It's hotter than hell out here. Let's have a rest," he said, as he sat down on the dusty ground.

Tom managed a weak smile, feeling the ache gnawing at his lower back. He paused for a moment, surveying the skeletal structure that would soon become another tenement in the crowded city. It was far from the picturesque homeland they had left behind in Ireland, but it was a life, nonetheless.

"All right, boys, break time's over! You two are slacking off again! I've half a mind to dock your pay!" barked their boss, Mr O'Malley, from across the site. His face twisted by anger and frustration. He was a short and stout man with ruddy cheeks and a temper that flared as quickly as a struck match. "Get back to work!"

"Ungrateful bastard," Dan muttered under his breath, shooting Tom a sidelong glance. "We're slavin' away while he sits in the shade, countin' his coins."

Tom sighed but said nothing, focusing on the task at hand. He couldn't afford to let his anger get the better of him; too much was riding on this job. Instead, he hoisted the beam up once more, feeling the familiar burn return to his muscles.

"Hey!" O'Malley shouted suddenly, storming over to them. "I told you two to move faster! What do I pay you for?"

"Pay us?" Dan scoffed; his face flushed with anger. "You call what you're givin' us wages? We can barely make ends meet with what you pay!"

"You're lucky I even gave you a job." O'Malley warned, his voice low and dangerous.

"We're working as hard as we can. The heat is—" Dan said, his reply cut short.

"Excuses!" The foreman spat. "You think I care about the bloody heat? Finish this job today or you're both out!"

"Out?" Dan echoed incredulously, lowering the plank. "We've been working 'round the clock, doing the work of three men each!"

"If you don't like it, there's plenty who'll take your place," O'Malley roared with rage.

"Like hell there is," Tom muttered, his anger flaring. Loyalty surged within him, a tide of protectiveness for his friend and the countless injustices they had faced from unscrupulous employers. "You've been taking advantage of us for months, paying us less than we deserve while we break our backs for you."

"Watch your mouth, Ryan," the foreman warned.

"Or what?" Dan challenged, stepping closer, his fists clenching at his sides. "You'll fire us?"

"Fine!" O'Malley snapped. "You're both fired! Get off my site!"

"Is that so?" Dan snarled. "Well, maybe we don't need your damned job. In fact, fuck you O'Malley, I'll show you, who's boss around here before we go. I took enough shite from you."

"Dan, calm down," Tom urged, placing a hand on his friend's shoulder, holding him back. He could feel the tension coiling in Dan's body like a spring. "It's not worth it." Tom realised that the last thing they needed was to be locked up in a jail cell for the night if Dan battered O'Malley.

"O'Malley, please," Tom pleaded, desperation clawing at his throat. "We need this work—"

"Too late, Ryan," the boss snapped, cutting him off. "You should have thought of that before you sided with your troublemaking friend. Now get off my site. You're both easily replaced. In fact, consider yourselves replaced. You're fired."

With a final scowl at their former boss, the two friends gathered their tools and trudged away from the construction site, the weight of their uncertain future settling heavily upon them. Tom felt an uneasy mixture of anger and despair churning in the pit of his stomach. His mind raced with worry, thoughts of his mother, Maureen, and his sisters, consuming him. How would he provide for them now? They could barely survive on their wages? What other options did they have?

How would he break the news to them? He had let them down, and the weight of that realisation settled like a stone in his chest. Tom clenched his jaw, the frustration boiling within him threatening to spill over.

Tom and Dan sat at the edge of a crumbling stone wall, faces streaked with sweat and grime as they stared at their hardened hands clenched into fists, the dirt beneath their fingernails a reminder of the work they had lost. Tom stared out at the distant horizon, where the sun was sinking low in a riot of oranges and reds, casting shadows that stretched across the dirty streets of Lower Manhattan and painting the sky with a beauty that seemed incongruous to the turmoil writhing inside him. They were once again jobless. The cruel irony of their situation was not lost on them; strong men with able bodies yet unable to provide for those who depended on them.

"Damn O'Malley," Dan muttered, kicking at a clump of dirt. "We deserved better than that."

"Aye," Tom agreed quietly, his mind racing with worry. "But what do we do now?"

"Something will come up, Tom," Dan said, determination flashing in his eyes. "We'll find another job. We always have."

"Maybe so," Tom agreed, his voice tight with emotion. "But I'm tired, Dan. Tired of being taken for granted, of struggling just to survive. There has to be something more out there for us. "God damn it," Tom muttered under his breath, slamming his fist against the wall. "This isn't how it's supposed to be... Will we find work, Dan? With this damn war starting, jobs are drying up, there isn't as much money around the city no more," Tom asked bitterly, his voice cracking.

"Maybe it's time we considered other options. Maybe there's another way," Dan mused, his eyes narrowed in thought.

"Like what?" Tom asked, curious despite his own weariness.

"Joining the army. The 69th Regiment, the Irish Brigade perhaps. I know plenty of lads who have signed up," Dan replied, his gaze unwavering.

Tom glanced at his friend; surprise etched on his face. "You're not serious?"

"Remember when we first came to America, Tom? How we dreamt of fighting for something bigger than ourselves, of making a difference?"

"Of course I do," Tom replied, a faint smile touching his lips. "We were going to change the world."

"Maybe it's time we made good on that promise," Dan said, his voice gaining strength. "It's a chance to prove our worth, to stand up for the rights of immigrants like us."

"War is a dangerous game." Tom warned, though the spark in his eyes betrayed his own longing for a purposeful fight.

"Life is a dangerous game, Tom, but at least in the army, we'd be fighting for something we believe in, and providing for our families at the same time."

"Look around, Tom," Dan said, gesturing to the city

that sprawled before them. "Jobs are scarce, and we're not the only ones struggling. The army would provide us with steady pay."

"Leaving our families behind, though..." Tom hesitated.

"Think about it," Dan insisted, laying a reassuring hand on Tom's shoulder. "We'd be fighting for their future, too."

Tom closed his eyes, feeling the pressure of Dan's hand anchoring him to the moment, to the decision that would shape their lives. He imagined his mother's face, her eyes weary yet full of pride. He then studied his friend's face, seeing the resolve etched into every line, and knew that Dan had already made up his mind. He thought of the countless times they had stood by each other's side, facing down adversity together, and knew he couldn't abandon him now.

"All right, Dan," he said finally, offering a weary smile. "If you're in, I'm in."

"We'll make a difference, you'll see. And when this war is over, people will remember the names Tom Ryan and Dan Sheehan."

"So, when are you thinking about signing up?" Tom asked.

"No time like the present." Dan smiled.

***

Sunlight filtered through the dust kicked up by passing carriages, casting an ethereal glow on the bustling streets of New York City. The streets were a blur of activity, packed with a sea of people from all walks of life. People of all ages and backgrounds as they hurriedly made their way to various destinations, each one with a distinct style and purpose. Carriages and horses navigated through the crowds, their hooves clacking against the cobblestone streets. Tall buildings towered above, each one packed with businesses and apartments. Their windows reflected the sun's rays and cast light on the bustling scene below that created an ever-changing landscape as the sun moved across the sky. The streets were alive with a rainbow of colours, vibrant clothing adorning people and bright flags and banners advertising shops fluttered in the light breeze. Large signs hung above the storefronts, beckoning customers with their bold letters and flashy images.

The smells of the city were a mix of enticing aromas of fried bacon, mustard and sauerkraut from food carts and restaurants. The smell of roasted coffee beans wafted from cafes, while the smell of warm baked bread tempted each passerby. Alongside that was the less pleasant scents of rotting trash and horse manure.

The streets were alive with a constant symphony of noises – carriage wheels rumbling, horses snorting, vendors calling out their wares, clanging and banging from construction sites and people chattering in different languages. English, German, Russian, Italian and Irish created a chaotic but familiar soundtrack. Church bells tolled and musicians played on street corners, adding their melodies to the mix.

New York pulsed with the energy of a city on the

brink of change. Every corner and alleyway seemed to hold a new adventure, a new story waiting to be discovered. Every step was a dance, every breath a symphony, and every heartbeat a reminder of the possibilities that awaited. The city had a rapidly growing population as the immigrants flooded in. It was coming close to one million inhabitants and beginning to rival London and Paris.

Tom and Dan navigated the throngs of people, their hearts pounding with a mixture of excitement and trepidation as they approached the recruitment office.

"Are you scared?" Tom asked, trying to sound casual but unable to completely mask the tremor in his voice.

"Only a fool wouldn't be," Dan admitted, rubbing his sweaty palms on his trousers. "But if we're going to do this, we'll see it through together, like always."

"Like always," Tom echoed.

The recruitment office loomed before them, it stood tall and foreboding, its dark stone walls towering over the bustling streets. Its sombre facade a stark reminder of the gravity of their decision. The entrance was adorned with a large oak door, the brass doorknob gleaming in the sunlight. Above the door, a sign in bold letters read, "Union Army Recruitment Office, Join the Fight for Liberty and Unity." Below it in smaller text read: 'Enlist today to preserve the union. Serve your country with honour and courage. Benefits include: competitive pay, clothing and rations provided, opportunity for advancement. Fight for freedom and justice. Defend the Constitution and preserve the Union. Enlistment officers available daily. Visit us today to serve your country!'

As they stepped inside, the noise of the city was replaced by hushed voices and the scratch of pens on paper. The walls were lined with wooden counters and shelves. Above them military posters and portraits of proud soldiers, all serving as a constant reminder of the gravity of their decision to enlist. Dusty windows let in little sunlight. Rows of wooden desks lined the room occupied by po-faced men in uniforms writing furiously with metal nib pens.

"Next!" called the officer behind the desk, beckoning them forward. Tom swallowed hard, tugging at his collar as they approached.

"Thomas Ryan and Daniel Sheehan, sir," he announced, his voice steadier than he felt. "We're here to enlist in the 69th New York Regiment."

"Very well," the officer replied, studying the two men closely before handing them each a stack of paperwork. "Fill these out and return them to me."

***

"Mr Ryan," a soft voice called out from the doorway, breaking him from his thoughts. A young nurse, her expression warm yet professional, entered the room carrying a tray with his afternoon meal. "I've brought you something to eat."

"Thank you, miss," Tom replied, trying to muster a smile as he accepted the tray. Food had lost much of its appeal in recent weeks, but he knew it was necessary if he wanted to regain his strength.

"Your progress continues to impress the doctors," she commented, pulling up a chair beside his bed. "They say you'll be walking again very soon."

"Good," Tom said, his voice laced with determination. "I need to get back on my feet. There are… things I must do."

"Like what?" she asked curiously, her eyes searching his face for clues.

"Visit my family," he responded, swallowing the lump that formed in his throat. "It's been too long since I've seen them. They need me."

"Family is important," the nurse agreed, her own eyes misting over with empathy. "They can provide solace during our darkest days."

"Indeed," Tom muttered, pushing aside the uneaten food on his tray. His mind drifted to his: sisters and his mother. He could almost hear their laughter, see their smiles, and feel their embrace. It was a comfort, one that he desperately needed to drown out the lingering echoes of war and loss.

"Mr Ryan," the nurse said gently, placing a hand on his arm. "You've been through so much, and you've come so far. Don't forget to lean on your loved ones during this time. They'll be your anchor as you continue to heal."

"Thank you," he whispered, squeezing her hand. "I will."

As the nurse left his room, Tom gazed once more at the cityscape outside his window. It may have seemed distant and cold before, but now, it held a glimmer of hope – the promise of reunion with his family and the chance to rebuild his life in the wake of all he had lost.

Chapter 3: A Sort of Homecoming
May 8th, Bellevue Hospital, New York

Tom stepped out of the hospital doors, his discharge papers clutched tightly in his hand as the morning sun momentarily blinded him. His body still bore the scars of battle, his right leg throbbed, his muscles weakened from too long lying on a hospital bed and overall, his movements were laboured. Four long years of fighting in the Civil War had taken their toll, but Tom was finally coming home.

As he made his way through the familiar streets of Manhattan, the streets were strangely subdued in the early morning light. Tom couldn't help but feel a sense of sombreness weighing heavily upon him. The city had changed in his absence, yet it remained a constant reminder of the life he had left behind. Tom felt removed from it all, his mind wandering back to the chaos of war. Would he ever escape those memories?

He walked past a bath house and decided to turn back, a good wash was in order. Inside, he looked up to admire the high ceilings supported by ornate columns. Rows of metal tubs, each filled with steaming hot water, lined the large room. The walls were adorned with posters advertising soap and other hygiene products. The predominant scent was a mix of chlorine, soap and the faint aroma of sweat. Men were disrobing and preparing to cleanse themselves. A small bald man in a tight striped waistcoat approached Tom. He asked him if he required a tub. Tom said he did, he paid him the charge and the waistcoated man led him along a line of baths with men scrubbing in until they reached a vacant one.

After undressing from his military uniform, he sank into the warm water. He winced as the water met his still-healing leg. He lifted a bar of pine tar soap and began to lather himself, feeling the dirt and grime wash away. The soap gave off a pungent odour.

The soundscape of the bathhouse was lively and diverse. There was a steady drip of water as attendants topped up the tubs with large jugs of hot water, accompanied by the occasional splash as someone stepped in. Conversations in various languages echoed off the walls as people from different ethnicities and backgrounds interacted. Patrons exchanged gossip, discussed politics, or haggled over the price of services. The clatter of metal as attendants moved buckets and ladles blended with the softer sounds of towels being wrung out or garments being hung to dry.

After his bath, Tom sought out a barber shop. His hair had become long and unkempt and his beard thick and unruly.

Guided by the murmurs of the city, Johnathan stumbled upon a quaint little barber shop nestled in a row of brick buildings on Broadway. Its wooden sign swung gently in the breeze, adorned with the words, "Wilson's Barber &

Shaving Parlour." The soldier pushed open the creaking door and was greeted by the comforting scent of sandalwood and lather. Inside, the shop was a symphony of scissors snipping and the low hum of conversation. The walls were lined with mirrors, reflecting the faces of men in various stages of grooming. A potbelly stove crackled in the corner, casting a warm glow across the room. Behind the counter stood Mr Wilson, the proprietor of the establishment. He was a thin man with a handlebar moustache and a twinkle in his eye that spoke of years of experience. He greeted Tom with a friendly nod, his scissors poised and ready for action.

"Good afternoon, sir," Mr Wilson said, his voice as smooth as the shaving cream he wielded. "What can I do for you today?"

Tom cleared his throat, suddenly feeling self-conscious under the barber's scrutinizing gaze. "I'm in need of a haircut and a shave," he replied, his voice rough from disuse.

"*Ah*, a soldier returning from the war, I presume?" Mr Wilson said, his tone sympathetic as he looked at Tom's war weathered uniform. "Well, you've come to the right place. Take a seat, and we'll have you looking like a new man in no time."

As Tom settled into the worn leather chair, he couldn't help but feel a sense of relief wash over him. Here, in this humble barber shop, he was just another face in the crowd – a welcome respite from the horrors he had witnessed on the battlefield. As the razor glided across his skin, he felt a sense of renewal, as if the cutthroat razor was slicing away the agony of the previous years.

Cleanly shaven and with a fresh haircut, he stopped at a bank to withdraw the last of his army pay. It was a considerable amount, considering he had not drawn it down in over two years. The one benefit of fighting at the front was that cash was not a necessity. Keeping alive was a necessity.

He stepped into the grand marble lobby of the First National Bank of New York, his army boots echoing against the polished floors. The bank was a symbol of the city's prosperity, its towering columns reaching towards the heavens like silent sentinels guarding the wealth within.

As he approached the teller's counter, Tom couldn't help but feel a twinge of nervousness gnawing at his gut. It had been over two years since he had last set foot in a bank, and he couldn't shake the feeling that he was somehow out of place among the well-dressed gentlemen and busy clerks. Behind the counter stood a young man with a mop of unruly hair and a pair of wire-framed spectacles perched precariously on the bridge of his nose. He looked up from his ledger with a polite smile, his pen poised and ready to take down Tom's request.

"Good afternoon, soldier," the teller said, his voice polite but tinged with a hint of impatience. "How may I assist you today?"

Tom coughed, suddenly feeling self-conscious under the teller's scrutinising gaze. "I'm here to withdraw the last of my army pay, it's been quite some time since I last accessed my account."

"Certainly, sir, may I ask for your full name, address and date of birth?"

"My name is Tom Ryan, born in Dromdoire, County Kerry, in Ireland, in 1836. I have lived in this great country since 1847, sir. My address is 138 Mulberry Street, Lower Manhattan." The address that Tom gave was that of his sister's home. He didn't own or rent a property of his own.

"Thank you," the teller replied as he jotted down the details. "Do you have any proof of identity? You do understand that we have to be careful, there are many dishonest people these days who try to take advantage, but I am certain, sir, that you are not one of those scallywags."

"Here are my United States Army papers, I hope they will suffice." Tom said as he took out an envelope from his coat pocket and handed them to the teller, who studied them for a few minutes before returning them.

"Thank you, Mr Ryan, we are all very grateful for your years of service in our army."

Tom replied with an awkward nod of his head.

The teller's eyes widened in surprise as he flipped through the pages of his ledger, his brow furrowing in concentration. "*Ah*, yes, here we are," he said, his tone brightening as he located Tom's account. "It seems you have quite a tidy sum waiting for you, Mr Ryan."

"There should be," the soldier replied, his gaze drifting to the rows of neatly stacked bills behind the teller's counter. It was a considerable amount, more than he had ever imagined he would possess in his lifetime.

"Mr Ryan," the teller repeated, his fingers flying across the keys of his adding machine. "If you'll just sign here, I'll be happy to assist you with your withdrawal."

Tom scrawled his signature on the dotted line, and as he tucked the wad of bills into his pocket and stepped back out into the streets of the city, he couldn't help but feel a glimmer of hope stirring deep within his soul. For in this moment, surrounded by the sights and sounds of a city reborn from the ashes of war, he knew that anything was possible.

He caught his reflection in a shop window and realised how tatty his uniform was. "Time for some new clothes, I reckon I won't be needin' this uniform no more," he murmured to himself. With his funds secured, he made his way to a clothes shop, determined to present himself well for his long-awaited reunion with his family.

Tom stepped into the quaint tailor shop at Waverly Place. The shop was a cosy oasis amidst the teeming city streets, its windows adorned with neatly pressed suits and colourful fabrics that danced in the late morning sunlight. As he approached the counter, Tom was greeted by a young man with a measuring tape draped around his neck and a warm smile on his face. The tailor's shop assistant, James, was a slender fellow with nimble fingers and an eye for detail.

"Good afternoon, sir," James said, his voice friendly and inviting. "How may I assist you today?"

"I'm in need of a new suit and shoes… the works," he hesitated. Tom wasn't used to clothes shopping.

James nodded in understanding, his fingers tracing the fabric of suits that hung on a nearby rack. "Well, you've certainly come to the right place," he said with a smile.

"We have a wide selection of ready-made suits that are sure to fit your needs."

Tom's eyes scanned the racks of suits, each one more finely tailored than the last. But it was a dark-green suit that caught his eye – it spoke of sophistication for a man that meant business.

"I'll take this one," Tom said, his voice tinged with a sense of determination. "And I'll need everything else to go with it – shirt, underwear, socks, shoes and a hat, if you have one."

James's smile widened as he began gathering the necessary items, his hands moving with practiced precision. "Of course, sir," he said, his voice filled with enthusiasm. "We have everything you need to complete your ensemble, right here in the shop."

As Tom tried on the various garments and admired himself in the mirror, he couldn't help but feel a sense of excitement building within him. Here, in this humble tailor shop, he was attempting to transform himself from a weary soldier into a man of refinement and grace.

As he stepped outside wearing his new clothes, with his old army uniform parcelled up in brown paper held under his arm, Tom couldn't help but feel a glimmer of hope stirring deep within his soul.

Being a fine May morning, Tom decided to walk the half-hour journey from Bradway to his sister's home in lower Manhattan. He headed south, passing Union Square and onwards through the neighbourhoods of Greenwich Village, with its narrow streets and charming brownstone buildings, to the cast-iron architecture of the commercial district of SoHo. Before traversing the financial centre of Wall Street, the New York Stock Exchange, and Trinity Church. Continuing southward, he reached the tip of Manhattan Island, at Battery Park, overlooking the harbour towards Ellis Island. He stopped and stared at it and recalled his arrival with his family there eighteen years ago.

He remembered how on the cold and wet February morning on board the creaking ship, they stood on the deck as the wind and briny waters lashed into their skin. The towering spires of New York City came into view on the horizon as his mother held him, the youngest of the family, tightly to her chest. It had been a long and arduous journey across the ocean, filled with sickness, hunger, and the great loss of his older brother Michael. But now as they approached Ellis Island, they dared to believe that a new beginning was within their grasp.

His father John stood by his wife's side, his rough hands gripping the railing of the ship as he gazed out at the sprawling metropolis before them. He had heard tales of America – of its magnificent cities, fertile plains, and boundless opportunities – and now, as he beheld the shimmering skyline of New York, he felt a swell of pride and determination rise within him.

As the ship pulled into port, the Ryans joined the throngs of immigrants crowding the deck, their eyes wide with wonder as they caught their first glimpse of the land that would become their new home. It was a welcome after seven arduous weeks on board the Black Ball Line ship that departed Tralee on January 2nd. The air was alive with the sounds of foreign languages and the cries of seagulls circling overhead, mingling with the *hum* of activity from the docks below.

Maureen Ryan clung to her children's hands tightly as they made their way through the crowded halls of the immigration station. Behind her, John followed close behind, carrying the bags containing their limited possessions, his eyes scanning the faces of the weary travellers around them in search of familiar kin. Finally, after what seemed like an eternity, the family reached the front of the line, where they were greeted by a weary-looking immigration officer with a clipboard in hand.

"Name?" the officer asked, his voice gruff but not unkind.

"John Ryan," John replied, his voice steady despite the nerves that churned in his stomach.

"And your family?" the officer pressed, gesturing towards Maureen and the children. Maureen stepped forward; her chin held high as she met the officer's gaze. "Maureen Ryan, and these are our children – Frances, Mary, and little Tom," she said, her voice trembling slightly with emotion.

The officer nodded, jotting down their names on his clipboard before gesturing towards the crowded waiting area. "Welcome to America," he said with a tired and sarcastic smile. "You're officially in the land of opportunity now."

While Ellis Island represented the gateway to a new life for many immigrants, it also bore witness to the hardships and struggles endured by those seeking refuge and opportunity in America. It harboured its own share of horrors. Upon arrival, immigrants underwent rigorous medical inspections to screen for contagious diseases. Those found to be ill or disabled faced the threat of being denied entry and possibly deported back to Ireland. Families were sometimes separated during the inspection process, causing immense emotional distress and uncertainty as loved ones awaited reunification. It was overcrowded, leading to cramped and unsanitary conditions, which exacerbated the spread of disease and illness such as cholera, typhoid and tuberculosis. So, if you arrived disease free, there was a good chance one would contract a disease during your stay. The processing of immigrants could take days, weeks, or even months, leading to long wait times in crowded and uncomfortable conditions. During this time some immigrants fell victim to exploitation by unscrupulous individuals, including fraudulent 'immigration agents' who charged exorbitant fees for assistance with the immigration process.

Tom turned his attention to the here and now as he was approaching his sister's home on Mulberry Street. Tom couldn't help but notice how much the neighbourhood had changed since he had left. Mulberry Street was a busy thoroughfare, alive with the sounds of horse-drawn carriages clattering by and the chatter of merchants hawking their wares from storefronts. The air was thick with the scent of simmering pots of stew, mingling with the earthy aroma of tobacco smoke. The people of the neighbourhood were a diverse mix of immigrants from all corners of the globe, but they were predominantly Irish.

As he approached his sister Frances's modest brownstone, it stood out among the row of buildings on Mulberry Street, its faded brick facade adorned with a wrought iron railing and a cheerful flower box overflowing with vibrant blooms. Tom's heart swelled with pride as he climbed the steps to the front door, but then he hesitated. It had been so long. Would they even recognize him? It had been four long years. He hoped that the letter he had posted while recovering in hospital had been received and that they were aware he would be calling. Each step brought him closer to the moment he had longed for yet dreaded in equal measure. His heart pounded with nervousness as he approached the front door, his hand trembling as he took a deep breath and reached out to knock.

The door swung open to reveal Frances standing on the threshold, her eyes widening in surprise at the sight of her long-lost brother. She was a striking woman, with auburn hair and warm hazel eyes that sparkled with joy and relief at the sight of him.

"Tom!" She pulled him into an embrace. "We've been so worried… Tom! Is it really you?" Frances exclaimed, her voice trembling with emotion as she threw her arms around him in a tight embrace. "I never thought I'd see you again!"

Tom held his sister tight, relief flooding through him, drinking in the familiar scent of lavender soap and freshly baked bread that clung to her skin. "I'm home, Frances," he whispered, his voice choked with emotion. "I'm finally home."

Inside the brownstone, the air was warm and inviting, with sunlight streaming in through lace curtains and throwing soft shadows on the worn wooden floorboards. The sound of laughter and chatter filled the air as Frances led Tom into the cosy parlour, where their mother sat nestled in an armchair, with a blanket wrapped around her by a blazing fireplace.

Their mother, Maureen, was a fragile figure, her once vibrant spirit dimmed by the ravages of time, the heartbreak of losing her husband John and eldest son Michael, and the worry that Tom might never come back from the war. She looked so much frailer than Tom remembered and much older than her fifty-eight years. She was a pale shadow of her former self, her cheeks hollowed and her breaths shallow and laboured, but when she saw him, her face lit up as she greeted her son with a weak smile.

"Tom… my lovely boy," she said faintly, her voice barely above a whisper as she extended a trembling hand towards her son. "You've come back to us." Tears welled in Tom's eyes as he knelt beside his mother's chair, his heart breaking at the sight of her frail form.

"I'm here, Ma," he said softly, his voice thick with emotion. "I'm here to stay."

He studied the deep lines on her face, the hollowness of her cheeks.

"We didn't know if you'd made it," she whispered.

Tom swallowed hard, overcome with guilt for having left them. "I'm here now, Ma," he said.

His sister Frances put a hand on his shoulder. "We're just glad you're back safe."

Tom nodded, trying to smile despite the lump in his throat. He stood, squeezing his mother's thin hand gently before letting go.

"It's good to be home," he said. Looking around, he noticed the absence of his other sister. "Where is everyone else?"

"Mary will be over later this evening. She is working until five this evening. My two boys are at school, Conor and John. They are really excited to meet you. Always talking about their brave uncle Tom, the war hero." Frances smiled.

"I'm no war hero, I was just doing my job, how is your husband, Frank?"

"He is fine, working away at the factory, all hours, you know Frank, not enough hours in the day for him," Frances replied.

Tom absorbed this, thinking of how much had changed since he'd left. His sisters had grown up, started lives of their own. And his mother.

Frances touched his arm, drawing him aside into the small kitchen. Her voice dropped to a whisper. "The war took its toll on mother. And then she developed a cough that just won't go away."

Tom's chest tightened.

Frances continued, "The doctor says it's consumption. She's weakened substantially this past year."

The news hit Tom like a hammer blow, his heart

heavy with sorrow and fear. He looked across at his mother. She gazed into the fire, the dancing flames shining on her drawn face.

"I won't leave her again," Tom said firmly. Frances searched his eyes and nodded.

"We'll get through this," she said, "together."

Tom set his jaw. No matter what lay ahead, he would remain by his family's side. They had suffered enough.

A few hours passed as Tom sank into a chair by the fire after enjoying a fine dinner, the day's events weighing heavily on his shoulders. Despite the joy of reuniting with his family, worries crept in. His mother's illness, his own uncertain future – where would he find work and a place to live? The struggle to simply survive in this city – it all pressed down on him.

Frances brought over a cup of tea. As she handed it to him, she hesitated.

"There's something else," she said carefully. Tom looked up, reading the conflict in her eyes. She sat down across from him.

"We received word last month that Uncle Brendan passed away."

Tom stiffened. "Uncle Brendan?" He hadn't seen his uncle since they'd left Ireland when he was just a boy. But he remembered the towering man with a booming laugh who had hoisted him onto his shoulders.

Frances nodded sadly. "The letter said it was sudden. His heart."

Tom's throat tightened with unexpected grief. He took a shaky sip of tea. His uncle had been their only family left in Ireland.

"He left us something in his will," Frances continued gently, "the farm in Dromdaire."

Tom's eyes widened. He recalled his uncle's sheep farm near the rocky coast, could it be theirs now? His mind raced, imagining his mother breathing the fresh Irish air, walking those hills again. Hope flickered inside him, then dimmed, when he realised that she would never survive the voyage.

Tom met his sister's gaze, he looked confused. She reached over and squeezed his hand with a reassuring smile.

"It's all a lot to take in," she said.

Tom sat in thoughtful silence as Frances tidied up the tea cups. His mind was still spinning with questions about the inheritance. What would become of the farm now? Would he have to travel to Ireland to settle his uncle's affairs?

After a few moments, he spoke up hesitantly. "Frances… can you tell me more about the farm? Did the letter say anything else?"

She paused, considering. "Not much more. Just that the farm and house are ours now. I suppose there are details to sort out. We have to contact a solicitor in Killarney."

Tom nodded. "It's hard to believe it's really ours. I have so many memories there as a boy." He rubbed his chin. "Makes me wonder if I should go see the place. Pay my respects at Brendan's grave."

Frances tilted her head. "Perhaps, but it's a long

journey and you have been through a lot."

"I know." Tom sighed. "Still, it was good land. Fertile soil, grazing pastures. It could be an opportunity for us."

Frances gave a sad smile. "Let's not get ahead of ourselves. But you're right, it may be a blessing in disguise. A chance to honour uncle's memory."

"I'll have to give it some thought," he said.

Chapter 4: Peace of Mind
July 11th, the Five Points

Tom lingered at the window, watching the rain patter against the glass. The streets below were empty, soaked in the humid July downpour. It had been two months since he'd returned home, yet he still felt adrift. He had managed to find a small flat in a tenement building to rent in Five Points. He kept in regular contact with his mother and sisters, calling over to them most days.

The tenement building he now called home was a weathered brick structure, its façade marked by years of wear and tear. Inside, his poky flat was weakly lit by a single gas lamp. The space was compact, with low ceilings and narrow windows that let in only a sliver of daylight. In one corner of the room stood a modest kitchenette, equipped with a rusty stove and a small wooden table surrounded by mismatched chairs. The walls were adorned with faded wallpaper, peeling in places to reveal the bare plaster beneath. A threadbare rug covered the scuffed floorboards, its edges frayed with age. Against one wall sat a lumpy mattress atop a rickety bed frame, its sheets rumpled and worn. A battered trunk served as both storage and seating; its surface covered with a layer of dust. A solitary window looked out onto the wet street below, offering a glimpse of life in Five Points.

With a sigh, he turned from the window. His small apartment suddenly felt smothering. Grabbing his coat and hat, Tom headed out into the wet night. Maybe he'd walk for a while, clear his head, reacquaint himself with the familiar sights and sounds of his youth. Five Points was a place of contrasts, where poverty and prosperity existed side by side.

In the late 18th century, Five Points was originally a middle-class neighbourhood with a mixture of Dutch and English settlers. However, by the later 19th century, it became a melting pot for immigrants, particularly Irish seeking a better life in America. Five Points experienced rapid urbanisation and overcrowding due to waves of immigrants settling in the area, attracted by the promise of jobs in the nearby factories and docks. The tenement buildings becoming densely packed and living conditions deteriorating rapidly. It gained a notorious reputation for its poverty, crime, and unsanitary living conditions, known as one of the most dangerous and impoverished neighbourhoods in New York City.

His evening walks would always end with a visit to a public house. He found himself drawn to the darker corners of the city, seeking solace in the bottom of a glass and the arms of strangers. Most nights he wandered from bar to bar, drinking to dull his memories of the war. But it was a temporary escape. Come morning, worry and anxiety would return. The question tonight on his mind was whether he should visit one of his regular haunts or find a new joint where no one knew his name, where he could sit unbothered with his ghosts.

He made his way to one of the local pubs called Mulligans. The exterior of Mulligans was dingy and run-down, with plaster falling from damp walls. Its windows covered in a layer of grime and dust. The interior was no better, a filthy establishment with sawdust-covered floors that absorbed blood, booze and vomit. The walls of Mulligans were covered in layers of peeling paint, revealing the remnants of past patrons' graffiti and scribbled-over advertisements. The bar was lined with old wooden stools, some broken, and a thick layer of filth covered the counter. The low tables scattered around were chipped and worn. The ceiling hung low and was stained brown with years of tobacco smoke, creating a cramped and claustrophobic atmosphere. The faces of the rowdy and dishevelled clientele were illuminated by the glow of the open fire, which cast everything in a faint light and gloomy atmosphere.

The scent of dampness, mould, stale beer and cigarette smoke permeated the air. As more drinks were consumed, the smell of alcohol became stronger, intermingled with hints of foul body odour from the crowded room and urine from the toilets. The smell of greasy food from the kitchen wafted into the bar, making mouths water and stomachs growl.

Yet despite the drab surroundings, the sound of drunken and raucous laughter echoed off the walls, accompanied by the clinking of glasses and bottles and thuds as patrons slammed down their drinks on the tables and countertops. In the corner, a group of musicians played Irish traditional music, their instruments creating a lively soundtrack for the evening. The chatter from groups of friends mixed with the shouts from drunken patrons, creating a lively cacophony that filled the air.

Pubs like Mulligans were like beacons of warmth and camaraderie in the cold, unforgiving city, offering refuge to locals and weary travellers. Mulligans, with its rowdy patrons, was a place where one could lose themselves in laughter and ale, a place where stories flowed as freely as the drinks. It was a microcosm of the neighbourhood, a chaotic yet comforting haven amidst the poverty that surrounded it. A sanctuary for the lost and lonely, and the raucous laughter could drown out any painful memories, at least for a few hours.

He ordered a pint of ale and settled into a corner booth, content tonight to bask in the warmth of familiar company. As the night wore on, Tom found himself surrounded by old friends and new acquaintances, each with their own stories to tell. Together, they laughed and drank, their troubles momentarily forgotten.

Tonight had been no different. Tom slowly rotated his aching shoulder, bruised from the brawl at Flynn's Tavern the night before. The whisky had fuelled his rage when the loudmouth on the next stool spouted off insults. At least the split knuckles from cracking the loudmouth's jaw and sore shoulder from the stool that hit him afterwards had given Tom something tangible to blame for the pain. Not like the invisible wounds carved deeper inside.

Tom trudged down the rain-slicked streets back towards his tenement, collar turned up against the rain that was still beating down. He wasn't paying attention to where his feet were taking him until he looked up to find himself outside the Emerald Isle Hall. Irish music spilled from the windows into the night. The exterior was bright, cheerful and welcoming, the arched windows adorned with flickering candles which emitted a warm glow.

Inside the hall, Tom observed strings of twinkling and glittering lanterns hung from the ceiling, giving the room a festive atmosphere. The stage was decorated with Irish banners and flags and a lone podium stood in the centre. The walls were adorned with posters of Irish revolutionary figures such as Theobald Wolfe Tone and Robert Emmet. People of all ages and backgrounds were packed tightly together, standing room only, and their faces were flushed with emotion as they listened attentively. They were dressed in a mix of ragged clothes, Union Army uniforms and finely tailored suits and dresses, creating a dynamic visual.

Curiosity drew Tom closer. As Tom got closer to the stage, pushing his large muscular frame through the crowd, he could hear the sound of a man's voice rising, speaking with passion and conviction, his hands moving dramatically as he spoke to the large crowd. Occasionally, the patrons erupted into cheers and applause, creating a jubilant atmosphere. Tom recognized the tall, imposing and charismatic speaker from the newspapers, he was James Stephens, the leader of the Fenians or Irish Republican Brotherhood. His voice rang out, clear and powerful, his words filling the room with an air of rebellion and hope.

Tom had heard about Stephens and the Fenians. He

knew that the Fenians were a society dedicated to the overthrow of British rule in Ireland and the establishment of an independent Irish republic. Tom had also read that Stephens was trying to raise money in New York from wealthy Irish-American donors for the cause. His primary aim was to recruit ex-Union soldiers for the IRB in the United States. Stephens clearly recognised the military experience and potential loyalty of these veterans. He was aware of the fervour for freedom that had driven many Irish immigrants to fight in the Civil War, and he believed that these veterans could be persuaded to continue their fight for liberty in their ancestral homeland. He saw in them a pool of skilled and battle-hardened recruits who could bolster the Fenian ranks and lend their expertise to the cause of Irish independence.

The Fenians' efforts to recruit ex-Union soldiers were met with varying degrees of success. Many veterans, disillusioned by the horrors of war and eager to return to civilian life, were reluctant to become embroiled in another conflict. Others, however, were drawn to the Fenian cause by a sense of solidarity with their Irish brethren and a desire to continue fighting for the principles of freedom and self-determination. Despite facing challenges and setbacks, Stephens and the Fenian Brotherhood succeeded in enlisting a significant number of ex-Union soldiers to their cause. These veterans brought with them valuable military experience, organisational skills, and a spirit of determination that would prove invaluable to the Fenians in the years to come.

The large crowd in the Emerald Isle Hall hung on

every word coming out of Stephens mouth.

"Ladies and gentlemen, tonight, as we gather in this hallowed hall, I am reminded of the unyielding spirit of our people, the sons and daughters of Erin, who have endured centuries of oppression and hardship at the hands of the British. But let me tell you this: the spirit of Ireland cannot be crushed, for it burns bright within each and every one of us, a flame that refuses to be extinguished!

"We stand at a pivotal moment in our history, a moment when the winds of change are blowing across Ireland and the call for freedom grows ever louder. The time has come for us to rise up and reclaim what is rightfully ours – our land, our heritage, our independence!

"For too long, we have languished under the yoke of British tyranny, our people subjected to poverty, injustice, and indignity. But I say to you tonight, enough is enough! The time for action is upon us, and we must seize this opportunity with both hands!

"We are not alone in our struggle. Across the Atlantic, our brothers and sisters in Ireland look to us for support, for solidarity, for hope. And you, the sons and daughters of Ireland living here in the land of the free, have a duty to answer their call, to stand shoulder to shoulder with them in their fight for liberty and justice.

"But let me be clear: our fight is not just for the people of Ireland but for all oppressed peoples around the world. We stand in solidarity with the downtrodden, the marginalised, the forgotten, for we know that their struggle is our struggle, and their victory will be our victory!

"So, I say to you tonight, let us rally together, let us unite in common purpose, let us march forward with courage and conviction, knowing that the cause of freedom is just, and our cause is just!

"Together, we shall overcome the forces of oppression, together, we shall forge a new destiny for Ireland, a destiny of freedom, of dignity, of prosperity for all!

"Arise, sons and daughters of Erin, arise and claim your birthright! The time for freedom is now, and we shall not rest until victory is ours! Too long have we suffered under British rule!" Stephens cried; fist raised. "Join our fight, lend your arms to the cause, and we will take back our homeland!

"God bless Ireland, God bless the USA, and God bless all who fight for Ireland's cause!

"Thank you."

The crowd erupted. Men surged forward to sign their names to the roster being passed around. Tom watched, with interest. Part of him longed to be part of something bigger than himself again. But the scars of war held him back.

Stephens caught Tom's eye. "You there, brother! Will you not join us and shake off the English yoke of oppression? Will you not free your nation?"

All eyes turned expectantly to Tom. He opened his mouth, an apology on his lips. But instead, he heard himself rasp, "I'm tired of fighting. I'm tired... of watching young men die."

Without waiting for a response, he turned and disappeared outside into the rain. All he wanted now was to find peace, to care for his family and honour the memory of those he had lost.

Chapter 5: A Dark Parade
February 4th 1886, Mulberry Street, Lower Manhattan

Tom's boots echoed down the cobblestone road of Mulberry Street, each step a heavy drumbeat against his chest. He paused before the familiar door, worn and stoic, steadying himself for what lay beyond the threshold. His knuckles white as he clutched the doorknob, hesitant to enter. A deep breath failed to quell the tremor in his hands as he rapped gently on the wood.

"Tom, you've come." Frances greeted him with a feeble smile as the door opened, her eyes red and weary, dark-shadowed pools of grief surrounding them. She moved aside, her presence a bastion amid the storm of sorrow. "She's upstairs."

In the cramped quarters of the home, the air was thick with a sombre weight. The chill of February seeped through the thin walls, chilling the bones of those who dwelled within. Tom could already sense the heaviness of the atmosphere pressing down upon him like a smothering blanket.

"Frances, how is she?" Tom's voice wavered, his throat constricted with emotion as he whispered to his sister, the sound barely carrying beyond the threshold.

Frances gestured towards the narrow staircase that led

to the upper floor. "She's upstairs. Very weak. It won't be long now."

With a heavy heart, Tom ascended the stairs, the creaking wooden steps echoing in the silent house. Ascending the narrow staircase felt like wading through a flood of yesterdays; each creaking step another moment gone. The dim light did little to chase away the ghosts that seemed to linger in the corners. As he reached the landing, he was met with the sight of his mother's bedroom door ajar, the flickering light of a solitary candle throwing dancing shadows across the worn floorboards. A sliver of the inevitable seeping out.

Pushing the door open gently, the scent of illness hung heavy in the air, mingling with the faint aroma of herbs and liniment. His eyes fell upon the figure lying in the bed, her frail form barely visible beneath the shrouded layers of blankets. Her face, pale and gaunt, her eyes closed in peaceful repose.

"Ma," Tom said gently, his voice breaking as he approached the bedside.

His mother turned her head weakly, her eyes dull with fatigue but still filled with a flicker of recognition. "Tom," she murmured, her voice barely audible above a whisper.

"Come here, my boy." A fragile thread drew him forward. The room was filled with the quiet dignity of an ending; death had already laid its claim, evident in the stillness that enveloped her form. Frances and Mary flanked the bed like sentinels, their faces drawn with sorrow, etched with the pain of impending loss. Mary reached out to clasp Tom's hand, her grip tight with silent solidarity.

"We're all here, Ma," Tom said softly, his voice trembling with emotion. "You're not alone."

Maureen managed a faint smile, her pallid lips trembling with the effort. "I've been waiting for you, Tom… there's something I need to tell you."

Tom leaned in closer, his heart heavy with dread. "What is it, Ma? What do you need to say?"

"Tom," Maureen beckoned with a feeble gesture, "Sit with me."

He sat slowly and carefully on the bed, he took his mother's thin and bony hand, a parchment map of their shared journey on her skin. The weight of her life pressing into his palm. Her eyes, once vibrant, now flickered with the fatigue of a waning flame.

Maureen's gaze drifted to the burning candle beside her bed, her eyes distant as though she were gazing into the beyond. "I don't have much time left, my boy," she said, her voice barely more than a whisper. "But before I go, there's something you must do for me."

Tom felt a lump form in his throat as he listened, his eyes stinging with tears. "Anything, Ma," he choked out. "Anything you ask of me."

"Promise me, Tom," she implored, each word a labour of love, "…promise you'll go back to Ireland. To your uncle Brendan's farm. There's life for you there… a new start. I heard from your sisters… that you have spent too much of your nights here in bars, drinking too much. It is no good for you, Tom."

Maureen continued to grasp her son's hand; her grip

feeble but determined. "You must go back home, Tom," she said, her voice barely more than a breath. "Back to Dromdaire. Take over the farm. It's yours now, yours and your sisters. Start anew, build a life for yourself. Find a good Kerry woman, marry her, settle down."

Tears welled in Tom's eyes as he listened to his mother's words, his heart torn between duty and desire. "But what about you, Ma?" he whispered, his voice thick with emotion. "What about Frances and Mary? I can't leave you all again. I was away for far too long, four years fighting in the damn war."

Maureen smiled weakly; her gaze filled with a mother's love. "They'll be fine, Tom," she said, "I am going soon, to be with your father John, your brother Michael and to be with my mother and father. We'll take care of each other. Your sisters are married here, they have families. They will be okay. But you… you have a chance for something more. Don't let it slip away."

"Ma, I—" Tom's voice cracked, the enormity of her request settling upon him like a mantle.

"Promise," she insisted, a mother's command that brokered no argument.

"I promise," he surrendered, the words sealing his fate.

"Good boy," Maureen said.

As Maureen's words faded into the silence of the room, Tom felt a wave of grief wash over him, his heart heavy with the weight of impending loss. He squeezed his mother's hand tightly, his fingers trembling with emotion.

"I love you, Ma," he whispered, his voice choked with

tears.

Maureen's lips curved into a soft smile as she squeezed Tom's hand weakly. "I love you too, son," she said, her voice barely more than a sigh. "Always."

And with those final words, Maureen closed her eyes, her breaths growing shallower with each passing moment. Tom watched in silent anguish as his mother slipped away, her frail form disappearing into the darkness like a fading memory. Beside him, Frances and Mary wept openly, their tears mingling with his own as they mourned the passing of their beloved mother. In that dimly lit room on Mulberry Street, amidst the chill of a February night, a family said their final farewell to a woman who had loved them more than life itself. And as the candle flickered and died, delivering the room into darkness, Tom knew that nothing would ever be the same again.

***

The morning of Maureen Doyle's funeral dawned grey and overcast, the sky heavy with the promise of looming rain. A horse-drawn hearse, draped in mourning black that seemed to absorb the light around it. With ornate but minimal decoration, it emerged like a shadow in the morning haze, a vessel of solemnity navigating the city's labyrinthine arteries with a quiet grace. The black horses, noble and steady, their breaths forming misty clouds in the chill February air, pulled the hearse with a regal dignity. The wheels of the hearse were sturdy and spoked, designed to navigate the cobblestone streets of the city with ease.

The sides of the carriage were tall and enclosed. The windows were small, allowing only faint glimpses of the interior. The hearse was a dignified conveyance, designed to transport the deceased with grace and respect. Within its confines, the simple wooden coffin rested in silent repose that held Maureen's earthly remains, a vessel of memories of a life once lived. Adorned with flowers, their petals kissed by raindrops. A homage to the fragility of existence, a fleeting reminder of mortality's grasp.

A driver sat elevated above the horses for a clear view of the road ahead. He was clad in drab attire befitting the occasion, a dark coat made of broadcloth, which fit snugly against his form. Underneath a matching waistcoat, fastened securely with polished buttons. Upon his head rested a hat, wide-brimmed and dark, shielding his face somewhat from the elements. The hat was decorated with a band of black ribbon. His hands, gloved in supple leather, held the reins with practiced ease, guiding the horses along the winding streets of the city with a steady hand. His gaze, though hidden beneath the brim of his hat, was focused and vigilant to the needs of the mourners. Overall, the driver exuded an air of quiet reverence, with movements measured and deliberate. He was the steadfast guardian of the departed on their final journey to rest.

As the dark parade wound its way through the narrow streets of the Lower East Side, it attracted the gaze of people on their journeys through their daily routines, each pausing to offer a silent nod of respect or a mouthed prayer. The streets themselves seem to hush in reverence, their bustling energy momentarily stilled by the sober procession.

The hearse solemnly glided towards the church. The dark silhouette of the vehicle against the pale winter sky was a striking contrast.

The hearse came to a stop at the foot of the steps leading to the entrance of the Church of St. Michael and All Angels. As it came to a halt, there was a moment of silence that seemed to fill the air, as if even nature itself was paying respects. All that was heard was the soft sway of barren branches in the winter trees along the avenue, which added a poignant melody to the scene.

St. Michael's imposing and towering gothic spires reached skyward like fingers in supplication, reaching out to pray and merging with the dark clouds above. A tangible plea to the heavens for comfort in the face of loss.

Then, the doors of the church creaked open, welcoming the mourners within, their hearts heavy with grief yet buoyed by the promise of solace and remembrance.

As Tom carried his mother's coffin alongside his two brothers-in-law and the undertaker, the weight of grief hung heavy upon his shoulders rather than the coffin, each step a painful reminder of the loss of his beloved mother. The candles on the altar shimmered as the coffin of Maureen Ryan slowly approached.

Within the church, the soft murmur of prayers could be heard from those gathered, their hushed voices conveying their respect and grief. The scent of incense mingled with the musty aroma of old wood, radiating a pall of reverence over the gathered mourners. The church bell tolled, its mournful chime adding to the solemn atmosphere.

The priest, Father O'Reilly, stood tall and lean at the altar as he prepared to deliver the funeral sermon. His face lined with age and experience; deep crevices etched into his skin like roads on a map. His gentle yet piercing eyes filled with compassion and empathy. He wore a traditional black cassock robe with a white collar that threatened to swallow him whole. His hands were clasped in front of him as he prepared to speak, his fingers intertwining in nervous anticipation. His grey hair was neatly combed back, and the light from the stained-glass windows kindled a warm glow on his weathered face. The rustle of his robes echoed through the quiet church as he adjusted them. His voice, deep and strong, resonated through the cavernous space of the church, carrying the weight of centuries of tradition and faith as he began his sermon.

"My brothers and sisters," he began, his voice steady. "Today, we gather to mourn the passing of a beloved member of our parish, Maureen Ryan. Though her earthly journey has come to an end, her spirit lives on in the hearts of those who loved her."

Every word he spoke was deliberate and purposeful, filled with emotion, reverence and compassion that brought comfort to the mourners gathered before him. Occasionally he paused to take a deep breath before continuing on. His words wove a tapestry of remembrance, painting a portrait of Maureen's life with reverence and grace. He spoke of her kindness, her generosity, and her unwavering faith, painting a picture of a woman who had lived her life with humility and grace despite the terrible sorrow she endured through her life. The mourners strained to hear his every word, hanging on to his every syllable.

"And so, my friends, let us commend Maureen Ryan to the mercy of Almighty God, trusting in his infinite love and mercy to welcome her into his kingdom of eternal peace."

The lines etched into the priest's cheeks and brow resembled the gnarled bark of an ancient oak, weathered by years of wind and storm and the furrow between his brows was deep like a riverbed, eroded over years of delivering sermons and consoling mourners.

As the congregation bowed their heads in silent prayer, the strains of a hymn filled the air, their voices rising in harmony as they paid tribute to the life and legacy of a beloved member of their community.

Outside, the rain began to fall in earnest against the cobblestone streets as the mourners made their way to the cemetery. Beneath the shadow of towering oak trees, they gathered once more, their faces turned upward toward the heavens as the priest offered a final prayer of committal.

"Earth to earth, ashes to ashes, dust to dust." he intoned, his voice filled with gravity as he blessed the ground that would soon receive Maureen's mortal remains. "May the angels lead you into paradise, and may the saints welcome you home to the eternal kingdom of God."

As the first cold shovelfuls of earth fell upon Maureen's coffin, a hush fell over the gathered mourners, broken only by the soft sound of weeping and the distant tolling of church bells. In that moment, beneath the grey skies of a February afternoon, a community came together to mourn the passing of one of their own, finding solace in the promise of eternal life and the hope of resurrection yet to come.

Tom stood by the graveside, staring downwards into the hole which was like a gaping maw ready to swallow him.

"Tom," Frances said softly, her hand on his arm, "remember what Ma said. It's time for you to find your way home."

Mary nodded, her eyes brimming with tears but resolute. "You've done enough here. Let Ireland heal you."

He looked between them, their faces mirrors of the strength and sacrifice they'd known. In their eyes, he saw the reflection of his own conflict – a war between duty and desire, the comfort of the known and the call of the unseen.

"Ma wouldn't have asked if she didn't believe it was right," Frances said, her practical nature a balm to his doubts.

"Go," Mary urged, her voice soft but insistent, "and take our love with you."

As the burial rites concluded, a chapter of Tom Ryan's life closed with the hard thud of earth upon wood.

Chapter 6: The Atlantic Coastal Line
March 2ⁿᵈ, South Street Sea Port

In the hush of a March morning, the docks of South Street Seaport awoke to the gentle lapping of waves against weathered wooden pilings, which created a soothing soundtrack to the busy atmosphere of the dock. The voices of dockers could be heard, their conversations blending together in a chorus of industry. The creaking of ropes and jangling of metal chains converged as they worked and echoed through the air. In the distance, the whistle of a ship's horn resonated through the harbour. Overall, the docks were like a symphony of salt and wood.

The East River glimmered in the early light, a silver ribbon that seemed to stretch endlessly into the horizon and carried secrets and dreams yet uncharted. Here, amidst the salt-tinged air, sailors and stevedores, their faces cracked by wind and sun, moved with purpose along the worn planks of the dock, their voices a chorus of industry. Above, the masts of tall ships stood against the sky, their masts reaching towards the clouds and rigging woven like an intricate web, woven by hands washed by brine and sweat. The sails were furled and waiting for their next adventure, the lure of unknown shores.

At the water's edge, rowboats bobbed gently in the current, their wooden hulls polished to a gleam by the hands of those who ply the river's ancient trade. From afar, the distant *hum* of the city blended with the cries of gulls wheeling overhead. On the dockside, crates and barrels lay in neat rows, their contents a tribute to the bounty of distant lands and the commerce that binds nations together. The scent of spices hung in the air, mingling with the tar, seaweed and rotting fish. For here, at the docks of South Street Seaport, the world began anew with each tide, and the dreams of a thousand voyages took flight upon the wings of the wind.

Tom stood on the bustling docks, the brisk March wind ruffling his coat as he scanned the crowded pier, his heart heavy with apprehension as he prepared to embark on his voyage across the Atlantic. Before him loomed the towering masts of the ship that would carry him to his ancestral homeland, its weathered hull bearing the name *The S.S. Great Republic*, a fitting moniker for a vessel bound for the shores of Ireland, for a country that aspired to be a republic. The ship was a clipper renowned for its size and speed, a venerable titan of timber and sail. The ship belonged to the Oceanic Line; a company known for its transatlantic voyages that connected the old world to the new.

He made his way through the throngs of passengers and crew, his eyes fixed on the gangway that led aboard the vessel. As he reached the ticket booth, he exchanged coins for a slip of paper that bore his name and passage details, a tangible symbol of his long voyage ahead. With ticket in hand, Tom ascended the gangway, the sound of his footsteps echoing against the worn planks of the ship's deck blending with the sounds of the excited chatter of passengers and the rhythmic creaking of the ship's timbers.

Making his way below deck, he found himself in the confines of the steerage quarters. A crew member directed him to his assigned berth. The steerage quarters were small and cramped. The dim lighting created a gloomy atmosphere, the only source of light coming from a few lanterns hung at uneven intervals. The small space was filled with rows of wooden bunks, each one hardly wide enough for a grown man to sleep on comfortably. The walls were plain and chipped, with peeling paint revealing the bare wood underneath.

The low ceiling seemed to press down on the rows of narrow bunks, making the space feel even smaller. The bunks themselves were plain and bare, with only a thin blanket and rough pillow provided. The cramped space was filled with the belongings of the passengers, some hanging from hooks, others stored underneath the bunks or in small, chipped, and worn wooden lockers lining the walls with various items of clothing spilling out from them. The wooden floors were scuffed, with little room to walk between the beds. The lack of privacy and size of the space gave it a claustrophobic feel.

The air was heavy and musty, with a strong scent of unwashed bodies lingering in the confined space. A hint of salt lingered in the air, a reminder of the ocean just outside the ship's hull. A faint odour of old food and cooking wafted from the communal kitchen nearby. The strongest odour was the foul stench of vomit from seasick passengers.

The constant creaking of the ship's timbers blended with the sound of passengers shuffling about in their cramped quarters. The occasional groan or muffled conversation broke through the pervasive quiet, accompanied by the distant sounds of waves crashing against the hull. Occasionally, a crew member's voice could be on deck.

With a heavy heart, Tom stowed his belongings away, his fingers lingering over the few precious mementos he had brought from home. His thoughts turned to his sisters, left behind in the crowded streets of New York, their faces etched in his memory like shadows in the fading light.

As the ship set sail, Tom lay on his bunk and thought of the six-week voyage that lay ahead and the uncertain future that awaited him on the distant shores of Ireland. With each passing minute, the distance between himself and his sisters grew wider, until they were little more than a distant memory on the horizon. And as the *Republic* ploughed through the dark waters of the Atlantic, Tom closed his eyes and surrendered to the embrace of the unknown. The creaking timbers of the ship provided a steady rhythm as Tom settled into his makeshift bed among the throngs of fellow passengers.

As the days turned into weeks, and the monotony of time fell over him like a haze. Tom found himself drawn to the deck; his eyes fixed on the distant horizon. The endless expanse of sea stretched out before him, a vast and unforgiving realm that held both promise and peril in equal measure. As the vessel cleaved through the vastness, he listened to the ocean's incessant wind, the creak of wood and the snap of canvas straining against the gales. Its wooden hull a steadfast guardian against the boundless Atlantic Ocean that churned beneath the hull of the ship, a restless and moody beast that rocked the vessel to and fro. Tom gripped the railing as he watched a thick fog envelop the ship, blurring the line between sea and sky. It all felt surreal, this journey back to Ireland – a place he had left as a child to escape famine, and now, with the distant echo of the Civil War still ringing in his ears, he found himself seeking solace in the land that had threatened his family with annihilation.

The conditions aboard the ship were harsh; filth and disease lurked in every corner, breeding a sense of unease among the passengers. Meals consisted of meagre rations of salted meat, hardtack, and dried peas, washed down with brackish water that tasted of seaweed and salt.

Despite the discomfort and privations of life aboard the ship, Tom found solace in the camaraderie of his fellow passengers. They hailed from all walks of life; their faces hardened by the harsh realities of existence. Here, amidst the cramped confines of the ship's lower decks, a community took root, bound together by the shared experience of the voyage. Conversations drifted like smoke on the breeze, mixing with the soft strains of music and the laughter of children as they played amidst the chaos of the crowded cabin.

As the ship's bow cut through the waves like a knife through silk, it was forever bound to the rhythm of the sea. For here, amidst the boundless expanse of the Atlantic, it was a pilgrimage of the soul. For those aboard the ship, the journey was not just a physical passage across the Atlantic but also a metaphorical journey of endurance, resilience and survival. It was a test of strength and fortitude, a rite of passage that would shape their lives and the lives of generations to come.

Tom clung to the hope that lay within his heart, the promise of a new beginning that beckoned him across the vast expanse of ocean. With each passing day, the anticipation of his arrival in Ireland grew. Would he find the belonging he sought, or would he be forever haunted by the spectre of the past?

He felt the weight of his mother's dying words, a sacred charge that propelled him forward even as doubt shackled his resolve. To forsake the land that had tested and forged him seemed a betrayal, yet the pull of blood and soil beckoned with a siren's allure.

Chapter 7: The Promise of the Days to Come
April 13th, Cork, Ireland

The sight of Ireland's coastline emerging from was like a balm to Tom's soul. As Cork materialised from the morning mist, a silhouette against the awakening sky, the ship reduced its sails and the bustling port drew closer, inch by painstaking inch. The juxtaposition was immediate and arresting. Gone were the towering edifices of steel and stone, the relentless churn of humanity; here, the embrace of open sky met the gentle undulation of emerald hills. A painter's palette of greens and browns spread before him, a canvas untouched by the soot and grind of the metropolis he'd left behind.

The ship groaned as it finally approached Cork Harbour, signalling the end of a long and arduous journey. Tom Doyle stood at the railing, his heart pounding as he caught his first glimpse of his homeland after six weeks at sea. The morning mist hung low over the water, casting a dreamlike haze over the harbour. Seagulls swooped and cried overhead, their calls mingling with the distant sounds of ship bells and the activity from the docks below. Sailors and dockers hurried about, loading and unloading cargo, their shouts and commands filling the air with a sense of purpose and urgency.

Disembarking with a duffle slung over his shoulder, Tom stepped onto the quay, inhaling deeply. The scents of peat and livestock converged in the air, an aromatic tapestry that spoke of simplicity and toil. Though busy, Cork carried a different rhythm to New York, one less frantic, more attuned to the languid pace of nature's own cadence.

His boots thudded on the wooden planks, each step resonating with finality and purpose. He paused, allowing himself a moment to survey the tableau of life around him – the fishermen mending their nets with deft fingers, the laughter of children chasing a runaway hen. It was a symphony of the everyday, a melody foreign yet strangely comforting to his war-weary heart. Here, at the edge of the Old World, Tom Ryan stood on the threshold of his new life.

"Welcome home, Tom Ryan," he murmured to himself, "Let's see what this place has in store for you."

As he made his way away from the waterfront through the winding and narrow streets of the city, lined with rows of elegant Georgian townhouses adorned with colourful façades and wrought-iron balconies. Tom's steps quickened with each familiar landmark he passed along the winding banks of the River Lee as it snaked its way through the city. The southern port city was alive with the sounds of commerce and industry. The sound of horse-drawn carriages clattering over the cobblestones resonates through the narrow lanes, their drivers calling out to pedestrians to make way. People ambled about, some carrying baskets of goods while others haggled at market stands.

The sound of church bells rang out, marking the passage of time as parishioners made their way to morning mass.

With the timbre of Cork's morning hustle at his back, Tom shouldered his way through the throng to the station. Emerging from the winding streets, the grand façade of Cork's train station came into view, standing proud and sturdy amidst the lively streets. As he stepped onto the platform, he was enveloped in a whirlwind of sights and sounds and the sharp tang of coal and steam assaulting his nostrils. The platform was a sea of movement, with people hurrying to and from trains. Men in tweed caps strode about, their voices raised in conversation, some lugging heavy trunks while others sat patiently on benches, waiting for their train. While women in long skirts and bonnets rushed alongside them, clutching parcels and children close.

The station was a sonata of clinks and clanks, as trains shunted together, and passengers rustled paper tickets. The screech of metal on metal filled the air, intermixed with the distant whistle of a train as it approached. The sound of footsteps and voices echoed off the stone walls, creating a constant *hum* that enveloped the entire space. Steam billowed from the locomotives as they impatiently waited to depart.

The station itself was a grand affair, its exterior made of sturdy but weathered limestone and crowned with a wrought iron roof that arched high above, supported by towering pillars that gave the station an air of strength and stability. From the platform, Tom could see rows of windows gleaming in the morning sunlight, projecting a warm radiance upon the throngs of passengers who queued patiently along the platform edge while smoke billowed from the chimneys of passing trains. Red and green train cars sat lined up on the tracks, ready to whisk passengers away on their journeys. Tom paused to take it all in as he scanned the crowd for a glimpse of his train, Tom's eyes were drawn to the station clock, its hands ticking steadily onwards as time marched on.

"Killarney!" cried the conductor, his voice cutting through the racket of people moving about the platform. The iron beast loomed before him, its steam breath mingling with the mist that clung to the station roof and whispered over tracks. The locomotive stood tall and proud, a massive machine with its sleek black body adorned with intricate patterns in trimmings of gold and deep blue, giving the impression of elegance and luxury. The train was an imposing structure, with its elongated shape stretching across multiple carriages. Its metallic exterior gleamed in the sunlight, the wheels spun, and smoke billowed from the stack, creating a mystical aura around it.

With a final glance back at the streets of Cork, Tom hoisted his bag onto his shoulder and mounted the steps of the carriage. As the heavy door clanked shut behind him, the engine let out a triumphant whistle and the train juddered to life. For in that moment, as the train began to pull away from the platform, Tom Ryan knew that he was embarking not just on a journey of miles, but on a journey of the soul – one that would take him far beyond the confines of Cork and into the boundless realms of possibility that awaited him amidst the lakes and mountains of Kerry. Though the journey from New York had been long and arduous, he couldn't help but feel grateful for the chance to begin anew in the place where his heart truly belonged. He felt a surge of adrenaline coursing through his veins, driving him forward with a newfound sense of purpose. His spirits buoyed by the promise of adventure that lay ahead.

As the train chugged along the tracks towards its destination, it left behind a trail of swirling smoke and steam. It emitted a steady, rhythmic rumble as it moved along the tracks. The hiss of steam provided a constant soundtrack as the engine powered forward. Springs groaned beneath him as the train emitted a steady *hum*.

The compartments were lined with worn leather seats and brass door handles, all bathed in a warm golden light from the large windows. He settled into his seat by the window. It seemed fitting that he should be able to watch the changing landscape as he travelled deeper into his ancestral homeland. He pressed his forehead against the cool glass, eyes tracing the undulating countryside that blurred into a watercolour wash of greens and browns. Hedgerows raced by in a blur, stitching together the patchwork quilt of fields and farms that stretched to the horizon. Dotted with the occasional cottage, smoke curling from chimneys like lazy serpents, the landscape held an unspoken promise. It was beautiful in a wild, untamed way that spoke to something deep within him.

***

As they neared Killarney, the train slowed to a crawl as it approached the station, and Tom's anticipation swelled like the thundering waters of a river after a storm.

"Welcome to Killarney," the conductor announced, as Tom alighted onto the platform and eventually out of the station, the flurry of activity washing over him, his senses alight with the rich tapestry of rural town life. The air was thick with the tang of turf fires and seasoned with the earthy aroma of livestock. Shopkeepers swept thresholds, and aproned women bartered for goods with sharp wit and laughter at market stalls brimming with fresh produce and handmade wares. Everywhere there was movement – life unfurling in every gesture and glance amidst this dance of the everyday.

Tom clutched his bag tightly as he threaded through the crowded streets, searching for the solicitor's office. His anxiety grew with each passing moment, gnawing at him like a ravenous beast. What if the inheritance was nothing more than a pittance, not enough to make a difference in his life? He unfolded the scrap of paper where he'd scrawled the address, the ink smudged by nervous fingers. Tom's pulse quickened as he scanned the street names, searching for the one that would lead him to the solicitor's office. His boots echoed on the pavement, each step a drumbeat of resolve and trepidation.

"Excuse me," he said, approaching a middle-aged

87

woman selling flowers by the side of the road. "Could you tell me where I might find the solicitor's office?"

"*Ah*, Mr O'Connell's place?" she replied, her eyes narrowing as she sized him up. "You'll want to head down this street here, then take a left at the bakery. It's just past the butcher's shop."

"Thank you," Tom muttered, tipping an imaginary hat out of habit more than necessity.

"You're welcome," came the response, accompanied by a nod and a curious squint at Tom's Yankee twang.

He followed the directions, his stride betraying a hint of urgency as the reality of his quest settled upon him. As he rounded the corner and caught sight of the modest brick building that housed the solicitor's office, the brass nameplate next to the entrance gleamed:

'Michael O'Connell, Solicitor

Est. 1835

Legal Counsel & Notary Public

Specialising in Property Law, Estates, and Contracts.'

Tom took a deep breath to steady himself. This was it – the moment that might determine the course of the rest of his life. With a mixture of excitement and unease, he reached for the handle, pushed open the door and stepped inside.

The door swung shut with a soft click behind Tom, cocooning him in the hush of the solicitor's office. The room, with its walls lined by shelves burdened with leather-bound tomes and documents, smelled faintly of beeswax and parchment – an aroma that spoke of order and antiquity. A large oak desk dominated the space, behind which sat a middle-aged man, bent over a document.

"Excuse me," Tom said hesitantly, "are you Mr O'Connell?"

The man looked up slowly, eyes squinting as they adjusted to the light filtering through the window. He was a tall, a thin man, his posture as straight as the spines of the books that surrounded him. His face was angular, with deep-set eyes and a prominent nose. With short greying hair that receded from his forehead. Dressed in a dark suit, he exuded an air of professionalism.

"Indeed, I am," Mr O'Connell replied, the voice sliced through the quiet. A spectacled gaze appraised Tom over a hooked nose.

Standing up and extending a hand to Tom he asked, "And you are?"

"I'm… Tom Ryan," he replied with a nervous stutter, extending a hand roughened from years of labour that seemed out of place in this realm of paper and ink. O'Connell accepted the handshake with a firm grip, his hand retreating almost immediately as if intimacy were an indulgence he could scarce afford.

"Oh, yes, Mr Ryan, your letter indicated you would be arriving soon. Please, have a seat."

"Thank you, sir," Tom said, lowering himself into a chair that creaked under the weight of his frame, dwarfing the delicate craftsmanship. He could feel his heart pounding in his chest, the anxiety building within him as he watched the solicitor settled behind the oak desk, fingers deftly parting the sea of papers until they rested upon a particular stack tied with a red ribbon.

"Let's get straight to the matter at hand, shall we?" Mr O'Connell said, rifling through a stack of papers. "Your late Uncle Brendan's estate… Your late uncle left you a rather sizable inheritance, including a house and a parcel of land near Dromdaire." Mr O'Connell began, his words meticulous as he outlined the breadth of the inheritance. Acres of farmland, livestock counts, boundary disputes long settled – the torrent of details washed over Tom.

"Did he leave any instructions or conditions?" Tom asked, trying to keep the tremor out of his voice.

"*Ah*, no, Mr Ryan. The property is yours outright, free of any encumbrances." Mr O'Connell reassured him, handing over a sheaf of documents.

"Could I get you please to sign this document sir," the solicitor said as he placed a manuscript in front of Tom and handed him his pen. Tom drew a breath, his fingers hovering before grasping the pen. It felt heavier than any rifle he'd held – ma weapon of a different sort that could sow futures or fell them with a stroke. His signature sprawled across the line, a declaration of intent and a tether to soil that had fed his bloodline for generations.

"These are the deeds to the house and land. And your uncle also left you a sum of money, which I have here." He produced a leather pouch, heavy with coins.

The deeds lay before Tom, their significance palpable as he lifted them. His hands shook as he accepted the deeds and the pouch. He was struck by the weight of the responsibility that now rested on his shoulders and felt a deep sense of gratitude towards his uncle for this unexpected gift. He felt a thrumming in his veins, a call resonating through the chambers of his heart – one that spoke of homecoming and the heavy mantle of stewardship.

"Congratulations, Mr Ryan," Mr O'Connell intoned. "You are now the rightful owner of the Ryan family farm in Dromdaire."

"Thank you, Mr O'Connell," Tom said, the timbre of his voice carrying a note of reverence, acknowledging the sacred trust being placed in his hands. "I can't tell you how much this means to me."

"Your uncle must have seen something in you, Mr Ryan," the solicitor replied solemnly. "He chose to entrust you with this legacy. I trust you will honour his memory."

"Indeed, I will," Tom vowed, his jaw set with determination. "I plan to restore the property and make it a home once more."

"Very well, may it bring you prosperity," Mr O'Connell said, his voice taking on a more formal tone. "If you have any questions or concerns, do not hesitate to contact me. And if you need assistance with any legal matters in the future, my services are at your disposal."

"Again, thank you," Tom said, rising from his chair. Clutching the deeds, feeling the solidity of the ground beneath him – ground that stretched far beyond the confines of this office, rolling in waves toward the western sea. With a nod of gratitude, he stepped back into the streets of Killarney, the folded documents pressed against his chest like armour against the unknown. He took a deep breath, steeling himself for the journey ahead. The reality of his new life was beginning to sink in, and with each step, a sense of belonging that had eluded him for so long.

Tom again navigated the cobbled streets of Killarney. His eyes scanned the storefronts for what he needed, a horse and waggon to carry him to Dromdaire. He made his way past the thatched-roof cottages as he sought out a local livery stable. He found Doyle's Livery Stable, nestled between a blacksmith's forge and a wool merchant's shop.

The livery stable was a large wooden building with a thatched roof that gave it a rustic and charming appearance. The walls were painted a warm brown colour, with the name 'Doyle's Livery Stable' painted in bold letters above the entrance. The stable had several large doors, each adorned with iron hinges and handles. Stalls lined the walls, with horses peering out curiously, while hay and sacks of feed were stacked nearby. The floor was covered in sawdust. The walls were lined with various tools and equipment. Saddles and harnesses hung from hooks on the walls, giving off an atmosphere of hard work and industry.

As Tom entered the livery stable, he was greeted by the strong scent of hay and horse musk. The pungent smell of manure mixed with the sweet aroma of grass and oats. The lingering scent of leather and polish could also be detected,

The sounds of horses snorting and whinnying merged with the creaking of the wooden stalls as they shifted their weight. The steady *clip-clop* stomping of their hooves on the dirt floor competed with the clanking of hammer on metal as the blacksmith worked on horseshoes in the nearby forge.

"Excuse me," Tom said to the liveryman, a wiry man with a weathered face and knowing eyes. "I'm looking to buy a horse and waggon."

"Yes, I see," the liveryman replied, sizing up Tom with a shrewd gaze. "What do you need them for?"

"Traveling to Dromdaire… and for farm work," Tom answered.

"Right, then. Follow me." Mr Doyle, a man with hands as gnarled as the oaks that dotted the Kerry landscape, led Tom to a small paddock where several horses grazed contentedly. "This one here is Rosie," he said, pointing to a sturdy chestnut mare with a calm demeanour. "She's reliable and strong. Perfect for a journey through the countryside."

She stood tall and proud, her strong muscles evident beneath her sleek fur. Her eyes were gentle, making her seem approachable and trustworthy. Her movements were graceful and sure-footed, and she carried herself with a calm and confident air.

"She looks perfect," Tom agreed, sensing the animal's steady nature. "Have you a waggon for purchase?"

"I have, take a look at that one outside the door," Doyle said as he pointed.

Tom examined the waggon carefully. He ran his hands over the wood, feeling the grooves and knots beneath his fingers, each a testament to journeys past. There were scratches and dents on the sides, signs of previous travels and rough roads. The waggon was made of sturdy pine with smooth, well-worn edges. It had seen many journeys, with scuff marks adding character to its exterior. The wheels were large and sturdy, ready to traverse any terrain. The waggon was painted a dark, rich brown colour. Its bed was spacious and flat, perfect for carrying goods and supplies. The edges lined with metal strips, adding reinforcement and protection. The seat was cushioned with faded green fabric, and there were small patches of cracked leather here and there. Despite its obvious age, the waggon was well-maintained with a strong frame that promised many more journeys.

"Rosie will see you right," Doyle declared, patting the mare's neck. "And the waggon's seen many a road, but she's solid."

Tom settled on a fair price without haggling. He loaded his belongings into the modest wooden waggon and hitched it to the mare. He climbed onto the driver's seat and set off on the winding road to Dromdaire.

The waggon wheels rumbled a syncopated rhythm on the stones, their wooden spokes pounding against the uneven surface. Each revolution echoed with a hollow thud, adding to the musicality of the journey. A steady beat like a drum as they rolled over the rough ground, punctuated by occasional jolts and bumps as wheels hit larger stones, producing a deeper clunk in the otherwise consistent rhythm. The repetitive sound reverberated through the surrounding landscape, mingling with the calls of birds and the soft rustle of leaves in the breeze.

He looked not to the left or right but toward the path that wound westward, beneath a sky streaked with the brushstrokes of departing day. As the miles stretched out before him, Tom marvelled at the ever-changing landscape. Rolling green hills dotted with grazing sheep gave way to rugged cliffs battered by the relentless waves of the Atlantic. A sense of awe washed over him as he took in the wild beauty. Mountains loomed on the horizon, their peaks shrouded in gossamer veils of cloud, and green valleys dipped into shadowed cradles, nurturing streams that sang over pebbles and rushes.

As dusk approached, the silhouette of Dromdaire materialised, a gentle smudge against the twilight canvas. Lights came to life in the windows of thatch-roofed cottages with whitewashed walls. People ambled along the footpaths, their gestures unhurried, their laughter weaving a melody with the evening breeze. Upon entering the town, Tom felt the weight of curious glances. They did not pierce or judge; rather, they wrapped around him like a shawl, threads of interest and speculation knitting together. A group of children ceased their play as they watched the newcomer with wide-eyed wonder. Men paused in their discussions, pipes momentarily forgotten under bushy moustaches, and women leaned closer in their gossip, their voices lowering to a *hum*.

"Who's that, then?" One voice carried, a blend of curiosity and welcome.

"Looks like a Ryan," another responded, a knowing lilt to the words.

Tom was tired, hungry and needed a wash. He decided to treat himself to a meal, a bath and a good night's sleep in a lodging house. The journey to his farm could wait until the morning. The mare would also need a rest after a three-hour journey.

"Is there an inn nearby?" Tom called out to one of the men staring at him, his voice betraying his weariness from the long journey.

"Down that way," the man replied, pointing to a modest tavern nestled among the homes and shops. "You can't miss it."

"Thank you," Tom said, his eyes meeting the man's curious gaze.

"Welcome to Dromdaire," a woman called out to him as he passed by her cottage, a friendly smile gracing her lips. "May your stay be blessed with good fortune."

"Thank you, mam," Tom responded.

Tom directed Rosie to the side of the road, bringing the waggon to a halt before a public house. He stepped down, his boots meeting the ground with a firmness that echoed his resolve.

For tonight, though, Tom simply tipped his hat to the gathering dusk, to the people of this town – his town. And as the first stars pierced the darkening sky, he felt the embrace of his heritage and the promise of the days to come.

Chapter 8: Heartland
April 14th, Ryan's Farm, Dromdaire

The following morning, Tom awoke with the sun, and after a breakfast, he made his way to the farm. It was only an hour's journey. The dirt path leading up to the property was overgrown with weeds and wildflowers, evidence of years of neglect. As Tom traversed the lane, the house came into view – an old stone cottage, its once-white walls now grey with age, and patches of moss creeping across its surface. The surrounding land, though unkempt, held a rugged beauty that stirred something deep within Tom's soul.

"By God, she needs some work, but I'll make her shine again," he muttered under his breath, determination burning in his eyes.

The iron gate groaned on its hinges, a melancholy greeting as he pushed it open, Rosie obediently following with the waggon in tow. Ahead, the farm lay draped in the quiet decay of abandonment, the house a slumped figure against the grey light of an April morning.

The once-proud stone walls wore a patchwork skin of moss and ivy, nature's embroidery on the fabric of man's neglect. Windows, clouded with grime, offered Tom no glimpse inside, reflecting instead the hollow sky. The roof sagged in places where slate tiles had slid away, like gaps in an old man's smile.

Tom stepped forward, his heart a drumbeat of determination beneath his ribcage. He ran a hand along the rough surface of the wall, feeling the chill of the stone seep into his skin. Here was a challenge not unlike those he'd faced before – a call to muster all he'd learned in life's battles.

"Right then," he muttered, squaring his shoulders as he surveyed the courtyard, where weeds had claimed sovereignty over cobblestones. Beyond, the barn's doors hung unevenly, creaking at the whisper of the wind that slipped through the gaps.

He approached the heavy door of the house, the key the solicitor had given him feeling substantial in his palm, an artefact of legacy. The lock turned with an echoing clunk, the door swollen from years of exposure to the elements, creaked loudly as he forced it open.

He stepped into the gloom, a shiver tracking down his spine. Inside, the air was stale and damp, the scent of decay clinging to every corner. Cobwebs festooned the corners of the rooms and hung from the rafters like tattered curtains, dust motes danced in the meagre light that fought through the dirt-stained windows. Floorboards groaned beneath his weight telling tales of years gone by. Furniture stood draped in white sheets, the ghosts of former days.

"Uncle Brendan." Tom breathed the name, imagining the man who had last called this place home. "Where do I even begin?" Surveying the disarray before him. He rolled up his sleeves and set to work, clearing away the debris that littered the floor, scrubbing away dirt from the windows, and dismantling the remnants of broken furniture.

As the day passed and darkness descended upon the countryside, Tom's thoughts turned to the task of building a fire. In the hearth, the remnants of a long-dead fire were cradled in the grate. Tom knelt before it, envisioning the glow of embers, the warmth that could once again fill this space. Gathering kindling from the remnants of some of the shattered furniture, his hands practiced in the art of coaxing flame from slumber. He soon had a small blaze flickering in the hearth, radiating a warm glow throughout the kitchen that danced with a newfound vigour, breathing life into the room.

His gaze travelled from the burgeoning fire to the rest of the room, to the staircase that spiralled upwards, its banister a coiled spine waiting to be polished back to life. He ascended and surveyed the sleeping chambers. Here, plaster cracked like dry earth, longing for the caress of care. Doors hung on weary hinges, yearning to swing true once more.

Though he longed for the comfort of a proper bed, Tom knew that the time for such luxuries would come later. For now, he settled into a rickety wooden chair next to the fire in the kitchen, his weary body grateful for the support. The room was filled with soothing warmth, and Tom's thoughts drifted to the challenges that lay ahead. The farm and the house were in dire need of repair, but he felt a strong sense of purpose as he considered the possibilities. This was his chance to forge a new life, to create something meaningful from the ashes of his past.

As sleep finally claimed him, Tom's dreams were filled with visions of lush green fields, a home restored to its former glory, and the echoes of laughter shared among friends and family. For the first time in weeks, he slept soundly, cradled in the embrace of the land that had called him back to his roots.

The first light of dawn crept through the gaps in the shutters, creating dappled patterns on the kitchen floor. Tom stirred, his muscles stiff from a night spent on the hard wooden chair. He rubbed his bleary eyes and gazed around the room, taking in the disarray but with determination etched into the lines of his face.

"Right," he muttered, rolling his shoulders to work out the kinks. "Time to get to work."

Reclaiming the house piece by piece: sweeping floors, airing linens, prying open stuck windows to let the breath of the countryside cleanse the stale air.

Tom set about organizing the tools he discovered in the shed at the rear of the house, a hammer, nails, a saw and other essentials for the task ahead.

"First things first," he mused aloud, surveying the state of the roof. "Gotta fix those leaks."

He hoisted a ladder against the side of the house, climbing up to inspect the damage more closely. The wind whipped around him, carrying the scent of damp earth and salt from the nearby sea. As he worked, carefully replacing broken slates and patching holes, he couldn't help but marvel at the beauty of his surroundings.

The farm stretched out before him; fields enclosed by moss-covered stone walls that seemed to have grown organically from the earth itself. Beyond lay rolling hills covered in a patchwork quilt of green, with the wild Atlantic crashing against the rocky shore in the distance. The sky overhead was vast and ever-changing, clouds scudding across it like a tempestuous sea.

Out in the fields, he walked the perimeter of the land, assessing the work to be done. Fences needed mending, soil required turning, and seeds awaited planting. With the sun reaching its zenith in the early afternoon sky, Tom paused, wiping sweat from his brow with the back of his hand. There was a rhythm here, a heart beating beneath the dereliction, a pulse he would quicken with his own hands.

As the days passed, Tom threw himself into the work, fixing floors and windows, clearing overgrown fields, and repairing fences. Progress was slow but steady. Each task he completed brought with it a sense of satisfaction, a tangible reminder that he was building something worthwhile. As the farm began to take shape, so too did Tom's connection to the land and its people. He found himself exchanging greetings with passing neighbours, swapping stories and advice over cups of tea or glasses of whisky in the dim light of the local pub.

Though the days were often long and gruelling, each night he returned to the now cosy kitchen, his body aching but his spirit soaring. It seemed that every trial he faced, from the fickle Irish weather to the stubbornness of the farm animals, served only to deepen his resolve.

"Bring it on," he declared one stormy evening, staring defiantly at the rain lashing against the windowpanes. "I can handle whatever you throw at me."

As Tom's first month back on Irish soil was completed, he firmly believed that the Ryan family legacy would not end with whispered memories in Dromdaire, but with the solid strike of hammer on nail, the sweet scent of fresh-cut hay, and the resilient spirit of a man determined to forge a new life from the old.

Chapter 9: Sweet River Flow
May 17th, Ryan's Farm, Dromdaire

The early summer sun was high in the sky as Tom wiped the sweat from his brow as he hammered the last nail into the newly repaired fence. Straightening his back, he surveyed his handiwork with a hint of satisfaction. The land was slowly coming back to life under his care. The tall grass around him swayed gently like emerald waves in the afternoon breeze.

He was making progress fixing up the land, but there were still supplies he needed. He knew that he couldn't continue his work without them. Tom hitched the waggon up to Rosie, and he headed towards town to purchase provisions from Martin Fitzgerald's hardware store.

Dromdaire was alive with activity, a welcome respite from the weeklong solitude he had endured on the farm. Tom observed it all, a slight smile coming to his face at the familiar scenes of daily life. He felt strangely invigorated by the cacophony. He pulled up his waggon on Main Street and walked the short distance towards Griffin's shop to pick up some flour, eggs and tea. Admiring the various shops and businesses that lined the path. He passed the RIC police barracks that stood tall and imposing, made of red bricks with sturdy columns lining the entrance. A large wooden door with a brass handle was guarded by two stern-looking officers in uniform. The Union Jack flag on its dark tiled roof fluttered in the breeze, a symbol of the town's connection to the British Empire. The windows had bars on them, giving the building a fortress-like appearance. Atop the barracks, a lookout tower provided a clear view of the town and its inhabitants. From the outside, the building exuded a sense of authority and power, reminding all who passed by of the imperial law and order it represents.

A sense of unease settled over Tom as an officer approached, his polished boots clicking as he walked.

"Oi, you there, stranger, who might you be?" called out a gruff voice. "State your name and business," the RIC man demanded, the tone of his voice leaving no room for argument.

The officer was tall and broad-shouldered, with a thick moustache that seemed to bristle with suspicion. He bore down on Tom, with his hand on his truncheon, his eyes narrowing as they scrutinised the stranger before him. His broad shoulders filled out the jacket, emphasising his formidable size. Every movement seemed to be calculated and purposeful. From the way he carried himself, it was evident that he was not one to be crossed.

Tom met the man's gaze. "Name's Tom Ryan. Just passing through for supplies," he said evenly. He knew men like this, suspicious of any new face but he wanted no trouble with the law.

"We don't like strangers and vagabonds in this town," the officer said. "Best keep your head down and be on your way quickly."

"I aim to," Tom replied, "I have no quarrel you fine folks."

"Where do you live?" the officer asked aggressively, his gaze unwavering.

"Over at Brendan Ryan's farm, about three miles from town," Tom answered hesitantly, feeling the weight of the officer's scrutiny. "I've been fixing it up."

"Keep your nose clean, Mr Ryan." The RIC man stared him down a moment longer before giving a curt nod and continuing his patrol, leaving Tom with a lingering sense of unease. He let out a slow breath, willing his nerves to settle, steeling himself against the intimidation and suspicion that had been thrust upon him.

After picking up the food provisions from Griffin's, Tom arrived at Fitzgerald's Hardware, the bell above the door announcing his entrance. The wooden floors creaked under Tom's feet as he entered. Rays of sunlight shone through the windows, illuminating the dust particles floating in the air.

A potbelly stove sat in the corner, radiated warmth and providing a cosy atmosphere. He paused for a moment, allowing his eyes to adjust to the dimmer interior. The scent of oil and wood filled his nostrils. Rows of shelves lined the walls, stocked with everything from nails and screws to ropes and lanterns. In spaces between the shelves, hand-written signs advertised different items and their prices. Tom's gaze found a young woman with striking blond hair, her vibrant locks cascading down her back in loose curls. She had a tall, slender figure and stood behind the counter with poise and grace.

She wore a simple blue dress, with a white apron tied around her waist, but it was clear that she took pride in her appearance, as her clothes were clean and well-fitted. She had delicate features, with a small nose and full lips with freckles scattered across her cheeks.

Her hands were quick and nimble as she carefully wrapped a length of wire in brown paper for an elderly customer.

"Just one moment, sir, I'll be right with you," she said, her voice warm and melodic.

Her friendly smile was contagious, brightening the room as she exchanged genial words with the old man before sending him on his way. Then she turned to Tom, gifting him with a radiant smile again that made his breath catch.

"Welcome to Fitzgerald. I'm Cathleen. How can I help you today?"

As he approached the counter, he hesitated, momentarily tongue-tied. He hadn't expected to encounter someone so lovely. "I, *uh*… I need some tools and other… equipment, I have a list – fixing up my farm," he stuttered as he passed Cathleen the list with a shaky hand.

"Wonderful. We've got everything you'll need," she said, her gentle voice putting him at ease as she began gathering supplies efficiently. She moved gracefully among the shelves, gathering the requested items and placing them on the counter. Tom couldn't help but admire the gentle strength in her movements, the confidence with which she navigated the crowded aisles.

"Are you new to the area?" Cathleen asked as she

gathered the last of the supplies Tom needed, her skirts swishing as she moved briskly around the shop.

"Yes, just arrived from America. Well… I've been here over a month. Name's Tom… Tom Ryan."

Cathleen's eyes lit up with interest. "Pleased to meet you, Tom. My da tells me it's quite a journey across the ocean. You're very brave to start a new life so far from home."

Tom rubbed his neck, unused to such warm regard from a stranger. "Appreciate that, miss. It hasn't been easy, but I believe in working hard for a better future."

Cathleen nodded. "That's a fine attitude to have. With some luck and perseverance, I'm sure you'll do well here."

Tom hoped she was right. Just her kind words raised his spirits and reaffirmed his decision to come back to Ireland. He was struck by a sudden curiosity about her life, the world she inhabited when she wasn't assisting customers in the hardware shop. He cleared his throat, willing himself to speak. "So, how long have you been working here?"

"Since I was old enough to reach the shelves." She giggled, a sweet sound that danced through the air. "My father had me learning the trade as soon as I could walk."

"Your father must be very proud of you," Tom remarked, genuinely impressed.

"Thank you," she said, blushing slightly at the compliment. "He's taught me everything he knows."

"Have you ever thought about doing more than just running the shop?" Tom asked, sensing there was much more to Cathleen than met the eye.

"Sometimes," she admitted, her gaze turning thoughtful. "But I'm not quite sure what that would look like yet. I suppose I'm still trying to figure it all out." She glanced back at Tom, her expression vulnerable yet hopeful. "What about you? What brought you to Dromdaire?"

"*Ah*, well," Tom hesitated, feeling a sudden urge to confide in her. "I recently inherited a farm not too far from here. I've been trying to fix it up, make it into something that my family could be proud of."

Cathleen's eyes softened at the mention of his family. "That sounds like quite a challenge, but a rewarding one."

"It is," he admitted.

As they continued to converse, Tom marvelled at how easily the words flowed between them. He found himself drawn to the kindness in her eyes, the warmth of her smile, and the intelligence that sparkled within her every word.

"Do you enjoy living here in Dromdaire?" Tom asked.

"Oh yes. It's a wonderful community. My family has been here for generations."

"It is a beautiful place," Tom agreed.

"It certainly is, the beach isn't far away, and there are beautiful lakes, Lough Currane and the Glanmore and the ruins of the old monastery. There is so much to see," Cathleen said excitedly. Tom considered telling Cathleen about how his family was originally from the area and that he knew every inch of the place, but he decided that it could wait.

"I look forward to exploring the countryside," Tom replied.

"I could show you around, if you'd like," Cathleen offered, a faint blush rose on her cheeks.

Tom felt his pulse quicken at the thought. "I'd appreciate that greatly."

They smiled at each other, both suddenly shy, unsure of what to say next.

"Is there anything else I can help you with?"

"Thank you, Miss Fitzgerald," Tom said, his gratitude genuine. "This should be enough for now."

"Please, call me Cathleen," she insisted.

"Very well. Thank you, Cathleen."

***

Tom found himself drawn back to the hardware shop more often than he would have imagined. Over the next few weeks, Tom made excuses to stop by, even when he didn't really need supplies. Cathleen always greeted him with a warm smile. She stirred something in him he'd never felt before. Tom found himself captivated by her beauty, her grace, quick mind and compassionate nature.

"Back again?" Cathleen asked, her eyes twinkling with amusement as she looked up from behind the counter.

"Seems I'm always needing something," Tom admitted with a sheepish grin.

"Or perhaps it's just good company you're seeking?" She teased, her laughter like a balm to his weary soul.

"Could be," he agreed, feeling the comforting warmth that came from being in her presence once more. Over time, their conversations had evolved, stretching beyond the confines of the hardware shop and into the intricate tapestry of their lives.

"Tell me about America," Cathleen said one day, her curiosity piqued. "What was it like growing up there?"

Tom hesitated, his memories tinged with both fondness and pain. "It was… different," he began slowly, searching for the right words. "There were opportunities, yes, but there was also hardship. My family, we struggled."

Cathleen listened intently, her empathy shining through in the gentle touch of her hand upon his arm. "You've come so far, though. You should be proud."

"Sometimes it's hard to see past the struggles," Tom admitted, grateful for her supportive words.

"Perhaps," Cathleen mused, "you just need someone to remind you."

As the weeks passed, their friendship deepened, each finding solace and support in the other's company. On one dreary afternoon, Cathleen confided in Tom, her voice shaking with emotion. "My grandmother, God rest her soul, she wanted so much for me. I sometimes worry I won't live up to her dreams."

"From what I've seen," Tom replied softly, placing a comforting hand on hers. "You're already more than she could have hoped for."

Their moments of vulnerability drew them closer, providing a foundation of trust that only grew stronger with each shared fear and hope.

"Have you ever thought about leaving Dromdaire?" Tom asked.

"Sometimes," Cathleen admitted, her eyes distant. "I always wanted too..." Cathleen stalled midway through her sentence.

"What... please, go on," Tom said softly.

"I'd love to study medicine in Dublin or London. But... but my father, he needs me here."

Tom nodded, understanding all too well the pull of duty and responsibility. "Just remember, you deserve to follow your own path, too."

"Thank you," she whispered, her eyes flickering with gratitude as she squeezed his hand.

"Would you care to take a walk with me after you close up for the day?" Tom asked after finally working up the courage.

Cathleen's cheeks turned pink, but her eyes sparkled, "I'd like that very much, Tom! I was hoping you'd ask me. I have an idea – let's go on a picnic this evening. It's such a beautiful Summer's evening. I love this time of year."

Tom grinned. "That sounds perfect."

"I know just the spot too, there's a meadow not far from here with a stream running through it."

"Sounds lovely."

"Let me just tell my father where we're going, and I want to pack a few things," Cathleen said as she put up the closed sign on the front door.

Ten minutes later she returned carrying a basket, and she had changed into a new dress.

"I hope you don't mind a bumpy trip on my old waggon." Tom laughed.

"We can walk, it's not far."

As they strolled through town, Cathleen pointed out places of interest like the old clock tower and the school she used to go to.

"I'm glad you came back to Dromdaire, Tom."

"So am I," he replied, "I haven't known such kindness since I arrived back in Ireland."

Cathleen looped her arm through his and gave a gentle squeeze. Tom's heart swelled. With her by his side, this place was starting to feel like home again.

"Come on," she urged, tugging at his hand as they began to walk along a worn path. "There's a spot I want to show you."

As they walked, their conversation flowed as freely as the wind through the grass, touching upon everything from the mundane details of their day to the grander dreams that filled their hearts. Tom found himself sharing stories he had long kept locked away, revealing fragments of his past he rarely discussed.

"America was so different," he told her, his voice tinged with nostalgia. "But Ireland, it feels like home."

"Home is where the heart is," Cathleen replied gently, her fingers brushing against his in a fleeting gesture of understanding.

"Indeed," Tom murmured, his thoughts echoing her sentiment as he allowed himself to become lost in the rhythm of their steps.

The path was a winding serpent, leading them deeper into a world of green and gold, an avenue lined with tall, majestic trees that formed a natural archway, their green leaves shimmering in the dappled sunlight. Small birds danced on branches as they sang a symphony of nature's harmonies, their colourful feathers adding vibrant hues to the scene. The rustle of trees' leaves in the gentle breeze added to the tranquil enchantment of it all.

The path led them to a secluded grove, the trees overhead created a canopy. It felt as though they had stumbled upon a secret world, untouched by the worries and strife that lay beyond its borders.

"Here we are," Cathleen declared, a note of triumph in her voice as she spread out a blanket beneath the sheltering arms of an ancient oak and enjoyed the fresh bread, cheese and apples Cathleen had packed.

After they had eaten, Cathleen tucked a wildflower behind her ear and lay back, gazing at the clouds drifting by. Tom's heart swelled looking at her. Tom settled down beside her, his shoulder brushing against hers as he leaned back against the tree trunk. A comfortable silence enveloped them, the kind that could only exist between two people who understood each other on a level deeper than words.

Tom looked out at the scene before him, the beauty of the landscape a balm for his weary soul. Beside him, Cathleen's eyes reflected the rich hues of the setting sun.

"Isn't it breathtaking?" she murmured, her breath a wisp of warmth against the evening chill. "I used to come here when I was little. It's always been a special place for me."

Tom nodded, as he turned to look at her, the delicate curve of her cheek illuminated by the fading light. "It is," he agreed, though he spoke not of the land but of the woman beside him. "Thank you for bringing me here," his voice low and filled with emotion. "It's nice to share this place with you."

Cathleen turned to face him, her eyes shining with sincerity. "I wanted you to see it, Tom. I wanted to share a piece of my heart with you."

This vivacious, clever woman who filled his days with joy. Unable to resist, he leaned over and kissed her softly. Cathleen's eyes fluttered open, first in surprise, then happiness. She pulled him close and returned the kiss. No words were needed to express what they felt in that perfect moment.

Cathleen sighed contentedly as they broke apart from the tender kiss. A blush crept across her cheeks as she met Tom's eyes.

"I hope that was all right," Tom said, suddenly bashful. "I've wanted to do that for some time now."

Cathleen smiled and squeezed his hand. "It was more than all right," she replied.

They sat in comfortable silence for a while, Cathleen's head resting on Tom's shoulder as they watched the clouds drift by. The meadow buzzed with life around them – bees flitting between flowers, it was a perfect summer's evening.

After some time Cathleen spoke, "Tom, can I tell you something?"

"Of course," he replied.

"I know we haven't known each other very long, but being with you just feels… right. You make me happy."

Tom's heart swelled at her words. "I feel the same

way."

They held each other close as the summer breeze rustled through the meadow. Both their hearts were full to bursting, thrilled at the love they had found in each other. Tom looked into her eyes, the feeling of warmth and connection palpable between them. As they sat there, wrapped in the beauty of the world and the solace of their friendship, Tom knew he had found something rare and precious.

"It's getting dark, we better go back, your father will have a search party out looking for you," Tom joked.

"I love it here; I don't want to go back… but I suppose you are right."

Tom couldn't help but agree. He didn't want to leave either. In the quiet serenity of this moment, he felt an unfamiliar sense of peace wash over him.

They packet away the blanket into the basket and began to make their way back to Dromdaire. Tom found himself acutely aware of the subtle warmth radiating from her body. Her presence seemed to amplify the beauty of their surroundings as they walked side by side.

"Tom," Cathleen said, her voice soft and melodic. "I've never told anyone this before, but I've always dreamt of traveling the world one day."

"Really?" Tom asked, genuinely intrigued. "Where would you go?"

"Everywhere," she replied, her eyes sparkling with excitement. "Paris, Rome, London… I want to see it all, experience everything life has to offer. Will you bring me to New York someday, Tom?"

"I will."

"Thank you."

As she spoke, Tom couldn't help but notice the way her cheeks flushed with excitement, how her delicate fingers danced in the air as if painting unseen images of far-off lands. He found himself captivated by her dreams, her passion and zest for life.

"Tell me about America, Tom," Cathleen implored; her eyes locked onto his. "What was it like growing up there?"

Tom hesitated for a moment, the memories of his past life coming back to him in vivid flashes. He found himself sharing stories of his childhood in America, of his family and friends, the struggles and triumphs that had shaped him into the man he was today. As he spoke, Cathleen listened with rapt attention, her eyes never leaving his face.

"Your life has been quite an adventure, Tom," she said softly, her hand resting lightly on his arm. "You've seen so much, endured so much."

Tom didn't respond and just sighed.

Their walk eventually led them back to the edge of town, where the warm glow of lamplight spilled out from the windows of the nearby houses. Tom felt the weight of the words that lay unspoken between them.

"Goodnight, Cathleen," Tom said softly as they reached her doorstep.

"Goodnight, Tom," She replied, her voice tinged with a hint of sadness.

As the door closed behind her, leaving Tom standing alone, he contemplated that the road ahead would be filled with uncertainty and challenges. But with Cathleen Fitzgerald in his life, the world would be a brighter place.

Chapter 10: Saints and Sinners
June 16th, Ryan's Farm, Dromdaire

Saturday

James Reid strode with a swagger that bespoke authority and ownership across the streets of Dromdaire. His eyes were cold, calculating, as if weighing the worth of everything he laid his gaze upon. His posture was impeccable, his tailored suit an extension of his own skin; he exuded an aura of dominance that left no doubt as to who held the reins of power in this corner of Ireland.

"*Ah*, Mr Reid!" called out a shopkeeper, attempting a warm smile but betraying a hint of nervousness. "A fine day, isn't it?"

"Indeed," replied James, barely sparing a glance at the man before continuing on his way. The shopkeeper's relief was palpable, as if he had just escaped an invisible snare.

James Reid had not been born into his power; rather, it had been carefully cultivated by his parents from a young age. As the only child of a well-to-do family in Dromdaire, he had been raised to understand the importance of wealth, influence, and control. His father, a shrewd businessman, had taught him the value of seizing opportunities and bending others to his will. His mother, a woman of high society, had instilled in him the art of charm and manipulation. Together, they had forged a formidable force, one that would shape the very fabric of their community.

In those early days, the young James Reid had been something of a local legend. His exploits, both real and imagined, were whispered about in hushed tones, passed down like folklore from one generation to the next. There were tales of how he had single-handedly saved his father's business from ruin, or how he had charmed the daughter of a rival merchant into revealing her father's secrets. And, of course, there were the more sinister stories: rumours of dark alliances and ruthless deeds carried out in the shadows.

But for James, these tales were not simply a matter of pride or vanity; they were a testament to the power he had been raised to wield. The lessons of his youth had etched themselves onto the very core of his being, shaping him into the man he was today, a man who would stop at nothing to maintain his grip on the world around him.

As he walked through the streets of Dromdaire, James Reid barely registered the deferential nods and hasty greetings that accompanied his every step. His mind was elsewhere, focused on the plans he had set in motion, the webs he had woven. For there was one thing above all else that James understood: in this world, there were those who held power, and those who cowered beneath it. And as long as he drew breath, he intended to remain firmly in the former category.

A gust of wind whipped through the streets, sending a shiver down James Reid's spine as he stood at the entrance of Stack's tavern. With a deep breath, he pushed open the door and stepped inside.

"*Ah*, Mr Reid!" The barkeeper greeted him with a forced smile, well aware of the landlord's influence in the town. "What can I get you?"

"Whisky," James replied curtly, making his way to a secluded corner table. As he observed the patrons around him, the laughter, the shared stories, something within him churned. He could not help but recall an early memory that had shaped his hunger for power and control. He was no more than ten years old, standing on the edge of his father's vast estate, staring out at the rolling hills and lush fields that stretched as far as the eye could see. Beside him stood his father, a stern man who had instilled in him the importance of maintaining control over one's surroundings.

"Remember, James," his father had said, gripping his shoulder tightly. "This is our land, our legacy. And it's up to us to ensure that it remains so."

From that moment on, James had made it his life's mission to do just that. He would stop at nothing to protect what was rightfully his while expanding his own reach, even if it meant manipulating and intimidating those who dared to challenge him.

"Your whisky, sir," the barkeeper interrupted his thoughts, placing the glass before him. James nodded in acknowledgment and took a sip, the liquid fire burning its way down his throat.

"Tell me," he began, eyeing the barkeeper with a calculating stare. "What news have you heard about the Ryan farm?"

"*Ah*, well," the barkeeper hesitated, clearly uncomfortable with the topic. "I heard that young Tom Ryan is doing quite well for himself. They say he has got his uncle's farm up and running again."

"Is that so?" James asked, feigning interest. In truth, he had been keeping a close eye on Tom Ryan's progress, envious of the young man's success and resentful of the threat it posed to his own dominance in the area.

"Indeed, sir," the barkeeper continued, sensing that he had no choice but to oblige the landlord's curiosity. "Some even claim that his methods could revolutionise farming in Dromdaire."

"Interesting." James took another sip of whisky, his mind already devising ways to ensure that Tom's potential success would not undermine his own power. "You know, I've been considering investing in new agricultural techniques myself. Perhaps I will call to visit Mr Ryan." As he finished his drink and rose from his seat.

***

Tom gazed out at the farm bathed in afternoon sunlight. The smell of a freshly cut pine tree mingled with the earthy scent of the fields. A pair of swallows swooped low over the grass, their wings skimming the tops of the blades. Tom felt at peace here, the land was etched into his bones. This was home. His muscles burned with the labour, but it felt good to see the fruits of his determination taking shape around him. He stopped to rest for a moment and spotted a lone rider coming up the pass to his farm. The rider emerged from the tree line, moving at an unhurried pace up the winding dirt road. Tom straightened himself and looked closer. A stranger, and one who didn't seem inclined to announce himself.

Tom strode into the centre of the road, planting himself before the rider. "You there!" Tom called out, shielding his eyes from the sun with his hand as a lone figure atop a horse approached. "You're on private property."

The man rode slowly, his eyes sweeping over the property as if he were surveying the lay of the land. He continued advancing for several strides before reining in his horse. He sat astride the beast with a languid sort of ease, continuing to survey the farm with a faint curl of his lip, ignoring Tom.

"Who are you? Do you realise that you are on private property," Tom stated sternly.

"Is it now?" the rider replied, not bothering to look at Tom as he spoke. His voice carried a distinct upper-class English accent, crisp, polished and condescending and utterly out of place in rural County Kerry. "And who might you be?"

Tom bristled. "I asked you first."

"More importantly, where do you come from?" The rider paused, finally meeting Tom's eyes, his tone dripping with disdain. "This farm seems rather… modest for a man of your presumed ambition."

"Enough with your games, my name's Tom Ryan," Tom said, annoyance creeping into his voice. "And this here's my land. Now, who are you and what do you want?"

"Come now, there's no need for hostility." The rider's pale eyes settled on Tom, betraying a hint of amusement. "…Very well," the rider sighed dramatically before introducing himself. "My name is James Reid, the largest landowner in this county. I've come to make you an offer, Mr Ryan. I wish to expand my estate and would like to purchase your land."

Tom sucked in a sharp breath. James Reid, the landlord who held claim to nearly every acre in the county. Tom had heard tales of the man's ruthlessness, how he gobbled up farms and livelihoods without a second thought. His stomach knotted with tension.

"Purchase my land?" Tom scoffed, digging his boots into the dirt as he stood his ground. "You're wasting your time, Mr Reid. This farm belongs to me. I won't be giving it up. This land isn't for sale."

"Is that so?" Reid's amusement faded, his expression chilling. "*Ah*, such a shame. You'll find I can be quite persuasive. It would be wise not to defy me. You should reconsider, Mr Ryan."

Tom stood firm, clutching his rage close lest it erupt to the surface. He had sacrificed too much, worked too hard to give up now. "I'll not be intimidated. Be on your way, Mr Reid."

For a long moment Reid merely stared at him, as if unused to such defiance. Then he gathered the reins and turned his horse about in a smooth motion. "You'll regret this, Mr Ryan." He called over his shoulder. "Mark my words."

Tom watched in silence as the landlord rode off down

the road and disappeared into the trees. His heart pounded against his ribs, a mix of anger and dread warring inside him. He knew then, with grim certainty, that this was only the beginning. Reid would not give up so easily. There would be trouble ahead.

Sunday

The congregation gathered for Sunday mass in the small, stone church in the heart of Dromdaire. Men and women, young and old, they all came together on this holy day, united by their faith and the shared hardships of life in rural Ireland.

Tom walked briskly through the heavy oak doors of the church. He dipped his fingers into the font of holy water, crossing himself as the smell of incense and candle wax filled his nostrils. He took his place in the hard, wooden pew near the back of the church. He glanced around the walls of the small chapel, sunlight streaming through the stained-glass windows creating a kaleidoscope of colours and glinting off the golden candlesticks at the altar.

Tom shifted on the unforgiving seat, his leg throbbing from his war wound acting up. He knelt and bowed his head respectfully as the priest led them in prayer, the ancient Latin phrases of the liturgy washing over him. The priest, Father Casey, was an elderly man with a gentle smile and eyes that held an ocean of compassion. His vestments a sombre black, his face creased with concentration. His voice rang clear and strong, each word

123

carrying with it the weight of history and the promise of salvation. He had the authority of a man who had seen generations come and go, nurturing the souls of his flock.

The congregation, an eclectic mix of farmers, shopkeepers and labourers was sparse this morning, scattered among the aged wooden benches. They whispered prayers, their voices a murmur beneath the priest's solemn intonations.

As the mass progressed, through the readings and homily, Tom's thoughts turned to Cathleen Fitzgerald, seated a few pews away. A smile pulled at his lips as he pictured her pretty face framed by waves of blond hair.

His mind wandered as the mass dragged on, thoughts returning to the dark days of the war, of friends lost and innocence destroyed. He shook himself back to the present when the priest announced the closing rites, rousing himself to receive the blessing.

"May the Lord be with you," Father Casey said, and the congregation responded in unison, "And also with you."

"Go in peace," the priest concluded, making the sign of the cross. The congregation echoed the gesture before rising as one, the creaking of pews and rustle of clothing filling the church.

The chapel emptied swiftly afterwards, the worshippers flowing outside onto the stoned yard outside, to chatter or hurry home for Sunday dinner. Their voices mingling with the gentle song of the morning breeze. Tom followed them outside, where the sky was clear and revealed an expanse of cerulean blue. He lingered near the chapel doors, hoping to catch a glimpse of Cathleen. There she was, laughing brightly with a few friends, their laughter ringing out like chimes on the breeze, while her father, Martin, stood watchfully nearby.

Tom approached Cathleen and her father; Cathleen broke into a radiant smile when she saw Tom.

"Good morning, Mr Fitzgerald," Tom said, extending a hand towards Martin.

"*Ah*, Tom!" Martin replied heartily, shaking his hand with a firm grip. "It's good to see you joining us for Mass.

"Thank you, sir. It's a beautiful morning, now that the rain has cleared," Tom said, turning to Cathleen. "Good morning, Cathleen, you look lovely."

"Thank you, Tom," she answered.

"I'm glad my Cathleen's found herself such a fine, church-going man."

Cathleen flushed prettily at her father's praise. "*Oh, Da*," she protested with a laugh. Spotting her friends, she touched Tom's arm. "I'll just be a moment."

As they watched her walk away, Martin clapped a hand on Tom's shoulder. "You know, Tom, I must say I'm glad that Cathleen has found such a fine young man to go out with. You've been through so much, haven't you? The famine, America, the war, and yet here you are back on Irish soil. You clearly are strong and resourceful."

"Thank you, sir, that's very kind. But those experiences have made me who I am today." Tom nodded, feeling a pang of sadness as memories surfaced of the hardships he had faced. He paused for a moment before he continued, "You've raised a wonderful daughter, Mr

Fitzgerald," Tom replied sincerely, his eyes still on Cathleen.

Martin smiled knowingly. "That she is. You treat her proper now, don't you be letting my little girl down now," he said with a laugh.

"I'd sooner walk through fire than hurt her, Mr Fitzgerald," Tom replied earnestly.

"*Aye*, I believe you would… Please, call me Martin," he said, offering a genuine smile.

Tom looked back at Martin, his expression a mixture of gratitude and resolve. The two men stood together in companionable silence, watching as Cathleen chatted animatedly with her friends. In that moment, Tom felt an overwhelming sense of gratitude for the community that had welcomed him home.

Cathleen returned then, slipping her arm through Tom's. Her touch was light and warm, stirring his heart. Together they made their way outside the churchyard, the prospect of Sunday dinner with the Fitzgeralds, a comforting thought.

Martin led Tom and Cathleen down the village road, chatting amiably about the unseasonably warm weather. As they walked, other churchgoers called out greetings.

"Good mornin' to you, Martin!"

"Grand day, isn't it?"

"Give my best to Margaret now!"

Martin tipped his cap in return, clearly a well-respected figure in the community.

Martin glanced over Tom's shoulder and waved. "*Ah*, there's my good friend, Shane Kelleher. Let me introduce you."

Tom turned to see a powerfully built man with ruddy cheeks and straw-coloured hair making his way towards them. Shane had the look of someone who spent his days tending land and cattle.

"Tom, meet Shane Kelleher," Martin said, gesturing to the farmer.

"Nice to meet you, Shane," Tom said, extending his hand.

"Likewise, Tom," Shane replied, gripping Tom's hand enthusiastically with a strength that spoke of hard labour. "I've heard much about you from Martin here, and I'm glad to finally put a face to the name. Your new to these parts?"

"Yes, sir, just moved here a few months back," Tom replied, not going into details about how he originally came from the area.

"What is it you do, Tom?"

"I'm a farmer, got some acres just east of town I'm working."

Shane's eyes lit up, "Well then, you should come along to the meeting tomorrow night. We're getting some local farm men together to discuss... opportunities in the area."

"Sounds worthwhile, I'd be happy to attend," Tom said feeling both humbled and excited by the prospect of connecting with his fellow farmers and to meet more of the community.

"Excellent!" Shane grinned broadly and clapped Tom's shoulder. "We'll see you there then. The old town hall at seven."

As they turned a corner, Tom caught sight of the Fitzgerald home, a modest two-story stone building nestled between rows of lush green hedges, smoke already wisping from the chimney.

"Here we are," Martin announced, "no place like home on the Lord's Day."

Cathleen hurried inside to help her mother while Martin showed Tom around the tidy yard and garden. Chickens clucked in a coop near the barn, and a plump cows grazed placidly in the pasture beyond.

"You've got a fine farm here," Tom remarked.

"*Aye*, we do all right for ourselves," Martin agreed proudly. "Hard work and faith, that's the trick."

Soon the savoury aroma of roasted meat wafted from the house, and Martin clapped his hands. "Let's not keep the womenfolk waiting! Margaret's a fine cook."

"*Ah*, we're just in time," Martin said with satisfaction, pushing open the front door to reveal a pleasant interior. A small fire crackled in the hearth, filling the room with a pleasant warmth. The walls were adorned with family portraits and trinkets from generations past, each object telling a story of the people who had come before.

"Thank you for having me," Tom said sincerely.

"Welcome, Tom! So pleased you could join us, you're always welcome here," Margaret exclaimed.

"Please, make yourself at home, Tom," Cathleen said, gesturing for him to take a seat at the dining table. The table was already set for dinner, with polished silverware and pristine white linens draped across its surface. "We're having roast beef. I hope that's all right."

"Sounds delicious," Tom replied, trying to hide his excitement at the prospect of a hot meal. It had been far too long since he'd enjoyed such comforts and the tantalising scent of roasted meat wafting through the air made his mouth water.

Margaret began passing platters of food – slices of tender roast beef, buttery boiled potatoes, carrots glazed with honey.

"This looks wonderful, ma'am," he said.

"*Oh*, go on with you now." Margaret tutted with a wave of her hand, but she looked pleased to have received the compliment.

Martin took a moment to say grace before they began eating. The food was hearty and delicious, and Tom couldn't help but savour every bite, appreciating the care with which it had been prepared. Between mouthfuls, he glanced up at Cathleen, who sat across from him. He couldn't help but notice her gaze lingering on him from across the table, her cheeks flushed from the heat of the fire. She looked beautiful in the fire light.

"How was your journey back to Ireland?" Martin asked, pulling Tom out of his reverie.

"Difficult, at times," he admitted, feeling the weight of memories from his voyage.

"Indeed," Martin agreed, "and we're glad to have you back among us. I think our community will benefit greatly from your presence."

"Thank you, sir," Tom replied, touched by the sentiment.

"Tom, there's no need for formality," Cathleen chimed in, her voice gentle yet assertive.

As they ate, the conversation flowed from the unseasonable warmth to the year's potato crop to the antics of various townsfolk. Martin recounted a hilarious mishap old Man Flanagan had got into with his donkey, and soon the table rang with laughter.

Tom found himself relaxing, warmed by the food and the Fitzgerald's' easy hospitality. He could see where Cathleen got her spirited nature from. Her parents were good people, hard-working but jolly. He was glad to be considered a welcomed guest in their home.

"To new friends and new beginnings," Martin said, raising his glass.

"To new friends and new beginnings," Tom echoed, raising his own glass.

As the conversation flowed throughout the evening, Tom felt an indescribable sense of contentment in the company of these good-hearted people. The hardships of his past seemed to fade away in the warm embrace of the Fitzgerald home, replaced by a newfound sense of purpose and belonging.

After the meal, Margaret and Cathleen cleared the table while Martin and Tom relaxed by the fire. Tom recounted the invitation he had received from Shane Kelleher.

"A meeting of local farmers, *Hmm*. Well now, that's very interesting…" Martin remarked, sitting up straighter in his chair as he tugged at his chin thoughtfully.

Tom nodded. "I confess I don't know much about it,

only what you overheard yourself."

Martin's interest was piqued. He leaned forward in his chair by the fire. "These new methods, I've heard whispers of change rippling through the county. Farmers talking of new scientific ways to increase crop yields and profits. *Aye*, modern agricultural science is making great strides. But many landlords are resistant to change, afraid it will disrupt the old ways and their power." Martin's eyes glinted knowingly.

Cathleen came over to refill their tea. "Da, you should go with Tom to the meeting tomorrow. Put your knowledge to use."

"Should I now?" Martin responded. "Well, I suppose I could. Been awhile since I flexed my thinking muscles properly." He grinned at Tom. "What say you, lad? Fancy some company tomorrow evening?"

"It would be an honour, sir," Tom said sincerely. Having Martin's wisdom and experience at his side would make him less nervous to speak up at the gathering.

***

Later that evening, Tom returned to his farm. He halted, staring in disbelief at the destruction that lay before him. Fences lay torn asunder, and crops, once standing tall and proud, were now trampled into the mud, their lifeblood seeping into the earth. His chest tightened at the sight, rage and anguish twisting into a knot inside him.

He knew at once who was responsible. Reid's threat from the previous day still echoed in his mind. "Damn you,

131

Reid," he muttered under his breath, clenching his fists in frustration.

Determined, he mounted his horse and rode toward James Reid's manor house, the imposing structure looming larger with each stride.

"Reid!" Tom bellowed, dismounting in front of the opulent residence, his voice echoing as it mingled with the rustling leaves of ancient oaks that lined the property. "I know you're behind this!" He pounded on the heavy oak doors until a servant appeared. "I wish to speak with Mr Reid. Now!"

Reid emerged a moment later, affecting a look of polite interest. "Mr Ryan. How may I help you?"

"You know damn well, know why I'm here," Tom spat. He shook with the effort to contain his anger.

"Whatever are you talking about, Mr Ryan?" An infuriatingly calm expression upon his face.

"Your thugs tore apart my farm!" Tom accused, his eyes burning with rage. "You couldn't force me to sell, so you decided to destroy what I've built instead! Was this meant to frighten me, to make me bend to your will?"

"I'm afraid I don't know what you're referring to." Reid's tone was mild, almost bored. "If there's been some trouble, I suggest you report it to the authorities."

Tom stepped forward. "I won't be bullied off my own land. You can threaten and sabotage all you like, but I'll not give it up."

"Mr Ryan, I assure you; I have no knowledge of any such acts," Reid replied smoothly, feigning innocence. "Perhaps it was merely the work of vandals or a rival seeking to cause you harm."

"Vandals?" Tom scoffed, his heart pounding in his chest. "You expect me to believe that?"

"Believe what you will, but I suggest you tend to your own affairs and leave mine alone." Reid warned, his tone icy as he turned to retreat into his manor house.

"Mark my words, Reid, you won't get away with this," Tom vowed, his voice simmering with fury.

Reid studied him for a long moment with an icy gaze betraying nothing. Then he sighed and waved a hand in dismissal. "Be on your way, Mr Ryan. I grow tired of your baseless accusations."

The door slammed in Tom's face before he could utter a reply. He stood staring at the wood grain, anger burning through his veins. Reid might hold all the power here, but he had underestimated his opponent. The fight had only just begun.

Chapter 11: Blood and Tears
June 17th, The Town Hall, Dromdaire

Arriving at the Fitzgerald's house on Monday evening. Martin greeted Tom warmly at the door. "Ready, my boy?"

"Sure." Tom was in no humour for conversation. He was still reeling from the events of the previous night.

Together they walked to the town hall. The air was heavy with the scent of peat fires and the promise of coming rain, but inside, the room buzzed with anticipation. Tom could see lanterns being lit inside and the murmur of voices drifting through the open windows. Taking a deep breath, he went up the steps and entered the building.

Inside, the hall hummed with spirited conversation as farmers greeted each other and found seats, others remained standing in clusters at the back of the hall. Shane Kelleher stood at the front, organizing papers on a podium. His face lit up when he saw Tom.

"Tom, glad you could make it! And I see you've brought a guest." He eagerly shook Martin's hand.

"Thanks for inviting me," Tom replied, his eyes taking in the scene before him: rows of wooden chairs filled with rough-hewn faces, men who had spent their lives toiling under the unforgiving Irish sky. He recognised some of them from church, others from his visits into town to the public houses.

Once the hall was full, Shane Kelleher walked to the podium and began to speak. "Let's get started, shall we?" Silencing the chatter and clapping his hands together. Standing before the gathering with an air of authority. "As you all know, we're here to discuss the possibility of peasant proprietorship. We've been under the thumb of landlords like James Reid for far too long. It's time for change."

A collective grumble rippled through the crowd at the mention of Reid's name – a man despised for his ruthless tactics and iron grip over the tenant farmers.

"Firstly," Shane continued, "I'd like to introduce Patrick Doyle of the Land League to address the crowd."

"Friends, you all know why we're here. For too long we've struggled under unfair rents and fickle landlords who show us no decency or respect," Patrick Doyle's strong voice boomed through the hall.

Murmurs of assent rose from the men. Tom listened intently.

"The time has come for change. There are ideas spreading, talk of something called peasant proprietorship. It would allow tenants to buy the land they farm, to own it themselves instead of renting it from cruel and heartless landlords. How will we get the money to buy our land back, you may be thinking. Well, the answer, friends, is that the British government will pay for it."

This was met with laughs and jeers from the crowd. One young man stood up and said, "Don't take us for fools. Why would the bloody British government give us the money to buy land from landlords?"

"I agree, at first I thought it was unbelievable as well," Patrick Doyle responded, speaking loudly over the chatter sweeping through the hall. "Michael Davitt and the Land League has used their influence through Parnell and the Irish parliamentary party to persuade Prime Minister Gladstone to introduce a Land Act that will provide loans to all tenant farmers to buy out their holdings. Imagine, friends, having the opportunity to purchase the land you work on, granting you full ownership rights and greater control over your livelihoods. Hundreds of landlords across the country have welcomed this plan as well because they are on the verge of bankruptcy. They have never recovered financially from the rents they lost twenty years ago during the famine. It suits them to sell their lands to their tenants. However, your local landlord James Reid has resisted this initiative, friends we must break the hold on the land this cruel tyrant has."

Excited conversations broke out at this. To own their land, not having to pay crushing rents… it was an inspiring concept. Tom's eyes widened, even though he was fortunate to own his own farm. He knew that James Reid would soon do his best to take it from him. The harrowing events that unfolded last night was just the first step.

As Shane introduced more farmers and their ideas, Tom could feel the energy in the room growing, a sense of hope and unity taking root. He listened intently, his mind racing with thoughts on how these techniques could be applied. The idea of defying Reid exhilarated him.

Tom watched as various farmers spoke up, each

sharing personal stories of hardship and mistreatment at the hands of their landlord.

"Enough is enough!" Cried an older farmer named Seamus O'Leary, his voice thick with emotion. "We have nothing left to lose and everything to gain."

"True words, Seamus," chimed in another farmer, Brendan Quinn. "We need to stand together and fight for our future. Our children deserve better than a life of servitude."

"Agreed," said Frank O'Shea, a young man with a fire burning behind his eyes. "We must take back ownership of the lands that were stolen from us by the British."

As the voices rose and fell around him, Tom felt a growing sense of urgency. He knew that he had something to contribute, his experiences abroad had taught him much about perseverance and the power of unity.

"Any other suggestions or comments?" Shane asked the crowd, his eyes lingering on Tom for a moment.

"Tom," Martin whispered beside him, sensing his internal struggle. "You have valuable insights to share. Don't let fear hold you back."

Tom hesitated as he weighed the possible consequences of speaking out, but emboldened by Martin's words and empowered by the energy in the hall, he found his voice and added his support. Tom decided it was time to make his voice heard.

Slowly, he stood up, his heart pounding in his chest as all eyes turned to him.

"Friends," he began, his voice steady despite his nerves. "I, too, have seen first-hand the cruelty of landlords like James Reid. He is trying to force me off the land I rightly own. But I have also witnessed the strength that comes from standing together and fighting for what is right. In America, where I lived for many years, I saw how people from all walks of life joined forces to challenge injustice and create a better future for themselves and their families. We can do the same here."

His comments were met with sporadic cheers from the crowd. This gave him the spirit to continue.

"James Reid cares nothing for us or our families, only forcing upon us crippling rent increases, and the constant threat of eviction," Tom declared, his voice ringing with conviction. "It's time we take matters into our own hands and demand fair treatment. Together, we can create a better future for ourselves and our children."

The room was silent for a moment, the farmers absorbing this new information. Then, one by one, they began to nod in agreement, murmuring words of support. Tom watched the faces of the men before him light up with hope and determination. Murmurs of agreement spread through the crowd, followed by enthusiastic applause. He could feel the tide turning in their favour as they united against a common enemy.

"Tom Ryan speaks the truth," Shane Kelleher declared; his expression resolute. "We must stand together against those who would seek to oppress us. Let us work towards a brighter future, one where we are no longer beholden to the likes of James Reid."

"Here, here!" echoed the others, their voices rising in unison, fuelled by a newfound determination and hope.

There was a collective sense of admiration and respect for this young man who had endured so much in America yet returned to fight for the betterment of his community. The chatter of men, passionate and determined, formed a symphony that resonated with Tom's own heart. The meeting ended late, but with a sense of hope and direction, change was coming, and Tom knew he wanted to be a part of it. By the meeting's end, he had earned the respect of all those gathered.

Tom and Martin rose from their chairs and began to exit the hall. The majority remained and continued to discuss with enthusiasm what they had heard from the speakers.

"You did very well, Tom. Very well indeed, you certainly got the attention of the crowd," Martin said, his eyes sparkling with admiration as he clasped Tom's hand warmly.

"Thanks, Martin, I was nervous as heck," Tom replied, "I am not one generally for public speaking, but the way James Reid has been abusing me, perhaps there is strength in numbers."

"Tom, wait a minute," Shane Kelleher called out, clapping him on the shoulder and intercepting him as he made his way towards the exit. "That was quite a speech you gave tonight. You have a talent for inspiring people, and we could certainly use someone like you in our ranks."

"Thank you, Shane," Tom responded, his cheeks flushing with pride. "I only spoke from the heart."

"You have a way with words, and you are passionate, you're able to rally people and help them see that together we can change things for the better, which is precisely why I'd like to propose that you become the chairman of our committee," Shane said, his eyes flashing with enthusiasm. "Together, we can rally our fellow farmers and push for the rights we've been denied for so long."

For a moment, Tom hesitated, considering the weight of the responsibility he was being offered. But as he looked around at the faces of those who had gathered in the hall, their expressions filled with hope, he knew he couldn't refuse. Though momentarily stunned, Tom gathered himself enough to humbly accept the critical role.

"All right, Shane," he agreed, extending a hand to his new comrade. "I'll do my best to help out."

"Excellent!" Shane exclaimed, shaking his hand vigorously. "We'll reconvene next week to formalise your position and continue planning our course of action."

Shane walked back to the podium to address the remaining crowd, "Gentlemen, I believe we've found our chairman!"

A round of applause erupted, and Tom felt a swell of pride in his chest.

***

Over the following weeks, the committee meetings continued, each one drawing larger crowds than the last. As the newly appointed chairman, Tom quickly became the main speaker, captivating the farmers with his knowledge and passion. As chairman, Tom worked tirelessly to organise meetings, draw in new supporters, and spread the concept of peasant proprietorship. His skills as a speaker blossomed, he knew how to inspire and unite people behind this movement.

With each passing week, Tom's criticism of James Reid became bolder, earning him the admiration and support of his fellow tenant farmers. Tom's speeches denouncing Reid electrified crowds. "Reid and his ilk have lorded over us for too long, taking what they please while we struggle!" Tom declared. "The time has come for us to claim the land that we have poured our blood and tears into for generations! James Reid has grown rich off the sweat of our brows and the toil of our hands yet offers us nothing but hardship and suffering in return," Tom proclaimed at one such gathering, his voice ringing out with authority. "It is high time we stand up to him and demand the rights we are owed!"

The farmers cheered Tom's bold, impassioned words, "Here, here!" the farmers cried, their voices echoing through the hall as they pounded their fists on the tables in agreement.

Tom's courage to directly challenge Reid made him a champion in their eyes. He found himself at the forefront of a movement that threatened to shake the very foundations of the oppressive system that had kept the tenant farmers in bondage for generations. Under Tom's leadership, the movement was gaining momentum, and he was becoming the face of their fight for justice and autonomy. As Tom's reputation grew, so too did his influence over the local tenant farmers. He was a beacon of hope in their struggle, a man who could guide them through the darkness that had long plagued their lives. As he stood before them, week after week, Tom hoped that together, they would not only defy their tyrannical landlord but also forge a new path toward a future filled with promise.

With each passing day, the tide turned further against James Reid, as the villagers united behind Tom in their quest for justice.

Chapter 12: The Lord of the Land
August 9th, The Reid Manor

Under the pale light of a waning moon, James Reid stood at his open study window overlooking Dromdaire. The moonlight glowing like a dark omen over the vast expanse of his estate. A chill wind whispered through the trees and the tall meadow grass, bearing with it the scent of impending rain and the whispers of secrets yet to be uncovered.

Standing, overlooking the sprawling lands that he held in his iron grip, his cold eyes surveyed the scene with a predatory hunger, as if he were seeking out any signs of weakness or defiance among the people who toiled beneath him. A gust of wind ruffled his neatly-combed hair, but it did nothing to disturb the calculating expression etched upon his face.

Inside his study, he poured himself a glass of whisky, the amber liquid reflecting the flickering candlelight.

"Mr Reid?" The hesitant voice of his butler, Edward, broke through the silence. "Your guests have arrived for the evening."

"Very well," James replied, tearing his gaze from the view before him. He turned and strode back into the drawing room, where several influential figures had gathered, each one eager to gain favour with the powerful landlord.

"*Ah*, gentlemen." James greeted them with a smile that never quite reached his eyes. "Shall we begin?"

As the group settled into their seats and engaged in hushed conversations, James listened with half an ear. He was always attentive to the murmurs of those around him, keen to exploit any opportunity to further his own interests. It was this ruthless ambition that had served him so well throughout his life, propelling him to a position of authority that few dared to challenge.

"Terrible news about Tom Ryan," James remarked casually to one of his guests, a local undertaker named Mr Longbridge. "I hear he's rallying support against me, trying to incite some kind of rebellion among the farmers."

"Indeed," Mr Longbridge replied, his brow furrowed with concern. "It's a dangerous game he's playing, no doubt. You must be worried, Mr Reid."

"Hardly." James scoffed, his lips curling in disdain. "Tom Ryan is a nuisance, nothing more. I've dealt with far greater threats than him before."

"Still, if the people rally behind him…" Mr Longbridge trailed off, leaving the implication hanging in the air.

"Then I'll have no choice but to teach them a lesson," James finished his sentence for him, his voice icy and resolute. "No one defies me and gets away with it."

As the evening wore on, James deftly navigated the web of politics and allegiances, planting seeds of doubt and suspicion among his guests. He knew that Tom Ryan's growing influence was a problem, but he also knew how to exploit the fears of those around him. The more they worried about Tom's intentions, the easier it would be for James to maintain control over the situation.

"Tell me, Mr Reid," said another guest, a lawyer by the name of Mr Hennessy, as they shared a glass of whisky in the corner of the room. "What do you plan to do about Tom Ryan?"

"Whatever is necessary," James replied, taking a slow sip of his drink. "He's a small fish in a very big pond, Mr Hennessy, and I've never been fond of sharing my territory."

"Nor should you be," Mr Hennessy agreed, nodding sagely. "A man like you shouldn't have to tolerate such insubordination."

"Indeed," James murmured, his mind already racing with plans and schemes to neutralise the threat that Tom posed to his dominion. It wouldn't be the first time he had crushed a rival beneath his heel, and he doubted it would be the last.

As the night drew to a close and the last of his guests departed, James stood on the balcony, his eyes fixed upon the distant glow of a solitary farmhouse. There, he knew, Tom Ryan was plotting and scheming even as he did the same.

But as the darkness closed in around him, James Reid felt no fear, and he would not rest until every last threat to his power had been snuffed out like the dying embers of a fire. He revelled in the knowledge of the strings he pulled, the lives he controlled, and the world that bent to his will. For James Reid was a master of manipulation, a man who understood the intricacies of power and control, and he would stop at nothing to protect his legacy and maintain his grip on the people of Dromdaire.

"*Ah*, there you are, Father," said his eldest son, Benjamin, entering the study and joining his father on the adjacent balcony with a casual arrogance that mirrored James's own. "Was your meeting successful?"

"Indeed," James replied, sipping his drink and savouring its warmth as it slid down his throat. "It seems our dear Mr Ryan is quite determined to challenge my authority." He set the glass down on the heavy oak desk next to the balcony, the sound echoing through the dimly lit room.

"Surely you can keep him in check?" Benjamin asked, a hint of doubt colouring his words.

"Of course," James assured him with a dismissive wave. "He may be ambitious, but he lacks the resources and connections to truly pose a threat."

As they spoke, footsteps approached, and the door opened to reveal James's wife, Sylvia. Her eyes scanned the room, immediately noticing the tension that hung in the air like a pall.

"James," she said softly, her voice laced with concern, "Is everything all right?"

"Nothing to worry about, my dear," he replied smoothly, his tone betraying none of the turbulence roiling beneath the surface. "Just discussing business."

"Very well." She hesitated for a moment before stepping closer, placing a hand on his arm. "But remember, there's more to life than power and control."

"Of course," James agreed, his words dripping with feigned sincerity as he placed a hand over hers, feeling the delicate bones beneath her skin.

"Sir." A voice called from the doorway, and he looked up to see his loyal servant, Edward, standing in the shadows. "I've received word that Mr Ryan is planning to meet again with several other local farmers tomorrow in the so-called Land League."

"Is that so?" James mused, his eyes narrowing as he contemplated this new development. "It appears our friend has grown bolder than I anticipated. We must ensure that his influence does not spread uncontrollably… Find me someone who can help me put an end to this… nuisance." His voice laced with disdain as he stared out the window at the gathering clouds.

"Certainly, sir," Edward replied, ever attentive, and nodded in affirmation, bowing respectfully before retreating from the room.

But before he could go, James added, "And make sure it's someone familiar with the law. I want this done legally, if possible. No need to dirty our hands if we don't have to."

"Very well, sir." With that, Edward retreated from the room, leaving James to brood over his plans.

As James Reid's wife and son filed out of his study one by one, each carried with them a sense of unease, the knowledge that their fate rested in the hands of a man driven by ruthless ambition. And as the black night deepened, it seemed as if darkness itself had taken root within James Reid's very soul.

***

James Reid, with hands clasped behind his back, stood tall on the steps of the courthouse in Dromdaire, his piercing eyes scanning the townspeople below him. This was his town, and anyone who met his gaze quickly lowered their eyes in deference.

Reid had not always been so imposing. As a child, he was slender and slight, often lost in the shadow of his broad-shouldered brothers. His father, a stern patriarch, had little patience for his youngest son's bookish nature. "No Reid man shirks his duties." He would thunder, sending the timid boy scurrying. And so, James Reid hardened himself, burying his sensitive soul beneath a shell of cold ambition. By the time his father passed, James had transformed himself into a cunning force, wielding power and influence beyond even his late father's imaginings.

Now, as Reid observed the scurrying townsfolk below, he allowed himself a thin smile. This was the life he had manifested through sheer will and relentless drive. The people here were his to command, the land his to own. And he would suffer no rival. A man like Tom Ryan, with his foolish notions, posed too great a threat. Reid's smile faded, his eyes narrowing. Ryan would learn his place soon enough.

With a swirl of his cloak, Reid descended the courthouse steps. The townsfolk shrank back as he passed, their shoulders hunched against the chill wind. But Reid stood tall, his presence absolute. He strode through the busy marketplace, the crowd parting before him like waves breaking upon a tall ship. Though he kept his eyes fixed ahead, he remained keenly aware of the hushed whispers and darting glances that followed in his wake.

As the day wore on, word spread quickly of James Reid's intentions to disrupt Tom Ryan's meeting in the town hall. The young upstart had become a thorn in Reid's side, stirring unrest among the tenants with his radical notions. Those who had hoped for a peaceful resolution between Reid and the local Land League branch realised that their wishes were about to be dashed upon the rocks.

When the time came, James arrived at the town hall accompanied by a solicitor named Mr Hargreaves. As the two men approached the gathered farmers, the weight of their presence seemed to suck the very air from the room.

Tom stood at the podium and watched Reid enter the hall, anger and frustration boiling up inside him. The man's arrogance was infuriating. Did he really think these people were just pawns to be manipulated and discarded at will? If Reid wouldn't listen to reason, there were other ways to fight back. He needed to rally the people, make them see that they didn't have to live under Reid's thumb.

Tom began to address the assembled farmers at the hall as he stared directly at Reid, who stood at the back of the hall defiantly. "James Reid cannot be allowed to intimidate us any longer! We must stand together, united against his unjust rule!"

The villagers murmured agreement, faces hardening with resolve. Here was the spark Tom had been hoping for.

If even a few brave souls united in defiance, it could catch fire and turn the tide against Reid's iron-fisted control.

Tom met each person's eyes in turn, "Change is never easy my friends, but if we do not act, our children will inherit only poverty and oppression. We owe it to them, and to ourselves, to fight for the just and free future we deserve!"

A rumble of assent rose from the crowd. Tom felt a fierce joy rising in his chest. If Reid thought he would back down easily, he was sorely mistaken. This was only the beginning. For the first time, he truly believed they could break Reid's stranglehold on this place.

"We'll start small but make no mistake, this is a fight we can win!" Tom continued. "We'll withhold a portion of our rents. His wealth and influence depend on our compliance!"

The villagers nodded, bolstered by Tom's words. He felt a swell of pride for these people who had suffered too long.

"It will get worse before it gets better. Reid will retaliate with force and cunning. We must stand resolute!"

Tom met the eyes of the tenant farmers. He saw their fear but also courage. They were ready.

"Stick together and do not waver. Our day of liberation is at hand!" Tom raised his fist and the crowd followed suit, voices joining in a defiant cheer.

When the cheering died down, there was a slow handclap from the back of the hall. The crowd turned to look. "Well, if it isn't our champion of the people," James Reid said, his voice dripping scorn. "Rousing more rebellion, I presume?"

"Just speaking the truth, Mr Reid," Tom replied.

"You've been spreading lies about me," Reid hissed, eyes glinting with malice. "Trying to turn my people against me. A very unwise move, Mr Ryan."

"The only lies here are the ones coming out of your mouth," Tom shot back. He was aware of the crowd gathering around them, of the hard glares and clenched fists. "You've bled this county dry for long enough. It's time for new leadership."

"I understand you've been making quite an impact on the community with your innovative farming ideas."

"I've been fortunate to have some success with my methods."

"Indeed, it seems you've caught the attention of many in Dromdaire," Reid said, "some might say you're becoming a threat to the established order."

"Threat?" Tom's eyebrows raised, his pulse quickening at the implication. " I'm simply telling these men their rights, as free citizens. Rights you seem intent on denying. I'm trying to improve the lives of those who work the land, not undermine anyone."

Reid stepped closer, emphasising the disparity in their heights. "Rights? The only right that matters here is mine, to collect the rent owed to me as landowner. Those who question that right will find their leases terminated."

A vein throbbed at Reid's temple, rage twisting his features. "Bold words. But you have no idea, the forces you're dealing with." His gaze slid to the villagers. "Turn against me, and you will all suffer the consequences."

The tenant farmers shrank back, exchanging anxious glances. Reid smiled coldly. "Run along now. And think carefully on where your best interests lie."

As the chastened men hurried away, Reid gripped Tom's shoulder. "As for you, Mr Ryan, take care your foolish crusade does not carry you someplace you'll regret. You see, Tom." Reid leaned closer, his eyes cold and calculating. "There's a delicate balance that must be maintained in this world, and when one person gains too much influence or power, it upsets that equilibrium."

"Are you suggesting I should cease my efforts?" Tom challenged, anger simmering beneath the surface, his hands clenching into fists.

"Cease? No, no." Reid laughed, raising his glass to his lips. "But perhaps consider the ramifications of your actions. For every farm that flourishes under your guidance, another may falter and the people of Dromdaire may begin to question the competence of their landlords."

"Perhaps they should," Tom retorted before he could stop himself. "If there's a better way to provide for our families, shouldn't we pursue it?"

"Bold words, Mr Ryan," James replied, his tone icy, not betraying the fury that smouldered beneath his polished exterior. "But heed my warning: do not mistake ambition for wisdom. There are consequences for challenging the status quo."

With that, he released Ryan, satisfied at having put the impudent whelp in his place. But inwardly, his thoughts churned like the dark sea.

"Mr Ryan," Reid continued, his tone dripping with

false cordiality. "It seems you've been busy discussing matters that concern my land. Would you care to share your… innovative ideas?"

"Reid," Tom replied, his voice steady despite the knot of anger tightening in his chest. "These ideas are for the good of the community. They'll help us all."

"Is that so?" Reid countered, feigning curiosity. "Well, we wouldn't want to stand in the way of progress, would we? Mr Hargreaves, would you be so kind as to review these… proposals?"

"Certainly, Mr Reid," Hargreaves said as he opened a black leather satchel and placed documents on a table next to the podium. As he poured over the documents, it was clear that he had been carefully chosen by Reid for his ability to twist the law to suit his master's desires. With each passing minute, the solicitor found a new and seemingly insurmountable legal obstacle to place in Tom's path.

"Mr Ryan," Hargreaves finally declared, "I regret to inform you that your plans are in direct violation of several land use regulations and contractual agreements. I fear that if you proceed with these methods, you and your fellow farmers will face severe legal consequences."

"That is ridiculous, the British government supports this plan for tenants to buy out their land. Gladstone himself has stated this," Tom pointed out.

"It is only a proposal by Gladstone, it will not pass the House of Commons and most certainly not the House of Lords," Hargreaves replied as he peered over the top of his spectacles at Tom.

"In fact, there appears to be a legal problem with your land, sir. The land you inherited from your uncle?"

"There is no problem with my land, I own it, fair and square," Tom said confidently.

"Indeed, there is a problem, Mr Ryan. A major problem. A discrepancy in the deeds. It appears that a portion of your land actually belongs to Mr Reid," Hargreaves explained, his voice tinged with delight.

"Thank you, Mr Hargreaves," Reid interrupted. "Now, Mr Ryan, I have a choice, I could be very selfish and send you a letter of eviction, or I could be generous and buy your farm off you for its correct market value."

"This is a farce, there is no problem with the deeds. I will get my solicitor. Mr O'Connell in Killarney to verify that. There is no way you are getting my land," Tom said as he thumped the podium.

"Mr Ryan, I was in contact with your solicitor Mr O' Connell, it was him who discovered that Mr Reid owns part of your farm," Hargreaves injected.

"After you bribed him probably," Tom said.

"Take your time, think about my offer. You can have the payment as soon as you wish, and you can go back to New York, where you belong, or I can have the RIC drag you kicking and screaming from your little house before they demolish it. Mr Ryan, I hope you'll see reason and accept my proposal," Reid said with a satisfied smile as he turned to leave the hall with Hargreaves behind him. As the door closed behind the two men, Tom clenched his fists, struggling to contain his rage. He knew that James Reid had orchestrated this outcome, manipulating the law and the people around him to maintain his stranglehold on the land and its inhabitants.

As Tom was about to leave the hall. He saw a number of large men approaching up the central aisle of the hall, Reid's men no doubt. He felt no fear, only steely determination. The time for submission was over. He recognized Burke, Reid's cruel enforcer, flanked by his usual gang of brutes. They must have caught wind of the villagers' meeting.

Tom stepped forward, he would not let these bullies intimidate him, not today.

"Evening, gents. Lovely evening for a stroll, isn't it?" Tom kept his tone light, belying the tension thrumming through him.

"Save it, Ryan. We got word you're stirring up trouble, putting ideas in people's heads," Burke growled. His beady eyes glared at the villagers.

"Just having a friendly chat with my neighbours. No law against that, last I checked."

"There don't need to be a law. Mr Reid don't take kindly to rabble-rousers and rebels on his land." Burke cracked his knuckles menacingly.

"Reid doesn't own these people. They got a right to speak their minds and I aim to protect that right."

Burke laughed derisively. "Still clinging to those American notions of freedom and justice. This here is Reid's area, and his word is law."

Ryan met Burke's sneer with steely resolve, "The law says no man can own another. These people's liberty has been denied too long under Reid's boot. That ends today."

Burke's expression darkened; any pretence of civility gone. He reached for the billy club at his hip.

"It's time you learn your place, boy."

Tom braced himself as the other men fanned out, cutting off any escape. He had known this confrontation was inevitable. Reid would not loosen his grip easily. But Tom was ready to fight for the spark of defiance and hope he had ignited in the villagers. For freedom, no price was too high. Ryan held his ground as Burke and the men closed in. He knew the odds were against him, but he refused to back down.

"This is your last warning. Leave now, or you'll be leaving on a stretcher," Burke growled.

Tom stood tall, "I don't scare easy. You want me gone, you're gonna have to drag me out."

Burke swung his club at Tom's head. Tom ducked and delivered a hard punch to Burke's gut. As the man doubled over, Ryan grabbed the club from his hand.

The other men rushed at Tom. He swung the club in a wide arc, catching one across the jaw. Another tackled Tom from behind, knocking him to the ground. Tom scrambled up and smashed his elbow into the man's face.

More men piled on, raining blows down on Tom. He fought like a man possessed, every hit fuelling his fury. But he was outnumbered. A heavy boot caught him in the ribs, knocking the wind from his lungs.

As Tom struggled for breath, Burke loomed over him. Blood dripped from a gash on the enforcer's brow. His eyes blazed with contempt.

"You just signed your death warrant, boy," he spat.

"Reid is going to bury you."

Tom glared up defiantly as two men hauled him to his feet. "Do your worst. I won't stop fighting till the people here are free."

Burke backhanded Tom hard across the face. Tom tasted blood but kept his feet under him.

"We'll see how long that fighting spirit of yours lasts in prison. He's got ways of breaking men like you." Burke sneered as he picked up his hat and wiped the blood from his face. "This is just a warning, take Mr Reid's offer or you will suffer the consequences."

"Tell your boss I'm going nowhere," Tom responded.

***

Later that Night

James Reid sat at his desk, ledger open before him, though he paid it no mind. His thoughts were focused solely on Tom Ryan and how the impudent young man had dared to challenge his authority. Reid would need to make an example of him, show the people what happened to those who opposed his rule. Ryan remained a problem to be dealt with, and soon, permanently. "Let this be a lesson to all who dare defy me," James whispered into the dark, "this land is mine, and I will not tolerate dissent."

Perhaps a public flogging? No, too risky it could stoke the embers of rebellion. Better to break Ryan's spirit in private, make him recant his treasonous words before the magistrate. Reid would see to it personally that the young idealist left his prison a humbled, compliant shell of a man.

The wind rattled the glass in the window behind him as if attempting to pry its way into the room, but he remained unyielding in his vigilance. Reid's study was dark, the heavy velvet curtains drawn. Shadows flickered across the walls from the fire crackling in the marble hearth. It was a room meant to intimidate, from the claw-footed antique furnishings to the mounted stag heads gazing blankly from the walls.

As dawn approached, James continued to pace his study, the thrill of impending triumph coursing through his veins like a powerful elixir. He imagined Tom Ryan's face, his pathetic dreams of independence crumbling around him. The first light of day began to seep through the heavy curtains, shining across the opulent furnishings of his study. But for James Reid, the darkness within was far more potent than the feeble light that struggled to penetrate it. His ambition, his lust for power, drove him ever forward, consuming everything in its path like the relentless tide. And as the sun finally broke free of the horizon, painting the world in hues of gold and crimson, one thing remained certain: there would be no stopping James Reid in his quest for absolute control.

A knock interrupted Reid's thought. "Enter," he called out impatiently.

His butler, Edward, appeared, face grim. "Sir, there's been an... incident at the old mill."

Reid's eyes narrowed. "Go on."

"A group of tenants have seized control of it, sir. They're refusing to work, demanding lower rents and better conditions."

Reid surged to his feet, face mottling with rage. "Who is responsible for this?" he thundered.

Edward shrank back. "W-we're still investigating, sir."

Reid swept past Edward; jaw clenched. He would root out and destroy whoever was behind this insurrection. Tom Ryan's rebellion would be crushed before it ever gained momentum.

He strode through the manor halls, servants scrambling out of his path. Dark fury roiled inside him as he mentally catalogued the punishments he would inflict. Death was too kind for these traitorous dogs. He would see them stripped, their bare backs flogged bloody, and left to rot in irons. Their seditious tongues would be ripped from their mouths. No mercy would be shown to those who dared challenge his authority.

At the front entrance, his carriage awaited. Reid barked orders to the driver as he stepped inside. With a snap of the reins, the horses surged forward, the carriage wheels clattering over the cobblestones. Reid's hands clenched around his cane as he gazed out the window at the passing countryside. His lands, his people. And some had forgotten their place. He would remind them.

The carriage turned onto a muddy road leading to the old mill. Up ahead, Reid spotted a ragtag group of peasants, armed with scythes and pitchforks. One caught sight of the carriage and shouted. The mob turned as one, brandishing their makeshift weapons.

Reid's lip curled in contempt. He rapped his cane

against the carriage roof. "Stop here."

As the carriage rolled to a halt, Reid thrust open the door. He stepped out slowly, surveying the crowd with a menacing glare. Fear rippled through their ranks and tools wavered in uncertain hands.

Reid's voice lashed out like a whip, "Return to your duties, now, and I may be merciful. Defy me further at your peril."

The mob hesitated, exchanging uneasy glances. Reid's fingers tightened around his cane. If they did not submit, he would teach them the meaning of suffering.

"What is it to be?" Reid demanded, "I know all of you, I know your homes, your wives, your mothers, your children. Do you want to end up in the workhouse or worse, starve or freeze to death in a cold, wet ditch?"

Slowly the mob began to disperse until only two men were left.

"The two brave ringleaders, I presume." Reid laughed mockingly. "Sean McMahon and Dermot Walsh, consider yourselves and your families evicted. At least it is summertime, gentlemen, fine weather to sleep along the roads. Go home and gather what you can from your cottages; they will both be rubble by noon."

Chapter 13: Predators and Prey
August 16th, The Ryan Farm

Tom awoke to an eerie silence. Usually, the farm was alive with the sounds of cattle, chickens clucking, and horses nickering in their stalls. But this morning, all was quiet. With a sense of dread, he trudged through the early morning dew, the weight of his boots sinking into the damp soil. The scent of freshly turned earth mingled with the faintest hint of decay. As he approached the grazing field, a sudden unease settled in his gut. "Something's not right," he muttered, scanning the pasture for signs of his cattle. A chill ran down his spine as he spotted a gruesome scene, the first carcass, its once-glossy hide now marred with ugly gashes and dark, congealing blood. Close by, two other cows lay dead in the field, and their calves with bellies slit open and entrails strewn about. Blood soaked into the grass, already attracting flies. His chest tightened at the sight, bile rising in his throat.

"Dear God," he whispered, horror etching itself onto his face as he hurried toward the fallen creatures. There was no doubt in Tom's mind that Reid was behind this monstrous act.

He harnessed his strongest horse to the waggon and began the grim task of loading the carcasses of the calves onto it. Once finished, he set off for town, jaw clenched in quiet fury. Every bump and jolt along the road stoked the fires of his rage. By the time he arrived, his knuckles were white around the reins.

Tom marched straight through the village, paying no heed to the startled looks of any passersby. At the RIC barracks, he banged a fist on the door and demanded to see the sergeant.

The sergeant emerged, blinking in surprise. "What's all the racket for?" His eyes fell upon the waggon and its gruesome cargo, and he blanched. "Jesus, Mary and Joseph…"

"I want to report a crime," Tom said tightly, "five of my cattle were slaughtered last night."

The sergeant scratched his head. "Well, now… that's terrible. But we've had some trouble with wild dogs in the area. I reckon that's what did your cattle in."

"That's a lie and you know it," Tom snapped. "James Reid and his men are behind this. I won't stay silent while he terrorises me and destroys my livelihood."

The sergeant shifted, refusing to meet his eyes. "Mr Ryan… it's best not to make such wild accusations, you have no proof. Mr Reid is a respectable man. He is no criminal, now be on your way."

"So, you are not going to look into this crime, no investigation?" Tom said, bewildered.

"I told you it was wild dogs," the sergeant responded firmly.

"Their stomachs were sliced open with a blade, its clearly not the work of dogs," Tom said, pointing at the carcasses.

"Don't waste any more of my time, off you go back to your farm," the sergeant said as he turned to go back into the RIC barracks.

"I should have known better than waste my time coming here. James Reid has you all on a leash," Tom shouted.

"Off with you now, Ryan, if you know what's good for you," the sergeant replied as he shook his fist.

In frustration, Tom mounted his waggon and then had second thoughts as he looked over at Stack's tavern. Tom hadn't drunk much since he left New York, but today he needed a whisky. He pushed open the heavy wooden door, taking in the familiar scent of spilt ale and pipe smoke. Conversations and laughter filled the dimly lit room.

"*Ah*, Tom!" Patrick, the tavern's owner called out, wiping down a pint glass with a well-worn rag. "Haven't seen you 'round here for a spell."

"It is one day I need a whisky or two," Tom replied, his voice heavy with resolve.

"Is there anything wrong, you look troubled," Partick observed.

Tom took a deep breath, gathering his thoughts before sharing his story. "James Reid's men destroyed my fences, trampled my crops," Tom said, his voice ringing with conviction. "Killed my cattle." The words flowed from him like water from a broken dam. As he spoke, his gaze met that of each customer at the bar, some nodding sympathetically, while others shifted uncomfortably in their seats.

"James Reid is a snake," Tom concluded, slamming

his fist against the scarred wooden counter. "And if we don't stand up to him, he'll continue to slither his way through our lives, poisoning everything he touches."

"Tom," Patrick said slowly, his brow creased with concern as he leaned forward, closer to Tom. "James Reid is a powerful man. You can't just go around accusing him without proof. It's too dangerous."

"Then what am I supposed to do?" Tom demanded, frustration seething in his chest. "Just stand by while he tries to drive me off my land. To ruin me?"

"Easy, lad," an elderly man next to Tom interjected, his gnarled hand gripping Tom's shoulder. "We're not sayin' we don't believe you, but there are families here who depend on Reid's favour for their livin'. It's not a simple matter."

"Every one of us has a stake in this," Tom insisted, getting braver as he drank more whisky. "If he can do this to me, he can do it to any one of you. He's a monster, and you're all too cowardly to stand up to him!" Tom roared, eyes blazing. "Mark my words, I will see justice done. If none of you have the spine to help, I'll handle Reid myself."

***

As Tom left the pub that evening, he was disappointed that nobody had offered to help him, but he understood the precarious position they were all in, caught between loyalty and fear. He climbed onto the waggon, turning toward home. The fields whipped past in a blur as a plan took shape in his mind. Reid wanted a war. He would give him one.

The wind whispered once more, carrying with it the promise of a storm yet to come. As Tom turned towards home, the first raindrops began to fall upon the parched earth.

That night, Tom kept watch over his farm, he knew Reid would send one of his hired thugs again. Under the hazy gaze of a moon partially hidden by clouds, he crouched behind the weathered stone wall that marked the edge of his property. The restless wind tugged at his coat. Shadows stretched across the land, concealing both predator and prey in their embrace.

"Tonight," he murmured to himself, fingers tightening around his rifle. "I'll catch them in the act and expose Reid for the bastard he is."

As the hours wore on, patience grew thin, and doubt began to gnaw at the edges of his resolve. He shook his head, banishing the creeping thoughts, and focused on the task at hand. It was then that he heard it, the soft crunch of boots on soil, punctuating the stillness of the night.

Tom's muscles tensed as he watched the shadowy figure approach, the thug's steps deliberate and careful. The figure crept across the field under cover of darkness. Tom gripped his rifle tight, following the silhouette. The man paused, glancing around before reaching into his pocket and producing a knife. With practiced ease, he set to work, slashing at the ropes that held the fence together, making his way toward the cattle pen.

"Got you now," Tom whispered, springing from his

hiding place like a lion pouncing upon its quarry.

Tom fired a warning shot, kicking up dirt at the man's feet. "Turn around slowly." The man froze, then did as he was told. As Tom emerged, rifle trained on his captive. He grabbed the thug's wrist, twisting it until the knife clattered to the ground. The man's face contorted in pain, his eyes wide with shock.

"Who sent you?" Tom demanded, his voice a low growl. "Tell me!"

"Reid! It was James Reid!" The man gasped, fear lending truth to his words.

"Of course it was." Tom's grip tightened further, anger blazing in his chest. "Did he order you to destroy my livelihood? To kill my cattle?"

"Y-yes! He wanted to force you to sell your land to him," the thug stammered.

"Those figures," Tom spat, disgust mingling with his rage. "And what if I were to turn you over to the police? Would that put an end to Reid's schemes?"

"*Ha*! Don't make me laugh." The man sneered, a twisted grin distorting his features. "Reid controls the RIC around here. He's the local magistrate. They'll never touch him. You really think they'll do anything to Reid? He owns them, just like he owns everything else in this country."

Tom's finger tightened on the trigger, rage boiling up inside him. He knew the man spoke the truth, there would be no justice to be found here. Not while Reid still clung to power. He was going to have to take matters into his own hands.

"Damn it," Tom mumbled, his heart sinking as the reality of his situation closed in around him. He released the thug, shoving him away with enough force to send him sprawling onto the dirt. "Get off my land and if I ever see you or any of Reid's men here again, I won't be so merciful."

"Ryan," he spat, "Reid's gonna have your head for this."

"We'll see about that," Tom said grimly.

The thug scrambled to his feet and fled, disappearing into the darkness from which he had emerged. Tom stood alone amidst the wreckage of his once-thriving farm, the weight of his predicament settling upon his shoulders like a shroud.

***

Fury burned within him as Tom stormed up the path to Reid's manor in the early morning light, his hands balled into fists at his sides. The grandiose estate loomed before him, its opulent facade a stark contrast to the devastation it housed within. He steeled himself, raising a fist to pound on the door.

"Reid!" Tom roared as the heavy oak swung open, his voice cutting through the crisp morning air. "You've gone too far this time!"

"*Ah*, Mr Ryan." Reid drawled, a cruel smile playing at the corners of his mouth. "To what do I owe this… unexpected visit?"

"Cut the act, Reid," Tom said through gritted teeth.

"Your men killed my cattle. You think you can scare me into selling?"

"Mr Ryan, you wound me with your baseless accusations," Reid replied, feigning innocence as he leaned casually against the doorframe. "I haven't the faintest idea what you're talking about. They must have been killed by wild dogs or a fox, perhaps."

"Wild animals don't slit throats and leave carcasses as warnings, Reid," Tom challenged, his eyes blazing with a rage. "You may control the law in this town, but I won't stand for this."

"Your determination is admirable, if misguided," Reid replied coolly. "But I assure you, I had nothing to do with the unfortunate demise of your livestock."

"Damn you, Reid!" Tom shouted, his voice cracking under the weight of his anger.

"Choose your words carefully, Mr Ryan," Reid warned, icicles dripping from his tone. "You tread on very dangerous ground."

"Whatever it takes, I will expose you for the monster you are," Tom vowed, his resolve unwavering despite the menace that hung in the air.

"Good morning, Mr Ryan," Reid said dismissively, turning his back on Tom as he retreated into the darkness of his manor.

As Tom stood there, staring at the closed door, he knew he faced an uphill battle. But he also knew that he couldn't afford to back down. His farm, his livelihood, and the future he envisioned with Cathleen depended on it.

Chapter 14: A Fire in the Darkness
August 20th, The Road from Dromdaire

The rain fell in sheets across the muddy road as Tom guided the horse and waggon home. The rain pelted the flat brim of Tom's hat, streaming down the sides and obscuring his vision. He squinted as he guided the horse forward, the waggon wheels churning through the mud. As the unyielding grey curtain of rain continued to fall. He spotted a lone and hunched figure trudging along, shoulders and head bent against the downpour. The man's-soaked clothing clung to him, and with each step, his boots sank into the mire.

Tom pulled up alongside the man. "Where are you headed in this mess?" The rain muffling his voice. "You need a lift?"

The stranger looked up, rain streaming down his gaunt and weathered face. His eyes, weary from exhaustion, met Tom's. His clothes were threadbare and his boots near worn through.

"Climb aboard, I can bring you a few miles on your journey," Tom said.

After a moment, he nodded gratefully and climbed onto the waggon, the wood creaking beneath his weight. The man's eyes lit with gratitude. "Bless you for the kindness. Thank you, sir," he said.

"Where are you going to on such a rotten day?" Tom

inquired.

"I'm Liam O'Sullivan," the man introduced himself, extending a hand. "I'm a labourer, looking for work. I'll walk as far as I need to find it."

"Tom Ryan," he replied, clasping Liam's hand firmly. "I could use some help on my farm. I've some repairs to do, can't pay much, but I can offer you food and a bed for a few days."

"Thank you kindly," Liam said, his voice rough like gravel. "I appreciate it."

They rode in silence until the waggon passed through the gates of Tom's farm. Liam took in the modest house and outbuildings with keen interest. Tom extended his earlier offer, "I can't pay much, but you'll have food and a roof."

Liam nodded. "That's all I need."

A few days later, under a sky still bruised from the recent storm, Tom and Liam worked side by side to rebuild the damaged shed on the farm. Their movements were synchronised, a silent dance reflecting their mutual understanding and shared determination. As they hammered nails and sawed wood, Liam's resourcefulness became apparent. Liam attacked each task with restless energy, devising clever fixes with the rusted tools at hand. His hands bore the calloused legacy of hard years, but his grit never wavered. He suggested innovative solutions to fix the shed, impressing Tom with his skills.

"Try fixing the crossbeam at an angle like this," Liam said, demonstrating his idea with a piece of wood. "It'll give the roof more support."

"Smart thinking," Tom agreed. Together, they worked in harmony, their muscles aching as the shed slowly took shape again.

Tom was impressed by the man's ingenuity. "You've got some clever solutions. I can see you've done this kind of work before."

Liam drove a nail into the new framing with a resounding bang. "*Aye,* you learned a few tricks when you've nothing but your hands and wits to get by."

"Your hands have seen plenty of work," Tom commented.

"*Aye,*" Liam replied, pausing briefly to wipe the sweat from his brow. "But it's honest work, and that's all I can ask for."

As Liam expertly notched a wooden beam with his saw, Tom couldn't help but admire the man's resilience.

Liam hummed an old Irish ballad as he sawed planks of wood. The tune conjured images in Tom's mind of misty glens and stout-hearted rebels. When Liam reached the chorus, Tom surprised him by joining in. The men's voices rose and fell in unison. When the song ended, they laughed together.

"You've got a good voice on you," Liam remarked.

"As do you," Tom replied, "my father used to sing that very tune while he worked. Hearing it reminds me of him. Those old songs are the best."

Liam nodded solemnly. "The old songs connect us to those gone before."

They soon had the shed patched up and sturdy. Tom studied his new farmhand, curiosity kindled. What had set this fellow on such a hard road? He hoped in time Liam might share his story. For now, Tom was thankful for the company and for his help.

The farm itself seemed to come alive again under their joined efforts. The scent of freshly cut wood filled the air, mingling with the earthy aroma of the fields. Birds flitted about in the nearby trees, their songs adding a melodic harmony to the rhythmic sounds of hammers striking nails and saws cutting through timber. For a while, Tom forgot about the last few weeks and the threat of James Reid.

***

That evening, after a shared meal of hearty stew and crusty bread, Tom and Liam sat on wooden stools by the glowing hearth as darkness fell outside.

"Did I ever tell you about the time I was caught in a storm on the Atlantic?" Tom asked.

Liam looked up from the fire, curiosity flickering in his eyes. "No, I don't believe you have."

Tom chuckled, the memories flooding back as he began to recount the tale. "It was during my voyage back from America. The waves were monstrous, crashing against the ship like giants. I remember gripping the railing, my knuckles white with fear, praying that we'd make it through the night."

"Sounds terrifying," Liam said, sharing a grin with Tom. "But here you are, still standing strong. You've seen your share of hardships, haven't you?"

"More than I care to admit," Tom replied, his voice

tinged with both pride and sorrow.

"Well, we all go through tough times," Liam said as he stared into the fire.

"Your help has been invaluable these past few days, Liam," Tom began, his voice warm with gratitude. "But I can't help but wonder what brought you to this place. You've got something in you that tells me there's more to your story."

Liam continued to look into the flames for a moment as if gathering his thoughts, the dancing light partially illuminated his face, the wrinkles etched by years of struggle. Then, with a deep breath, he began to share his tale.

"When I was a lad in Tipperary, myself and my father, God rest him, tried to stop English soldiers from evicting a family into the snow on a Christmas Eve, casting them from the only home they knew. They all froze to death that Christmas, every single one of them, mother, father, grandmother and five children." Liam's voice took on a fervent tone.

"A week later our father was taken from us—" His voice faltered, the pain still fresh in his heart.

"Taken?" Tom echoed, concern furrowing his brow.

"Arrested by the Peelers," Liam clarified, his jaw shaking. "Because he had fought against the British soldiers during that terrible eviction. He was accused of being a rebel. I never saw him again; I don't know what happened to him. They must have killed him. We never found his body. I was only fourteen."

The two men fell silent, the weight of the story settling

heavily upon their shoulders.

"I swore vengeance that day. I became involved with the Fenians, Tom. The Fenians gave me a chance to fight back."

As Liam spoke of his experiences with the brotherhood, his words rang with passion and conviction. He recounted daring acts of fighting, clandestine meetings under the cover of darkness, and the injustices he'd witnessed at the hands of the oppressors. Each word seemed to resonate within Tom, stirring something deep inside him.

"Over the years," Liam continued, "we've engaged in various forms of resistance. We've sabotaged British infrastructure, smuggled arms from abroad, and provided support to our people who suffer under their rule." He paused, gauging Tom's reaction, before adding, "…We've also infiltrated their ranks, gathering intelligence crucial to our cause. Another time, our brothers in America launched a series of raids into British Canada, hoping to draw the attention of the empire away from Ireland. The raids were a thorn in the side of the British, and they demonstrated our willingness to fight, even on foreign soil."

Tom silently listened with interest.

"Many have suffered greatly for the cause," Liam said, his eyes shining with fierce determination. "But we cannot let their sacrifices be in vain. Ireland deserves to be free, and I am willing to fight until my last breath to make it so."

Tom listened intently, his mind racing with the implications of Liam's revelations.

"Your dedication to the cause is admirable, Liam," Tom said, his voice heavy with emotion. "But I must ask, are you not afraid of the consequences? Of the danger you're putting yourself in?"

"Of course, I've known fear," Liam replied, looking Tom straight in the eye. "But it's a small price to pay for the chance at a better future for our people. I will gladly face any danger if it means seeing Ireland free."

As Tom mulled over Liam's words, he couldn't help but feel a growing sense of admiration for the man and his unwavering dedication to the Fenian cause.

Liam stared into the flickering flames, his expression turning grim. "I've been moving from place to place for years. The redcoats are always on my tail."

"Your courage is inspiring, Liam," Tom said solemnly, his eyes reflecting the fire's glow. "Yours is a dangerous road, and I cannot fault your loyalty to Ireland."

Liam looked up, his eyes blazing. "We won't rest until Ireland is free. No matter the cost, I'll keep fighting for independence, even if it means my death."

Tom was taken aback by the intensity of Liam's conviction. This was no idle dream but a sacred vow that anchored the man's very being. Tom had never yearned for a cause with such fiery devotion. He envied the clarity of purpose it gave Liam, even as he feared where it might lead him.

Liam nodded, the firelight carving deep shadows across his weathered face. "Mark my words, one day we'll drive the English from this land. And when Ireland is free, it will have been worth any sacrifice," Liam hesitated, weighing his words carefully. "I've seen what violence can do, Tom. I've lost friends and family to it, just like you have. But sometimes… sometimes, I can't help but think that it's the only language our oppressors understand. One thing is certain – we cannot stand idly by while our people suffer. We must act, and if that means taking up arms, then so be it."

The two men sat in companionable silence, each lost in his own thoughts as the fire crackled and danced before them. The weight of history and the desire for a brighter future hung heavy in the air between them, binding them together in ways they were only just beginning to understand.

Chapter 15: Winter is on Its Way
October 30th

As the weeks and months passed and summer gently slipped away to be replaced by the golden leaves of autumn, Tom and Liam continued working together, their friendship growing stronger as they worked the farm fields together. And even though clouds still loomed overhead, the warmth of camaraderie between them seemed to bring a little light in the darker months of the year's end.

Tom marvelled at how Liam's expertise made swift work of rebuilding a stone wall that had been knocked by yet another attempt by Reid and his hired thugs to sabotage the farm. The man was clearly no stranger to hard graft.

Liam's hands moved with precision and strength as he lifted and placed heavy stones, fitting them together perfectly, carefully filling in the gaps with smaller rocks to create a sturdy wall, weaving a structure from crumbling pieces of stone. His body seemed to flow seamlessly with the task, his skilled movements almost graceful. Despite the weight and size of the stones, Liam made it look effortless. His muscles flexed with each lift. As the wall rose higher and higher, it was clear that his expertise was truly admirable. Sweat glistened on his brow, but he didn't seem to tire at all. The result was a strong and sturdy stone wall, standing tall and proud, as if it could withstand any force thrown its way. It was clear that Liam's years of experience were evident in the work he was doing.

"Thank you, Liam," Tom said, his voice barely audible above the strong wind blowing through the almost bare branches. "For helping me out over the last number of months, I'm sorry that I haven't been able to reward you better financially."

"No need to thank me, Tom, it's been a pleasure. You kept me well fed and provided me with a warm a dry room to sleep in. For that I am very grateful."

"Well, I still feel I should repay you for all your hard work, Liam. When I sell some of the cattle next month, I will pay you, I promise."

"As I said, there is no need of payment, you have been more than good to me, my friend… well, there is one thing you could do for me."

Tom nodded, his brow furrowing as he anticipated the favour Liam would request.

"Tom," Liam began, his voice hesitant yet determined. "I've been thinking. You've been a good friend to me, and I can't thank you enough for giving me a place to stay and work. But there's something else I have to ask of you. Something for you to consider," Liam took a deep breath. "I want you to join the Fenian Brotherhood with me."

Tom stiffened, alarm rising within him. The Fenians were hunted by the authorities. If he joined, everything he'd built here could be destroyed.

"I can't, Liam," he said quietly, "it's too dangerous. I could lose the farm."

"Tom, think about it," Liam urged. "The Fenians fight for the people, for the land, for freedom. That's worth more than any one person or farm. And who's to say the RIC or Redcoats they won't come for you eventually? James Reid will stop at nothing to control this farm." Liam's eyes blazed. "Our people have suffered too long under British oppression! You know their cruelty better than most. Will you not stand with your own?"

Tom stiffened, his heart pounding as he weighed the risks and consequences of such a decision. It was true that he loathed James Reid, and the prospect of revenge had a certain allure. But joining the Fenians meant putting not only his life but also Cathleen's at risk. The thought of losing everything he'd worked so hard for filled him with dread.

"Revenge on James Reid is tempting, Liam," Tom admitted, his voice laced with uncertainty. "But I have responsibilities here – to my farm, to Cathleen. I can't just walk away from them."

Tom's thoughts swirled like a tempest, duty and self-preservation pulling him in opposite directions. He knew Liam was right – James Reid would never rest until he had absolute power. And yet, joining the Fenians meant embracing a life of danger and uncertainty.

"Tom," Liam said, his gaze never wavering from Tom's face. "I know you have the heart and the courage to fight for our people. Your experiences in the American Civil War – they've made you stronger, more resilient. We could use a brave heart like you with your military experience."

As Liam continued, Tom felt a spark of recognition within him. The same determination that had carried him through countless battles now surged through his veins once more. He began to see how his past struggles could serve this new purpose, a purpose that resonated deeply with the core of who he was.

"Your skills as a soldier, your resourcefulness under pressure… these are invaluable assets to the Fenians," Liam insisted, gripping Tom's arm tightly. "We need men like you, Tom. Men who will stand tall against the enemy, who will not be swayed or broken by the hardships they must endure."

Tom paused for a moment, allowing the weight of Liam's words to sink in. He felt the familiar stirrings of patriotism and longing for a better future take root within him.

"Tell me, Liam," Tom said, leaning forward. "What have the Fenians actually done to bring about this dream of an independent Ireland?"

Liam's eyes ignited with a zealous fire as he recounted tales of past Fenian actions. "One of our most daring acts was the raid on Chester Castle. A group of determined Fenians infiltrated the castle and stole a stack of rifles, right under the noses of the British garrison. They managed to transport the arms back to Ireland, where they were used to bolster our ranks and strengthen our resolve."

Tom admired the audacity of the raid, the bravery of those who had risked everything for the cause. As Liam spoke, Tom was transported to the battlefields of his past, his days in the Civil War. He recalled the camaraderie among the soldiers, the shared purpose that bound them together.

"Every day, Tom, Fenians work tirelessly behind the scenes, organising, planning, and preparing for the moment when we can finally strike back and reclaim our land. We smuggle arms, train our people in the ways of war, and gather intelligence on the movements of our enemies."

Tom sat next to Liam, perched on the stone wall, listening with growing interest. He considered the commitment and courage of those men and women, who risked so much for a cause greater than themselves. He recalled his own struggles and sacrifices, and a fire ignited within him, a burning desire to stand alongside the Fenians, to contribute his strengths to the fight for Irish freedom.

"Tom," Liam said, passion burning in his voice. "The Fenians seek not only to free Ireland from British rule but also to create a republic where all citizens have a say in their own governance. A nation where our people can live without fear or oppression, where they can cultivate their land, preserve their culture, and raise their children in peace. I know that you are heavily involved in the local Land League branch. I have heard you are a powerful speaker. But words can only get you so far. The only thing the damn British recognise is physical force. The Fenians are willing to lay down their lives for Ireland, to fight until their last breath if need be," his eyes glistened with a mix of admiration and sorrow. "Many have already done so."

Tom stared at Liam, the intensity of his gaze bore into

Liam like a chisel carving at stone, focusing on Liam's words as if they were lifelines thrown to him in a turbulent sea. He imagined the danger those Fenian men faced daily, the risk of capture, torture, or worse, yet they persevered, driven by a fierce loyalty to their homeland and an unquenchable thirst for freedom. He felt the burden of responsibility settle upon his shoulders. The weight was heavy but familiar, a load he had carried before. In the depths of his mind, memories stirred, memories of comrades lost, battles won and lost, and the relentless pursuit of a cause that had once consumed him. Tom's heart pounded with adrenaline and uncertainty. He had fought in the Civil War, seen first-hand the devastation wrought by war. But he also knew what it meant to stand up for one's beliefs, to defend those who could not defend themselves.

"Let me think about it, Liam," Tom said finally, his voice strained with the weight of his decision. "Thank you for sharing your passion with me. I am truly honoured to be asked, and I promise you, I will consider your offer seriously. I just need time to think about it."

"I understand," Liam replied, clapping a hand on Tom's shoulder. "Just remember, Tom, our fight is for the greater good. For an Ireland free from tyrants like James Reid."

Liam's grip on Tom's arm loosened, and he leaned back, his expression a mix of relief and gratitude. "Take your time, Tom. Reflect, and when you're ready, you let me know."

As the sun dipped below the horizon, the two men

rose from sitting on the stone wall, their faces bathed in the glow of the dying light. They clasped hands, a silent pledge of loyalty and friendship. As they made their way back towards the house, Tom knew that his life had changed irrevocably, that the fire within him had been stoked anew.

Later that night, alone in the darkness, he wrestled with his thoughts, the silence of the night punctuated only by the beating of his own conflicted heart. The night crept in around them, echoing with a thousand ghosts of the past. The familiar nightmares of war threatened to rise from the depths of his memories, but he fought them back. This was a different fight, one for the soul of a nation and the lives of its people. It was a heavy burden to bear.

Tom couldn't help but feel that the bond between Liam and him had shifted. The camaraderie they'd shared while working side by side was now tainted by the shadow of the Fenian cause, and though Tom valued their friendship, he couldn't ignore the whisper of doubt gnawing at the edges of his mind.

***

The next day, Tom stood by the edge of the yard, leaning against the wooden fence as he watched Liam tend to the horses, his eyes filled with a mixture of admiration and uncertainty. He knew that time was running out for him to make his decision, but still, his heart was torn. The words of Liam echoed in his mind, whispering of a possible future where Ireland was free from the likes of James Reid.

Tom paced along the fence, turmoil raging inside him. He yearned to stand up for Ireland, but the risks were immense. If he was captured or killed, what would become of Cathleen and the farm? His gut twisted at the thought of leaving her alone and unprotected.

"Tom," Liam called, noticing his friend lost in thought. "You've been quiet all day. Is everything all right?"

"Everything's fine," Tom replied, forcing a smile. But even as he said it, he could feel the weight of uncertainty bearing down upon him like a blacksmith's hammer on red-hot iron.

"Are you sure?" Laim asked, sensing Tom's unease as he stepped up beside him. "I know you're conflicted about joining the Fenians, but there are some things I'd like you to consider."

"Your words have stirred something inside me, Liam," Tom admitted, his voice low and contemplative. "I'm grateful for your friendship and your wisdom, but joining the Fenians… It's not a simple choice."

"Think about those who've come before us, those who've fought for our freedom. Men like Robert Emmet and Wolfe Tone," Liam said, his voice impassioned. "They believed in an independent Ireland, free from British rule. Don't their sacrifices mean something?"

"Of course they do," Tom replied, "but times have changed, Liam. We can't keep fighting the same battles over and over again. Is it really worth putting our lives on the line for a cause that may never be won?"

"Is your farm, your home, not worth fighting for?"

Liam shot back, his eyes wide with intensity. "James Reid has taken so much from you already. Are you just going to stand by and let him take the rest? Have you no pride?"

"There's more at stake here than just my pride, Liam," Tom said sternly.

"Tom, I know you're worried about Cathleen and the safety of your farm, but the Fenians aren't just about revenge," Liam urged, his tone softening. "We're fighting for the rights and freedoms of all Irish people. If we don't stand up against men like Reid, who will? Your farm won't matter if Ireland remains under the boot of British rule," Liam said fiercely. "We have to be willing to sacrifice for the cause."

Tom turned to him. "Haven't we sacrificed enough already?"

Liam's eyes clouded with memories. "Some gave more than others. My father died at the hands of the Redcoats. I won't let his death be in vain."

Tom fell silent, humbled by the anguish in Liam's voice. He thought of his own parents, starved and driven out by the British. Was it not his duty to continue their fight?

"Maybe there's another way," Tom suggested, his brow furrowed in thought. "A path that doesn't lead to more bloodshed. Like what the Land League and Parnell and the Home Rule party are trying to do."

"Tom, I've seen what the British are capable of." Liam said, the memories of past injustices etched into his face. "We can't trust them to change their ways without a fight."

"Then let it be a different kind of fight," Tom argued, his voice firm with resolve. "One where we don't risk losing everything we hold dear."

"Are you certain that's possible, Tom?" Liam asked, doubt clouding his eyes. "Can we truly achieve freedom without taking up arms?"

"I don't know," Tom admitted, gazing back at the rolling hills. "But I can't help but believe that there must be another way."

Liam sighed, a hint of resignation in his voice. "Perhaps you're right, Tom. Maybe there is another way. But if we don't stand together now, I fear we may lose the chance to make a difference."

"I'll need more time to think on this, but know that your words have not fallen on deaf ears." Tom's mind spun with indecision. If he joined the Fenians, it would also place him in grave danger and destroy the world he'd built here if he failed. His heart was torn between duty and self-preservation. He knew that a decision lay before him, one that could change the course of his life forever. "I want to see Ireland free someday. But this farm, it's all I have. If I lose it…" he trailed off, emotion choking his words.

Liam seemed to read his thoughts. "We can help you get revenge against Reid for what he did to your farm and livestock. His reign of terror will end."

Tom froze mid-step, temptation flaring. To finally make Reid pay… it was a profound desire. But could he risk everything for it?

"The days are getting shorter, the nights are getting cold, winter isn't far away," Tom sighed.

"Time's not waiting for us, Tom," Liam said softly, placing a reassuring hand on his friend's shoulder. "No matter what path you choose, know that I will support you. I'll stand by your side, whatever happens, and if by the grace of God something should ever happen to me… Say I had to go on the run for a while, call into Jack O'Connor's pub in the town and ask to speak with Cormac Moynihan… Right, I better get on and do some work; you don't want to listen to me talking all evening."

As Liam walked away, Tom was left to ponder the weight of Liam's words and the sacrifices of those who'd come before him. The question remained: what path would he choose, and would it lead to the freedom and peace he so desperately sought?

Chapter 16: Ribbonmen
November 19th

Oh, you Ribbonmen of Ireland,
long may you reign,
may you roll in joy and splendour
till you raise your flag again.

We were going down by Segimore
looking for some fun,
sure, that was the very night
we took the Orange drum.

Oh, you Ribbon boys of Ireland,
long may you reign,
may you roll in joy and splendour,
till you raise your flag again.

She hates our religion,
and our ways very much,
and she gives her curse to any man,
and turns and goes to church.

The morning mist clung to the land like a shroud, damp and chilling. Tom stared out over the hills surrounding his farm, a heaviness weighing on his heart. Shouts and cries of alarm shattered the still morning air. Tom spotted a horde of men galloping down the hill with reckless abandon, their horses' hooves kicked up clods of earth as they charged down the hill, their silhouettes eerily dark against the brightening sky. They seemed to materialise out of thin air, their figures hazy and indistinct like phantoms. The scene was like a painting of an ancient battle come to life, their weapons flashing in a menacing dance.

The thundering hooves of the horses echoed across the land, the sound growing louder as they got closer and closer, the rhythmic beats like a war drum. The men shouted and yelled, their voices carrying through the air like a battle cry. The sounds all blending together into a terrifying cacophony.

Tom's heart dropped like a stone in his chest watching as the riders moved with sinister purpose, setting fire to his out houses, trampling his crops, and killing those animals unlucky enough to be caught in their path. Chickens squawked and scattered; a goat bleated frantically. Tom's pulse roared in his ears. These monsters were destroying everything he'd worked for, ripping apart his livelihood while he stood by, powerless.

Tom clenched his fists, his heart pounding with a mixture of rage and fear as he ran towards the chaos. He could see the faces of the men who'd come to destroy everything he held dear, their expressions twisted into cruel sneers as they revelled in the destruction they wrought.

Tom spotted Liam crouched behind the barn,

motioning to him. As a raider grabbed Tom's arm, Liam leapt out and knocked the man to the ground.

"Tom!" Liam's voice cut through the cacophony, calling him back to the present. "We can't fight them off alone!"

"Then what do you suggest we do?" Tom shouted over the din of the attack, his voice tight with frustration.

"We need help, don't try to stop them. Know, they will kill you, there are too many of them. We will get our time," Liam said as he held Tom back.

"So, I just stand here and watch them destroy my farm," Tom cried out.

Liam had no response to give, he felt just as helpless as Tom as they watched the carnage and destruction all around them.

Ten minutes later, the horde had ridden off back up the hills where they had first appeared from. The entire raid lasted no more than twenty minutes, but all around were the remains of the attack. Dead animals lying on the ground, smoke billowing from the wooden sheds. Tom was heartbroken, he didn't know how many more times he could endure these attacks, how many more times he could rebuild and restock his farm.

Liam's eyes darted around the devastation before locking onto Tom's. "I have friends who could help," he said, his voice low and urgent. "A secret society called the Ribbonmen. They could destroy part of Reid's property, give him a taste of his own medicine."

Tom hesitated, his desire for vengeance warring with his sense of duty. The thought of bringing more violence into their lives seemed reckless, but how much longer could he endure these relentless attacks?

Swallowing hard, he gave Liam a curt nod. "Contact them," Tom finally said, the words tasting like ashes in his mouth. "But tell them not to harm innocent people. Only Reid's men and his property."

"Understood." Liam nodded, a grim determination settling over his features as he turned to carry out Tom's instructions.

As Liam disappeared into the tree line, Tom prayed he hadn't just made a deal with the devil. But there was another part of him, deep down, that thirsted for vengeance. The vision of James Reid's thugs attacking his farm burned within him like a smouldering ember. And as much as he tried to ignore it, that ember threatened to ignite into a full-fledged blaze.

Watching his farm burn, he knew he couldn't withstand these attacks forever. If law and justice couldn't protect them, what choice did he have but to take matters into his own hands?

***

A week later, under the blood-red moon, Liam stood at the edge of James Reid's vast estate, his heart pounding in anticipation. The Ribbonmen had gathered in the shadows, their faces obscured by dark masks and the night. With a silent nod from Liam, they moved as one, swift and purposeful, like a vengeful storm. As they approached the stables, he caught a whiff of hay and horses. Silently, they opened the barn doors and herded the expensive thoroughbreds out into the pasture. Then, they piled hay bales inside and set them alight. Flames licked up the dry wooden walls as the barn was engulfed.

The flickering light of the torches danced off the faces of the men who swarmed around the outhouses as they methodically set fire to them. The structures were quickly consumed by the flames, leaving behind billowing clouds of thick, black smoke. Other Ribbonmen moved with precision, expertly cutting through fences and releasing livestock into the chaotic night. In the distance, terrified screams could be heard, an ominous sign that some of Reid's men had met a horrific fate. The night sky illuminated with orange and red hues. The power of fire and rebellion on full display.

Next, they moved toward the manor house. Liam kept watch as two men picked the lock on the front door and slipped inside. Muffled shouts rang out, then silence. Moments later, his companions emerged, bloody daggers dripping in their hands.

The wind carried the scent of burning crops and vengeance, fuelling the fire in Liam's chest. He felt a twinge of regret at the loss of life – but this was war.

Back at the Ryan farm, Cathleen wrapped her shawl tighter against the night chill. Tom turned to see fear and doubt clouding Cathleen's eyes. Gently, he took her hands in his own.

"Do you think Liam and the others are safe?" she asked softly.

Tom gazed at the distant glow of the burning estate. "I pray they are. But we've started something now that cannot easily be undone."

Chapter 17: The Rising of the Moon
December 2nd

The RIC officers stormed onto Tom's farm, rifles cocked and ready. Liam peered out the window of the small stone cottage, his heart pounding. There could be only one reason for their presence. Somebody had informed on him.

He raced to the back door, flinging it open. Panic surged through him like a lightning bolt, and without hesitation, he sprinted away from the farm, cutting through tangled brush and leaping over low stone walls in an attempt to evade capture. His chest burned as he gasped for air, his legs pumping furiously. He had nowhere to go, nowhere to hide. They were gaining on him, their boots thudding against the ground as they gave chase.

"Halt, or we'll shoot!" One of the officers bellowed.

A bullet whizzed by Liam's head as he ran on, kicking up dirt at his feet.

"Stop, O'Sullivan!" an officer shouted, but Liam refused to relent. He knew the fate that awaited him if captured by the RIC. His breaths were ragged, and his heart pounded in his chest as adrenaline fuelled his desperate flight.

"Take aim, men!" ordered the sergeant, and the sound of rifles being raised filled the air. Several shots rang out, and a searing pain tore through Liam's lower calf. His leg buckled beneath him, sending him tumbling to the ground. He cried out, clutching his bleeding leg. There would be no escape now. The officers were upon him in seconds, securing his hands behind his back and dragging him along the ground.

"Thought you could outrun the law, did you?" The sergeant sneered, shoving his rifle into Liam's back. "You're under arrest for crimes against the Crown."

They hauled him off towards their waggon, tossing him in the back like a rag doll and they rumbled down the road towards Dromdaire. Liam gritted his teeth against the agony in his leg, which was pumping blood, steeling himself for what was to come. He would never break. He would never give them what they wanted.

***

The officers hauled him into the RIC barracks and through a hallway lined with cells, the walls stained with dirt and grime. A lone oil lantern threw eerie shadows on the officers' faces, which were twisted with cruel intent. The officers were large and intimidating, clad in dark uniforms and leather boots.

Liam was thrust into a small, windowless cell. The cell was sparse and almost bare, with only a rickety bed against the wall. He lay in agony on the cold, damp floor for what seemed like an hour as blood poured out of the gunshot wound in his leg as he awaited the inevitable. The stench of urine and faeces was overpowering in the small cell, making Liam gag. It mixed with the metallic scent of blood coming from his gunshot wound.

The cell door creaked open. The officers filed in, cracking their knuckles as they entered, their eyes filled with malice. There was a strong smell of alcohol off them.

"Take him to the interrogation room," the sergeant barked.

The interrogation room was a small, cramped space with a single table and two chairs, one of which had restraints attached to it.

"You're going to tell us everything you know about the Fenians," the sergeant said in a low, menacing tone. "One way or another."

He lunged at Liam, fists swinging. Pain exploded across his face and body as the beating began in earnest. Liam braced himself, refusing to cry out. He would never give in. He would die before betraying his comrades.

"O'Sullivan," an officer began. "We know you were responsible for the recent attacks on James Reid's estate. We know you're involved with the Fenians and that you organised the Ribbonmen attack on Reid's property."

The officers pummelled him relentlessly, each blow landing with brutal force, demanding information, but Liam remained silent. Darkness crept into the edges of his vision as he slipped towards oblivion, his body broken and bloodied. Liam gritted what was left of his teeth against the pain. The Fenian cause was worth dying for. And die he would, before he gave them a single name.

"Give us the names and addresses of other Fenians you know," they demanded, their voices cold and unyielding. The torture continued for another twenty minutes as his body weakened.

"Tell us what we want to know!" The sergeant roared as he stomped down hard with his boot on Liam's bloody leg, causing a bone to snap, but Liam's only response was a roar from the agonising pain and then a defiant glare up at the sergeant. In those final moments, as life slipped from his grasp, he mumbled through smashed teeth and a bloody and broken jaw his final words, "*Erin go bragh*, Ireland forever."

And so, Liam O'Sullivan died at the hands of the RIC, unbending and unwavering in his devotion to the cause he held dear.

*****

The Next Morning

Tom trudged through the forest, collecting firewood. His mind wandered as he walked, thinking of Liam and wondering when he would return. He thought that perhaps he was gone for good to escape capture. He was surprised that he had left his few belongings. Perhaps he had to leave in a hurry, he contemplated.

The forest floor was covered in branches and twigs that had come down due to a recent storm, and he soon had a large bundle in his arms. The bundle fell from his grip when, in shock, he froze in his tracks. There, amongst the gnarled roots and fallen leaves, was Liam's lifeless and mangled body – dumped unceremoniously in a ditch. Tom ran forward with a cry, dropping to his knees beside the corpse. Liam's lifeless eyes staring up at the sky. Rage and sorrow warred within him as he gazed at his friend. He had to clench his fists to stop them from shaking, anger burning in his gut like molten lead. They would pay for this. The bastards who did this would pay.

"Damn them," he whispered through gritted teeth, tears welling up in his eyes. The grief threatened to swallow him whole, yet it was tempered by a seething anger that refused to be quelled. His mind raced, trying to make sense of what had happened, how they could have found Liam, and why they'd left his broken body so close to home. Was it a warning? A cruel taunt? He couldn't shake the feeling that he was meant to find Liam here, a grim reminder of the danger he faced.

Tom knelt beside Liam, his hands trembling as he gently closed his friend's lifeless eyes. He felt a crushing weight settle upon his chest, an unbearable sadness that threatened to suffocate him. But beneath that sorrow, there was a steely resolve forming, a determination to avenge Liam's death. It was up to Tom now to make it right, to get justice for his fallen friend. The bastards who did this would pay. He swore it on Liam's lifeless body, rage burning in his heart like a wildfire. The men responsible for Liam's death were going to suffer for what they did. Tom would see to that personally.

Gently, he lifted Liam's body from the ditch and hoisted it onto his shoulders as he made his way slowly back to the farm and laid him in the barn. He washed the blood and dirt from his friend's face, straightening limbs and combing hair. When Liam looked as peaceful as possible, Tom sat beside the body, grief etched into every line of his face. He would give his friend a proper burial.

"Rest easy, Liam," Tom murmured, his voice thick with emotion. "I swear I'll make this right."

With great care, he carried Liam's body to a nearby field. There, beneath a winter sky streaked with clouds, he dug a grave for his friend. As he placed the last shovelful of earth onto the mound, he fashioned a simple cross from two ash branches and pressed it into the soil.

"May you find peace now, Liam," he whispered, wiping away the tears that traced lines down his dirt-streaked face.

***

Determined to learn the truth behind Liam's death, Tom travelled into town to meet with Cathleen. Her eyes were red when he found her sitting alone on a chair in the yard at the back of the hardware store. She jumped up when Tom approached and grasped him tightly.

"Tom, thank God you are okay. I was so worried about you," she said, her voice trembling. "Liam was arrested last night and taken to the RIC barracks. I heard that they killed him."

The words struck Tom like a thump in the stomach, fuelling the fire of his resolve. His jaw clenched, and his eyes narrowed. "I swear on my life, Cathleen, those brutes will pay for their actions."

He knew that his life would never be the same again.

He could no longer stand idly by while those in power continued to bring pain and suffering to him and those around him. Liam's death had been the final straw, and it was time to act.

"Tom," Cathleen said softly, placing a hand on his shoulder. "What are you going to do?"

He turned to face her, his eyes burning with resolve. "I'm going to find every last one of those bastards who had a hand in Liam's death, and they will suffer."

"Tom, be careful. You can't do it on your own. There are too many of them. I don't want to lose you," Cathleen pleaded.

"Don't worry, Cathleen, I know what I am doing. I have faced greater odds before. I promise you I will get through this with the skin on my back."

***

Tom walked up the main street of Dromdaire with purpose, his hands balled into fists inside his pockets. Every step stoking the flames of vengeance within him. By the time he reached the town centre, rage simmered beneath his skin, threatening to boil over. He spotted Constable Doyle exiting the post office, a smug grin on his round face. Tom quickened his pace, shoulders back and chin high.

"Well, if it isn't Tom Ryan. Come to turn yourself in, have you? Save us the trouble of hunting you down like the dog you are."

Tom stopped in front of Doyle, meeting his gaze with

unbridled contempt. "I've come to tell you I know what you did. I know you killed Liam O'Sullivan, you murdering bastard."

Doyle scoffed. "And what are you going to do about it?" He stepped closer, pushing out his chest, attempting to intimidate Tom. "You have no proof. No one will believe the word of a fool like you over an officer of the law."

"I don't need proof," Tom's voice was low and steady. "I don't need anyone else to believe. All I need is to make sure you pay for what you've done."

"Is that a threat?" Doyle's hand moved to the truncheon at his belt. "You'd do well to watch your tongue, boyo, if you want to keep it in your head."

A grim smile twisted Tom's lip. "Consider it a promise."

He shoved past the constable and continued down the road, leaving Doyle spluttering behind him. The constable and his comrades had signed their death warrants. Soon Tom would deliver the sentence.

Ten minutes later, Tom approached a public house at the end of Cooper's Lane, pausing outside to take a steadying breath. He looked up at the sign over the door that said O' Connor's public house. When he stepped through the door, a hush fell over the crowd. Men in threadbare coats glanced up from their drinks. He stood confidently at the bar and spoke, "Can somebody direct me to the owner of this place, Jack O'Connor?" There was a silence for a few moments, and then there was a sigh, and after a few moments' words spoken from a stocky man with a thick beard, sitting in the corner on his own, smoking a pipe and reading a newspaper.

"That me."

Tom strode over and sat down on a low stool opposite to him, away from the listening ears at the bar.

"I want to join up," Tom said. His voice was steady, betraying none of the turmoil churning inside him.

"Join what?" O'Connor said, still looking down at his newspaper.

"The brotherhood… the Fenians… Liam O'Sullivan told me to speak to you, he said you could put me in contact with Cormac Moynihan."

"Liam O'Sullivan was beaten to death by the Peelers last night," O'Connor said.

"Don't I know? I just buried his broken body a few hours ago on my farm, where he was dumped," Tom stated angrily.

The publican lifted his eyes and studied Tom; lips pursed, "And what makes you think you're Fenian material, lad?"

Tom's hands tightened at his sides. "I have experience. I fought for the Union in the Civil War in America."

The publican's gaze sharpened, flickering over Tom's worn but determined face.

Finally, he nodded and extended a hand. "You've the look of a man with purpose. And God knows we could use more like you. To be honest, lad, I have heard all about you from poor Liam. He told me that you would eventually be calling."

Tom grasped the O'Connor's hand. "Thank you, Jack. What happens now?"

"I'll set you up with a Cormac for a meeting."

Chapter 18: The Bold Fenian Men
December 3rd, Red Cove Strand

They think that they have pacified Ireland.
They think that they have purchased half of us
and intimidated the other half.
They think that they have foreseen everything,
think that they have provided against everything;
but the fools, the fools, the fools!
– they have left us our Fenian dead,
and while Ireland holds these graves,
Ireland unfree shall never be at peace.

Patrick Pearse

Tom Ryan's tall figure moved cautiously over the jagged rocks. The wind howled around him, whistling through caves, playing a mournful melody, as if the ocean itself was singing a sad song. He pulled his billowing coat tighter as the biting wind whipped him, cutting through the fabric of his coat and chilling him to the bone. The churning waves relentlessly crashed against the shore and created a deep roar that filled the air, white foam spraying against the dark rocks. The sky a deep grey above the rugged cliffs that jut out from the land like ragged teeth. He took a deep breath, letting the salty air fill his lungs, his own thoughts lost in the chaos of nature's song.

As he came upon the designated spot, he saw a figure, their back turned away from him. Tom's heart raced as he tried to steady his nerves. He knew that this encounter could change everything.

"Hello," he said, his voice low and rough from the tension. The figure turned around, revealing a face that was familiar.

"Evenin', Tom, we've been expectin' ya."

"Shane." Tom nodded, recognising him from the Land League meetings.

They stood in silence for a few moments, the crashing waves the only sound between them.

"I need to speak with Cormac Moynihan."

"Come on, then." Shane led Tom through the craggy terrain until they reached a small cave. The entrance to the cave was concealed by overhanging rocks, with only a small opening that led inside. The dim light from lanterns illuminated the rugged walls, revealing the huddled figures of several men gathered around a makeshift table. Maps and documents littered the table, their edges curling from exposure to the damp air. Each man had a look of determination on his face as they hunched over the maps, tracing routes with their fingers as they discussed their plans. The sound of parchment scratching against parchment could be heard as they continued to plan and strategise in their secluded hideout.

One man towered over the others; his broad shoulders seemed to fill the small space of the cave. A long, fiery red beard cascaded from his chin, his curly hair that framed his face was wild and unkempt, adding to his rugged and intimidating appearance. His muscular build and weathered skin revealed a life of physical labour and adventure. He emanated an aura of power and leadership. Tom assumed that he must be Cormac Moynihan.

"This is Tom Ryan," Shane announced.

Cormac looked up from the maps, his piercing blue eyes held a hardened determination.

"Pleased to meet you, Tom; I've heard much about you from Liam, God rest his soul," Cormac Moynihan said as he reached out to shake Tom's hand. "You're a long way from America."

"I am."

"What brings you to our humble gathering?" Cormac leaned back, folding his arms.

"I want to join your cause so I can kill the bastards that beat Liam to death," Tom said, getting straight to the point.

A murmur rippled through the group, but Cormac silenced them with a wave of his hand. "You have experience fighting, don't you, Tom?"

"Four years in the American Civil War," Tom confirmed, memories of death and destruction flashing before his eyes. "I've seen more bloodshed than any man should."

"Your determination is admirable, but are you prepared to face the consequences?" Cormac questioned him, his voice heavy with concern.

"I owe it to Liam to do this," Tom replied, a knot forming in his throat.

Cormac studied Tom for a moment, their gazes locked

in an unspoken exchange. Finally, he nodded. "You are welcome to join the Fenians, Tom. Your military experience will be invaluable to us. Liam recommended you to me months ago. I know you can be trusted. Are you prepared to pledge your allegiance to the Irish Republican Brotherhood?"

"I am," Tom said, accepting the offered hand. As he shook Cormac's firm grip, a sense of purpose washed over him.

***

Two weeks later, Tom stood at the edge of a field, watching as a ragtag group of Fenian fighters, an assortment of men, young and old, ran through combat drills. Their movements were clumsy and uncoordinated, betraying their lack of discipline and experience.

Tom shook his head, fingers tightening around the brim of his cap. Tom felt the weight of his responsibility settle on his shoulders. He had his work cut out for him.

When Shane Kelleher raised his hand, signalling the end of the drills, Tom stepped forward. The men turned to face him, curiosity etched into their weathered faces.

"You call that training?" Tom asked, unable to keep the derision from his voice. "My dead grandmother could put up a better fight, and she's been in the ground for forty years."

"Listen up," Tom said, his voice laced with grit. "We have much work to do and little time to waste. Our enemy is organised, well-equipped, and relentless. To defeat them, we must become disciplined, skilled, and merciless."

He paced in front of the assembled men, his eyes never leaving theirs. "Our focus will be guerrilla warfare. Hit fast, hit hard, vanish without a trace. We'll utilise the landscape, our knowledge of local terrain, and our cunning to outmanoeuvre and outsmart our foes."

"Discipline," Tom emphasised, beating his fists off each other. "Without discipline, we're just a mob, easily scattered and defeated. With discipline, we're a force to be reckoned with."

A few of the men bristled at his tone, but Tom ignored them. "If you want to stand a chance against the Peelers and the Redcoats, you need to take this seriously. Now pair up and we'll start again."

No one moved, the men exchanged wary glances, reluctance clear in their stances. Tom sighed, folding his arms over his chest. "Did you not hear me? Pair up, or you'll wish you had."

When they still didn't react, Tom walked forward and grabbed two men by their collars, shoving them together. "Like I said, take this seriously, or get out now. I won't waste my time on men not willing to train."

The men stared at him, stunned into silence. Then, slowly, they began to pair off, sheepish looks on their faces. Tom nodded, a spark of satisfaction easing the tension in his chest. "Good. Now, we start with the basics. And this time, I want to see some discipline and teamwork. Our lives will depend on it."

He began barking orders, putting the men through

their paces. "Teamwork," Tom insisted, as they practiced moving in formation. "When we act as one, we're greater than the sum of our parts. Trust each other, support each other. Remember, your comrade's life may depend on you."

As Tom began demonstrating the basic techniques of hand-to-hand combat, he stole glances at the expressions of his fellow Fenians. He saw a mixture of enthusiasm, fear and determination. The training would test their limits, but he knew it was necessary.

The weeks of training turned into months, and the Fenians' combat skills improved under Tom's watchful eye. By the end of the drills, their movements had sharpened, a newfound sense of purpose etched into their stances. The men learned to fight with their fists, knives and rifles, adapting to various situations and terrains. Their camaraderie deepened as they trained together.

Tom stood tall among the Fenian platoon; his eyes focused intently on their movements as they executed the drills he had taught them.

"Keep your elbows tucked in, O'Connor," Tom instructed, addressing a burly man with a thick beard. "You'll have better control over your aim."

"Like this?" O'Connor asked, adjusting his stance. His brow furrowed with concentration, sweat dripping from his forehead.

"Better," Tom confirmed, nodding approvingly.

Tom found solace in his newfound purpose. As he watched the men train, their bodies growing stronger and their minds honing their tactical skills, he felt an ember of hope begin to burn within him. Tom's thoughts strayed to the people they fought for, the families who had lost loved ones to the RIC and Redcoat brutality, the children who would grow up knowing only oppression and fear if nothing changed. It was for them that these Fenian men trained so diligently, pushing themselves to the limit each day under his guidance.

"Stay focused, men," Tom reminded them, his voice firm yet encouraging. "Remember why we're doing this. Remember what's at stake. We fight not just for ourselves, but for our families, our friends, and our homeland. Our cause is just, and our determination unyielding."

As the sun dipped below the horizon, the sounds of gunfire continued to ring out across the valley. Each shot a testament to their growing proficiency, and each shot carried with it the weight of a nation's hopes and dreams.

As they stared out across the rugged landscape, each man contemplating the sacrifices they would make for freedom, Tom knew that he had found a new family among the Fenians. They were united by their love for Ireland, their desire for freedom, and their willingness to risk everything to achieve it.

At night, as they gathered around a fire, Tom shared tales of his time in the American Civil War, sharing stories of daring night-time raids that turned the tide for his comrades in arms. He spoke of the strategies he learned and the horrors he witnessed. He stressed the importance of stealth.

"Stealth," Tom whispered to the men huddled close by the fire. "We must become shadows, ghosts that strike fear into our enemies' hearts. If we can't be seen, we can't be stopped."

In the quiet moments between training and planning, Tom's thoughts often drifted to Dan and Liam. The memory of his two friends fuelled his resolve, pushing him to teach the Fenians everything he knew about war and survival. He couldn't bring Liam or Dan back, but he could help prevent others from suffering the same fate.

Chapter 19: My Bloody Valentine
February 14th 1867, Dromdaire

Tom huddled with Cormac Moriarity and Shane Kelliher around a dimly lit table in the kitchen at the back of O'Connor's pub, pouring over a rough map of the RIC barracks.

"We go in through here," Tom said, tapping the back entrance. "It'll be guarded, but if we time it right, we can take the guards by surprise."

Shane frowned. "And if we can't? It'll be a death trap, trying to force our way in."

"Have a little faith," Tom said, "with the training the men had, we can overpower them. But speed and stealth will be key."

Cormac rolled up the map and stood. "Get some rest. We move out at midnight."

As they filed out, Shane lingered behind to speak to Tom. "Do you really think this will work?" he asked quietly, "I don't fancy getting myself killed over a fool's errand."

Tom clasped his shoulder. "If we die, at least we die free men. But if we succeed…" A fierce grin lit his face. "Ireland will remember your name."

Shane stared at him, then hesitantly nodded. "Right.

"Good man," Tom said. The two of them left,

disappearing into the gathering dusk.

***

A thick mist enveloped the Fenian camp as Tom stood at the centre of the gathered men, his eyes scanning their faces, which were barely visible through the haze. Their voices were hushed, their movements purposeful, as they unloaded crates of weapons and supplies from a creaking wooden cart. The weight of responsibility pressed heavy on Tom's chest, as he knew that these rifles had been procured at great risk by their network of sympathisers and supporters in Clann na Gael.

"Look at this, Tom," called out Ciaran Buckley, hoisting a gleaming rifle up to his shoulder. "Fresh from America, just like you."

Tom couldn't help but smile as he approached Buckley, taking the rifle in his hands and admiring its craftsmanship. As he inspected the weapon, the other Fenians gathered around. He could see the uncertainty in their eyes, the flicker of doubt that threatened to consume them if left unchecked. He knew he had to remind them of what they were capable of, of the heroism that coursed through their very veins.

"Remember, lads," Tom began, his voice steady and commanding, "…these rifles are more than just weapons. They are symbols of our determination to take back what is rightfully ours. We owe it to those who have suffered to use them wisely and effectively."

The men nodded solemnly, understanding the gravity

of their mission.

"Listen up!" Tom called out, his voice cutting through the anxious murmurs that rippled through the crowd. The men fell silent, turning their attention to their leader as he continued, "I know we're all feeling the weight of what's to come, but we mustn't let it overwhelm us. Each of you has a role to play in the upcoming operation. Tom continued. "Some of you will be responsible for securing our escape route, while others will create diversions or provide cover fire. Every man's contribution is vital to our success. Believe in yourself, men," Tom said, clasping a firm hand on Buckley's shoulder. "Believe in the cause and in the men standing beside you. We've trained long and hard for this moment, and we'll be ready."

He paused, letting his words sink in, before continuing with renewed fervour. "Think of Brian Boru, who united the clans of Ireland against the Vikings, driving them from our shores. Or Hugh O'Neill, who challenged the might of the English crown and rallied his people in defence of their lands and their faith." Tom's gaze never wavering from the men before him. "Each one of us carries within us the legacy of these great warriors," Tom declared, his voice rising in crescendo. "…And it is our duty, as sons of Ireland, to honour their sacrifices by standing up against the tyranny that oppresses our people. We may be facing insurmountable odds, but we are not alone. Our cause is just, and our hearts are full of courage. We will fight with honour and with purpose, and we will bring justice to those who have wronged us."

As Tom spoke these words, he felt a strange sense of

calm wash over him. Despite the lingering uncertainty that gnawed at the edges of his mind, he knew that he had done everything in his power to prepare his men for the battle ahead. And as he looked out upon their faces, illuminated by the flickering glow of the lanterns that pierced the night's darkness, he could see the same resilience and resolve that had carried him through the darkest days of his own life.

The men listened intently, their expressions shifting as Tom wove tales of their shared history, each story imbued with a sense of pride and purpose that seemed to flow from him like a river. As they absorbed his words, their shoulders straightened, their grips tightened and their eyes burned with the fire of determination.

"Tom's right," shouted Kavanagh, his fist rising into the air. "We're part of a proud tradition, lads! Let's show them what we're made of!"

"Damn right!" Shane Kelliher chimed in, the energy in the crowd surging with each affirmation.

"Then let's channel this passion, this resolve, into our attack on the RIC barracks," Tom said, his voice steady once more, his gaze locked onto each man in turn. "For Liam O'Sullivan, for our families, and for Ireland herself."

"Here's to Liam," Buckley added, raising an imaginary glass in a toast.

"*Aye!*" The Fenians roared in unison, fists clenched and hearts pounding with anticipation as the hour of reckoning drew near.

As Tom surveyed the men before him, he saw not just fighters, but brothers united by a common cause. And, for the first time since embarking on this mission of vengeance, he allowed himself a moment of hope, hope that, together, they might yet secure justice for all they had lost.

His men stirred, spines straightening as anger kindled in their eyes. Tom seized their rising fury and stoked it higher.

"They have oppressed us for too long!" he cried. "Taken our land, our liberty, our lives! But now we have drawn the sword – and we will not sheathe it until Ireland is free!"

A roar rose from the Fenian men, fists rising in the air. Tom let their cries wash over him, filling him with fierce pride. They were ready now, hardened and bonded by blood.

Tom raised his hands and silence fell. "We'll strike at midnight, when the guard change is at its weakest," he said, his eyes burning into each man. "We go to strike a blow against the tyrants. And we will keep striking, again and again, until they are driven from our shores, or we perish in the fight!"

***

That night, a chill wind swept through the hills, rattling the windows of the abandoned farmhouse where the Fenians had gathered. Tom stood outside, gazing up at the stars. His breath hung in the air like a ghostly whisper. His mind drifted to his own family, miles away in America. He wondered if they would understand why he had taken up arms once more, trading the horrors of the Civil War for this new, equally dangerous battlefield. But as he looked around at the men beside him – all of them bound by a fierce loyalty to each other and their cause – Tom knew that he could not have chosen any other path. He shook his head, forcing himself to focus on the task at hand. There would be time for reflection later, now was the moment for action, for retribution.

He went inside, where the men were checking their weapons and sharing quiet words of encouragement. Tom stood watch over them as they made their last preparations. The delicate clinking of ammunition and the rhythmic whir of sharpening blades punctuated the air, a symphony of readiness that spoke to the gravity of their imminent mission. For all his stoicism, Tom could not deny the coil of anxiety that tightened within him as he surveyed each man's face. He knew what weighed on their minds, the fear of failure, the burden of their shared responsibility, but as he had done so many times before, he braced himself and forged ahead.

"Keep your wits about you, lads. We've trained long and hard for this moment, and we're more than ready. Trust yourselves and trust each other."

They turned to look at him, their leader, for a final boost of morale, for some reassurance it was going to all work out in their favour.

"Remember," he called out, his voice steady despite the trepidation that gnawed at his thoughts. "Check your weapons twice. We can't afford any mishaps."

"Right you are, Tom," Kavanagh replied, carefully

loading his rifle with the precision of a seasoned warrior. "Everything's got to be perfect."

"The tyrants of our country believe they have beaten us into submission. They think we have given up, that the spirit of Ireland has been crushed. But they are wrong. Within each of us burns an undying flame, the flame of freedom. And tonight, my friends, we will unleash the full fury of that flame," Tom said as a fierce grin lit his face as he unsheathed his knife. "So, sharpen your blades, load your rifles, and prepare to show the Peelers the error of their ways."

A roar went up from the Fenians, shaking the rafters.

"To arms!" He shouted, raising his knife.

"To arms!" Came the echoing cry.

The Fenian men exchanged resolute nods, their eyes gleaming with conviction. Bolstered by this display of unity, he led them out into the night and onward, as they marched toward the outskirts of Dromdaire. The attack on the RIC barracks was about to begin. Tom's mind raced over the details of the plan, searching for any flaws or oversights. But after weeks of preparation, he was confident in their strategy. The real test would come very soon.

He led his squad through the darkened streets of the town, their boots thudding softly on the road. They moved as one, a force of retribution, the moon cast a silvery sheen on the cobblestones. The tension amongst the men was palpable, the air thick with anticipation and resolve. His mind was clear and focused; every shadow and sound sharpened his senses. The men followed silently behind him, a coiled spring of barely contained energy, ready to snap into action at the slightest provocation.

"Stay close," Tom murmured. The very air seemed to be holding its breath, the silence of the night an oppressive weight upon them all.

The barracks loomed ahead, lamplight glowed in a few windows, silhouetting the constabulary inside. Tom knew that the officers would fight fiercely to defend it.

As the Fenian platoon took a brief respite, Tom surveyed the landscape, planning out potential scenarios for the attack on the RIC barracks. He knew that the element of surprise would be crucial to their success, and that every man would need to play his part flawlessly.

He gathered the men in a close huddle, the wind whipping at their coats and carrying the scent of impending rain. He glanced up at the brooding sky, its dark clouds amassing like an ominous portent of the battle to come. Tom turned to face his comrades; their faces obscured by the shadows they had become one with. His stern eyes scanned each man, ensuring their readiness for the task ahead. He knew that their loyalty was unwavering, but he also understood the gravity of what they were about to undertake. He noted the grim anticipation on each face, they stood on the brink of either triumph or defeat. He searched for any signs of fear or doubt but found only iron determination.

His chest swelled with pride. They might perish tonight, but they would die as martyrs for Ireland's freedom. And their memory would live on, inspiring future generations to take up the fight.

"Listen closely," he began, his voice low and urgent as he outlined the plan once more. "You all know your roles. When the church bell tolls midnight, we attack. O'Connor', what have you learned about the guard rotations?"

"Every two hours, they change shifts," O'Connor replied, his voice low and measured. "Four men patrol the outer walls while two more stand watch inside."

"Good." Tom nodded, committing the information to memory. He glanced at the other members of his reconnaissance team, huddled together on the hillside. "Let's move closer. We need a better view of the entrances and possible escape routes."

As they crept through the underbrush, Tom's mind raced with plans and strategies. Every detail mattered, from the timing of their assault to the positioning of his men. A single misstep could spell disaster for their mission.

"Over there," whispered Flynn, pointing towards a narrow alley that ran alongside the barracks. "That door leads to the officer's quarters. It's bolted from the inside, but I reckon we can force it open with a crowbar."

"Excellent!" Tom said, making a mental note of the potential entry point. "What about the main entrance?"

"Guarded round-the-clock," Buckley chimed in, "but I think I've found a blind spot in their patrols. If we time it right, we can slip past them and into the courtyard."

"Timing will be crucial," Tom mused, his mind already calculating the intricacies of their attack. "When the guards change shifts, there's a brief few minutes when they'll be distracted. That's our moment to strike."

"Kavanagh," Tom said, his voice low and urgent. "You take the rear entrance. Make sure there are no surprises."

"Understood, Tom," Kavanagh replied, nodding firmly.

"McMahon," Tom called out, gesturing to a wiry young man with a sharp gaze. "You've got the steadiest hands I've ever seen. I want you on sniper duty, picking off any RIC officers who try to rally their men."

"Understood, Tom," McMahon replied. It was a role he had been practicing diligently, honing his skill with the rifle until he could hit a coin at a hundred yards.

"Keane, you and O'Shea will lead the first wave," Tom continued, pointing to two muscular men who exuded confidence. "Your job is to breach the front door and create an opening. The rest of us will follow, providing cover fire and drawing their attention."

"Leave it to us, Tom. That door won't know what hit it," Keane boasted, cracking his knuckles, while O'Shea grinned and slapped him on the back.

"Good," Tom said, his gaze sweeping over the rest of the men. "The remainder of you will be split into two teams. Team A, led by me, will follow Keane and O'Shea inside. Team B, under Cormac's command, will circle around-the-back to cut off any escape routes."

Tom drew his pistol, raising it high. His men followed suit, rifles and shotguns clutched in sweaty hands. Then he turned back to the barracks.

The bell began to toll in the distance, its sonorous peal

shattering the quiet. The hour of reckoning had arrived at last. He turned to the men and whispered. "Remember the plan. We strike fast and hard, show no mercy. Stay vigilant. Soon, they will know our wrath. Let's make history tonight, lads."

Each man nodded to show they understood. A murmur of agreement rippled through the ranks. "Good," Tom whispered, "let's move. God be with you – and with Ireland!"

As if in response to his words, a sudden cold gust of wind tore through the gathering with the scent of damp earth and decaying leaves, sending chills down their spines and ruffling the tall grass that surrounded them. Tom could feel it too, the electricity in the air, the anticipation that thrummed through every fibre of his being.

The men exchanged determined glances; their spirits lifted by Tom's unwavering conviction. Taking one last moment to gather himself before the chaos that was sure to come, Tom took a deep breath. With hearts pounding and adrenaline coursing through their veins, Tom and the Fenians surged forward, weapons raised. And as the Fenians melted into the shadows, poised to strike like a coiled serpent, each man braced himself for the battle that lay ahead, souls ignited by the flames of vengeance and justice that had brought them all together.

The shadows clung to Michael Keane like a second skin, concealing his presence as he waited for the perfect moment to strike. He could feel the cold steel of the knife in his hand, its weight strangely comforting as it promised retribution. He turned his attention back to the guard at the entrance. The man was idly whistling a tune, completely at ease at his post. It was a complacency that would cost him dearly.

"Patience," he reminded himself, his breaths coming in shallow and rapid. "Wait for the signal."

As if on cue, the distant church bell tolled midnight. That was it, time to attack. With a predatory grace, he burst from the shadows, his knife-wielding hand shooting out with lethal precision. Before the unsuspecting guard at the entrance even knew what hit him, Keane's blade had sliced through the tender flesh of his throat, silencing any cry for help. The hot spill of blood washed over Keane's hands, a visceral reminder of the life he'd just extinguished. Pat O'Shea used a crowbar to prise open the front door of the RIC barracks.

Tom gave the signal, and the remaining men flooded forward out of the darkness. The police guarding the barracks scrambled to action, fumbling with their rifles as the Fenians descended upon them.

Gunfire erupted on all sides, the sharp crack of pistols and shotguns mingling with shouts and screams. Tom fired at an officer taking aim from a second-story window, hitting him square in the chest. The man tumbled backwards out of view. The barracks was breached, the first wave of Fenian men were inside. Tom swung around just in time to see a policeman rush at him, bayonet fixed to his rifle. He sidestepped and slammed the butt of his pistol against the man's temple, sending him crashing to the floor.

The men swarmed into the barracks, rifles cracking as

they shot their way through the ground floor. Tom plunged into the chaos with a knife and pistol. The moonlight glinted off the stained blade in Tom's hand, dealing death with cold efficiency as he threw himself into the fray. He moved like a spectre his eyes scanning for the next threat. His heart pounded as he fought, but his mind remained clear and focused. Each enemy that fell was a victory, each death bringing him closer to avenging Liam. A bullet whizzed past his ear, and he returned fire, dropping another policeman. His heart pounded as he fought his way further into the barracks, every sense hyper alert. They had the element of surprise and superior numbers.

"Keep pushing, remember the plan. There is still work to be done," Tom roared, his own anger boiling over as he recalled the countless injustices his people had suffered at the hands of their oppressors. "Make them pay for what they've done!" He growled, his voice barely audible over the cacophony of gunfire and anguished cries. His pistol barked in response, felling an enemy who'd risen from behind an upturned desk, rifle raised.

"Enough!" The cry tore itself from his throat as he stood over a defeated officer, his boot pressing down on the man's chest. "Tell your devil that we will not be silenced!"

"Constable Doyle, you one of the bastards that killed Liam O'Sullivan, beat him to death in this station."

"We were just following orders," the officer responded through his tears.

"Whose orders… who gave the order to arrest and kill Liam O'Sullivan?" Tom demanded.

"It was… James Reid."

"I thought so, that snake Reid."

"Please," the officer choked out, terror flickering in his eyes. "I-I didn't want any part of it."

"None of us did. But here we are, drowning in the blood of our people. And you chose your side," Tom replied coldly, as he took aim at the officer's head and fired.

The guards upstairs had been caught unawares, dying before they could even raise their weapons in defence as they tumbled from their beds, desperately fumbling for their weapons in a futile bid to save themselves from the storm of rage that had been unleashed upon them.

The fighting was over in minutes, leaving a dozen Constabulary dead or dying. Tom stood over the corpses, they were broken, defeated and yet, he could not bring himself to feel pity for them. Their hands were stained with the blood of his brethren, and there could be no mercy for such crimes. Chest heaving, he turned to his men. "The tyrants now know we will not be silent!" He shouted. "We have drawn first blood – and it will not be the last!"

A cry of victory rose from the Fenians, the barracks echoing with the sound. The storm that had been brewing outside seemed to be in concert with their newfound strength. Justice had been served tonight. But Tom knew that this was just the beginning.

As the sounds of battle faded into an eerie silence, blood pooled around Tom's boots, the metallic scent of it filling the room as he assessed the carnage wrought by their righteous fury. The Fenians stood victorious, their faces a grim mix of satisfaction and exhaustion. The flames of rebellion had been kindled within their hearts, and the battle to free their homeland from tyranny would rage on, long after the echoes of tonight's violence had faded away. This was but the first step in their fight for freedom, and though the path ahead was uncertain, one thing was clear: they would never again bow before the tyrants who sought to enslave them.

"Tonight, we have made them bleed," Tom declared, his voice ringing with conviction. "And I swear, by all that is sacred, we will not rest until our land is free."

As the cheers continued, Tom looked around at his men. He knew they would follow him to hell and back, if need be, for each of them carried their own ghosts and wounds inflicted by the oppressive regime.

Tom allowed himself a moment to breathe. The adrenaline had begun to ebb, leaving a hollow ache in its wake. *Was it worth it?* whispered a small voice in the back of his mind. They had killed police officers and declared open war on the Crown. There would be no mercy shown to them now.

Tom knew there was some other business to take care of before the town was swarming with Redcoats.

Chapter 20: My Name is Vengeance
February 15th, Dromdaire

Tom Ryan hurried through the narrow streets of Dromdaire, his heart pounding with a mixture of adrenaline and fear. The successful attack on the Royal Irish Constabulary barracks had been a triumph for the Fenians, but Tom knew that their victory would be short-lived. British soldiers would soon descend upon the town, seeking retribution for their fallen comrades.

Tom made his way swiftly towards Cathleen Fitzgerald's home, his footsteps muffled by the soft, damp earth beneath him. His stomach growled angrily, and he was bone-weary, his feet aching and his clothes blood-spattered. But physical discomfort barely registered in Tom's mind. All his thoughts centred on Cathleen. She was in danger because of him. A mixture of anxiety and guilt churned within his body with peril looming over them like a dark cloud. He knew he had to ensure her safety at all costs.

"Forgive me, Cathleen," he murmured under his breath, his voice barely audible above the rustle of leaves and the patter of raindrops. "I never meant to bring you into this."

He crept through back alleys and gardens, avoiding the main streets. He paused outside the Fitzgerald's home, listening intently. Hearing nothing amiss, raising his fist, he rapped sharply on the wooden door. Moments later, it swung open to reveal Cathleen, her eyes wide with concern as she took in his dishevelled appearance.

"Tom!" she whispered, "what are you doing here? It's too dangerous… Are you hurt? You are covered in blood."

"I'm fine, Cathleen, but we don't have much time," Tom replied, his voice urgent. "Redcoats are coming. They'll tear this town apart looking for the men who attacked the RIC barracks. I fear for your safety if you stay here. Go to Cork, bring your mother and father with you. I will meet you there as soon as I can."

"My parents aren't here, they travelled to a funeral in Killarney this morning. They won't be back for two days… Where will I know where to find you in Cork?" Cathleen asked, scratching at her head with confusion.

"Book into a hotel near the harbour, I will find you there, I promise."

Cathleen's gaze flickered with uncertainty, and she took a step back, clutching the edge of the door for support. "I'll go, Tom, but only if you promise me you'll be careful."

Tom reached out, gently cupping her cheek in his hand. "I promise, Cathleen… Now you must go; there is a coach leaving for Cork in twenty minutes. Redcoats will be swarming this place by morning."

Cathleen searched his eyes. After a moment, she nodded. "Let me pack my things." She turned and went inside the house. With a heavy heart, Tom watched as Cathleen gathered her few belongings. Ten minutes later, she re-emerged, a shawl wrapped tight around her as she carried a small bag and hurried out into the night.

They crept down the darkened street, darting from building to building. Cathleen stumbled on the uneven cobblestones, and Tom caught her arm. Her pulse fluttered under his fingers like a caged bird.

At last, the coach station appeared. As they hurried inside, Tom felt Cathleen sag against him. Her whisper brushed his ear. "What if they find you?"

Tom turned, tilting her chin up. "They won't." Though uncertain himself, he infused his voice with reassurance. For a moment Cathleen searched his face again. Then she squeezed his hand and walked through the station doors without looking back.

Five minutes later, Tom watched the coach rattle away into the night, carrying her to safety, he prayed. But his own path remained unclear. Shadowed by the growing threat of violence and reprisal. The air was thick with tension, and he could feel the weight of the impending arrival of the British Redcoats. Time was running out, and he had to act fast.

***

The moon was a pale disc hanging low in the sky as Tom rode towards his farm. Hoofbeats echoed off the road as the wind whispered through the tall trees, carrying with it an undercurrent of something darker, more sinister, setting his nerves on edge. The night pressed close around him, filled with unseen threats. "Damn it," he said under his breath, glancing over his shoulder for the hundredth time. He couldn't shake the feeling that he was being followed, though he saw no one on the deserted road behind him.

He urged his horse into a faster pace, racing against the growing sense of dread that coiled tight in his chest. He planned to gather some fresh clothes and money and disappear to Cork for a time until things settled down.

As he approached his home, the sight of the familiar stone walls brought little comfort. Instead, he felt the weight of all he stood to lose pressing down upon him like a heavy burden. As the farmhouse came into view, unease prickled his neck. Had that been a glimmer of light in the window? He slowed his approach, one hand drifting toward his revolver.

"Stay here," he whispered to his horse, tying the reins to a nearby tree. He moved cautiously, listening intently for any signs of danger. Inside his home, he quickly gathered his belongings.

The sound of footsteps outside snapped him back to the present. Heart pounding, he reached for the pistol tucked into his waistband, his fingers closing around the cold metal handle with practiced ease. He barely had time to react before the first thug burst through the door, a vicious snarl twisting his features.

"Thought you could outrun us, did you?" The man sneered, lunging at Tom with a knife clenched in his fist.

Tom dodged the attack, landing a solid blow to the thug's jaw. He heard the crunch of bone and the man crumpled to the ground, unconscious. Three more men surged into the room; their eyes filled with malicious intent.

"Reid sends his regards." One of them spat, raising a pistol and firing in Tom's direction.

"James Reid." The name was a curse on Tom's lips as he ducked behind a table, barely avoiding the shot. He returned fire, picking off two of the remaining attackers. The last man charged at him, but Tom was quicker, grappling with him and ultimately sinking his blade into the thug's chest.

Tom could smell smoke. He looked up to see that smoke was pouring into the kitchen from overhead, he guessed that there were more men outside and they had occupied themselves by torching the roof. He slowly went outside and peered up at the roof of his home. Flames licked the thatch, casting a hellish glow. The nearby barn was already engulfed, horses screaming. He ran over to try and free them.

A shotgun blast shattered the night. Tom threw himself onto the ground as buckshot peppered the dirt. Shadowy figures converged from the trees. He drew his handgun and fired back, dropping one assailant. Another loomed from the darkness, swinging a club. Tom deflected the blow and slammed his pistol into the man's face. More gunfire flashed as they exchanged shots. Gritting his teeth, Tom downed two more before spotting the leader taking aim. He seized the dropped club and hurled it, catching the man full in the chest. Getting back to his feet, he managed to make it to the barn door. He opened it, allowing the terrified horses to run free.

Tom could only watch as his home burned, the

firelight reflecting in his cold eyes. The fire consuming the thatched roof with a ravenous hunger. It was too late to save it now.

"Damn you, Reid," Tom muttered, surveying the destruction. "This ends now."

Anger and vengeance burned hot within him as he mounted his horse, determination setting his jaw as he rode towards Reid's home.

***

The storm outside battered the windowpanes, raindrops pelting the glass in a steady rhythm. Tom's boots, heavy with mud from his hurried approach, stood before the formidable oak doors of Reid's manor. With a creak, the doors opened, and Tom took a deep breath, steadying his nerves. stepped into the dimly lit study where James Reid stood waiting, a fire crackling behind him. The door slammed shut, echoing through the room like the distant rumble of thunder.

"Well, well. If it isn't the illustrious Mr Ryan," his voice was smooth as silk, belying the venom underneath.

Tom met his gaze unflinchingly, "Reid."

They stared at each other, a battle of wills unfolding in the space between them. The unwavering stare of the young man who'd risen from the hardships of his past, against the cold, calculating gaze of the man who held the fates of so many in his iron grip. The tension rose like a noose tightening around Tom's neck, but he would not be cowed. Not today.

"You seem to have forgotten your place, Mr Ryan. Allow me to remind you." Reid's lips curled into a sneer. A flicker of unease passed over Reid's features before his mask of arrogance slid back into place. He straightened to his full height, looming over Tom in a display of dominance.

Tom stood firm against the implicit threat, his resolve absolute. "Yer time is up, Reid." Tom roared, his fists clenching at his sides. His jaw tightened, muscles flexing beneath the rough stubble that covered his face. "I'm here to put an end to the suffering you have inflicted on the people of Dromdaire."

James scoffed, "How noble of you, Mr Ryan. But you're just one man."

"I won't back down, Reid. You can't break me. All of your hired thugs are dead, the RIC officers are all dead. There is no one to protect you now."

"Is that so?" Reid inquired, taking a step closer to Tom, their faces mere inches apart.

"You've underestimated me before," Tom warned, his eyes never leaving Reid's. "And now you'll pay the price."

The room seemed to pulse with the energy of their standoff, each man refusing to bend to the other's will. Outside, the storm roared on and as the rain continued to fall, it was clear that this battle had only just begun.

A single bead of sweat trickled down Tom's temple, the only outward sign of his mounting tension as he held James Reid's calculating gaze. The grand room in which they stood was filled with opulence and wealth – a testament to the power Reid wielded over those who crossed him. Yet, Tom's resolve remained unshaken.

"Have you forgotten who I am, Ryan?" Reid said, his voice like ice. "I can crush you and everything you hold dear."

James Reid's nostrils flared, sensing that his usual tactics would not intimidate this man. Frustrated, he resorted to physical force. With a snarl, he lunged at Tom, aiming a fist at his face.

Tom's instincts, honed from years of battles, kicked in. He deftly sidestepped the blow, retaliating with a punch of his own that connected with a solid thud against Reid's jaw.

"Is that all ye've got?" Tom taunted.

"Damn you!" Reid spat blood, reeling from the impact of Tom's fist. He launched another attack, fuelled by desperation to maintain his control and dominance. "Your pathetic spirit means nothing to me!" Reid hissed; his face contorted with rage.

Tom struck back, his fist connecting with James' face once more. The sound of impact echoed through the lavish room.

Reid stumbled back from the blow, shock and fury warring on his face. He touched his jaw gingerly, examining the blood that coated his fingers.

"You'll pay for that, you insolent fool!" Reid roared.

He charged at Tom, unleashing a flurry of punches. Tom deflected the blows, fighting back with practiced efficiency. He ducked and pivoted, using Reid's momentum against him to land several hits of his own.

Reid was taller by about two inches, but Tom had the advantage of speed and skill. Still, it was a brutal match, and Tom could feel his knuckles swelling and bruises forming along his ribs.

With a yell, Reid grabbed Tom and slammed him against the wall. The wood panelling splintered under the impact as the air rushed from Tom's lungs.

Gasping, Tom wrestled free of Reid's grip and stumbled away. He blinked through the haze of pain, struggling to catch his breath.

The glow of firelight danced across Tom's sweat-slicked skin. His muscles strained beneath the coarse fabric of his shirt as he threw another punch at Reid, every fibre of his being fuelled by the desire to avenge Liam's death.

"Is this all you have?" Reid laughed, deflecting Tom's blow with surprising agility for a man of his age and status.

"You'll pay for what you've done!" Tom growled through gritted teeth, throwing himself forward in a reckless lunge. Their bodies collided with the force, sending them both staggering into the mahogany bookcase that lined the room.

Reid let out a guttural grunt as the heavy volumes rained down upon them, their leather-bound spines cracking underfoot like the bones of those who had suffered beneath his rule. "You're a fool if you think you can stop me." He spat blood, shoving Tom back with brute strength.

As the fight continued to unfold, antique chairs splintered beneath the weight of their grappling bodies, richly woven rugs were trampled and torn underfoot, and delicate porcelain shattered against the walls like fragile dreams dashed upon a stone.

"Enough!" Reid roared, his face flushed with rage and exertion. He attempted to regain control of the situation by standing upright and fixing Tom with a venomous glare, but the younger man would not be intimidated.

"You've taken so much from us," Tom panted; his eyes locked on James as he struggled to catch his breath. "But I'll not let you take any more."

"Your defiance will be your undoing," Reid warned, his voice shaking with fury. "You'll never win."

"Perhaps not," Tom conceded, his chest heaving with the effort it took to remain standing. "But neither will you."

With that, Tom drew upon a reserve of strength he hadn't known he possessed and lunged at James once more, their fists colliding in a crescendo of violence that seemed to shake the very foundations of the stately manor in which they fought.

The scent of blood and sweat hung heavy in the air. Tom could feel his heart pounding in his chest like a war drum, the rhythm urging him onwards as he faced down Reid, whose eyes gleamed with malice and desperation.

"Give it up, Reid," Tom snarled. "You're finished."

"*Ha!*" James spat, wiping the blood from his mouth with the back of his hand. "You think you can just waltz into my home, lay waste to everything I've built, and walk away unscathed? You're deluding yourself, boy."

"Am I?" Tom retorted, "I've come this far, haven't I?"

"Indeed," James conceded, his voice dripping with disdain. "But your little crusade ends here."

With a speed that belied his age, Reid lunged at Tom, his fist aiming straight for the younger man's face. But Tom was ready. He deftly sidestepped the blow, and as James stumbled forward off-balance, Tom seized his opportunity.

Drawing on every last scrap of energy within him, Tom sent a crushing uppercut into James' exposed jaw. The impact reverberated through the room like a cannon blast, and for a brief moment, time seemed to slow as Reid's eyes rolled back in his head and his body crumpled to the ground in a heap.

"James Reid, meet justice," Tom murmured, his breaths coming in ragged gasps as he surveyed his defeated foe.

Reid was bleeding heavily from his nose and mouth, but his eyes still held a dangerous glint. He pulled a pistol from a cabinet drawer and aimed it at Tom.

"This has gone on long enough," Reid said confidently. "It's time I put you in your place once and for all."

Tom tensed, his heart throbbing as he stared down the barrel of the gun. After everything, he couldn't die like this. Not when Cathleen still needed him. Tom hurled himself at Reid. The gun went off with a deafening crack, the bullet grazing Tom's arm. They tumbled to the floor, grappling for the pistol. Tom fought with a fury born of desperation. Finally, his fingers closed around the hilt of the gun. He wrestled it from Reid's grasp and pressed the cool metal to his enemy's temple.

"It's over." Tom panted as he squeezed the trigger.

"Have some mercy, Tom… I can give you money, anything you want… land… money… whatever you want."

"No mercy… Erin go bragh," Tom whispered as he pulled the trigger.

The echo of gunfire faded away, leaving only the sound of his heavy breathing and the crackling of the dwindling fire. With one final look of defiance at the dead remains of James Reid, Tom knew that justice had been finally served.

Chapter 21: In the Shadows of Pursuit
February 15th, Laharan

Tom made his way back to the safe house in Laharan to reunite with his Fenian comrades as they celebrated their recent victory. He felt drained from the night's events, and he knew that there was no time for resting. He would soon have to lead his men away from the area to avoid being slaughtered by Redcoats who would have a taste for Fenian blood on their lips. Standing a little apart from the revelry, he surveyed the scene with a mixture of pride and unease. He couldn't shake the feeling that their triumph had been too easy, that fate was preparing to exact a heavy price for their audacity.

"Tom!" Kavanagh called out, beckoning him over to have a drink. "Come on, man! Tonight's not the night for brooding!"

"Perhaps you're right," Tom replied, forcing a smile onto his battle-hardened features. He took several swigs from a whisky bottle as the men laughed heartily and sang songs.

"Give us a song, Tom, it's your turn." Doyle laughed.

"Sorry, lads, I have the voice of a crow," Tom said with a smile.

"Okay, will I suppose it's my turn again?" Kavanagh said as he pushed out his chest. But just as he was about to take a step forward to begin, a young messenger boy burst into the kitchen, his face pale and streaked with sweat.

"British soldiers!" He gasped, breathless from his sprint. "They are already in Dromdaire, they are burning it to the ground.

A hush fell over the once festive crowd as they turned to listen intently to the messenger's words. Tom felt his stomach drop, the elation of victory instantly replaced by a sickening dread. He knew this moment would come, but he'd hoped they'd have more time.

"Killarney has been reinforced and is heavily guarded," the boy continued, fear evident in his trembling voice.

Tom exchanged a troubled glance with the other men of the Fenian platoon before stepping forward decisively. It was clear that any plans they'd made to continue their fight needed to be abandoned immediately. Their priority now was to ensure the survival of as many of their comrades as possible.

Tom straightened his shoulders, pushing down the despair that threatened to overwhelm him. Now was not the time for doubt or fear. His men were looking to him for guidance, trusting in his leadership to see them through this crisis. He would not fail them.

"All right, everyone, listen up!" Tom shouted, the faces of the men turned towards him expectantly, hope and desperation mingling in their eyes. "Comrades!" His voice rang out clearly across the makeshift camp. "The British are coming to snuff out our bid for freedom before it can truly ignite. But they will not find us easy prey to slaughter. Attacking the RIC barracks in Killarney as we had planned is no longer an option! Our main focus now has to be survival. We need to escape and evade capture!" Tom's words were met with a cacophony of protest and disbelief, but he raised his hand for silence, his resolve unwavering, his eyes blazing with determination.

"Believe me, I understand how you feel. But we must face reality. Charging headlong into a heavily fortified barracks would be nothing short of suicide! We owe it to ourselves and our fallen comrades to live and fight another day. We came here to strike a blow against injustice, and strike we did. Now we must slip back into the shadows for a time, avoid the might of their army until we can regroup and renew our struggle. With any luck, we'll be able to slip through their fingers unnoticed."

The murmurs of dissent died down as Tom's stern gaze swept over the crowd. He knew that many of them had been dreaming of glorious victory, of driving the British from their homeland once and for all. But those dreams would mean nothing if they were all dead.

"Make no mistake, this is not the end. We will live to fight another day. Now quickly, gather your things. We leave straight away. And may God watch over us all."

"Tom's right," Doyle added. "We've come this far, and we won't let them take us without a fight. But we must be smart about it."

The men sprang into action, their weariness forgotten in the urgency of the moment. Tom watched them prepare, pride and hope flickering amidst the darkness. They would make it through this. Freedom was never easily won.

Tom gathered his trusted lieutenants, Doyle and Kavanagh, and began dividing the men into smaller groups, each with an appointed leader. Caution and stealth would serve them better now than force of arms.

"Remember, avoid the main roads where the Redcoats will be patrolling in force. Stick to the forests and mountain paths," Tom ordered.

The tension in the air was palpable as the Fenians split up, each man knowing that his life depended on their ability to remain hidden from the Redcoats. There were no goodbyes, only grim nods of understanding and fierce determination.

"Meet back here in five days," Tom instructed the leaders. "Be cautious and stay hidden. Godspeed to you all."

The groups slipped away in succession until only Tom's band remained. He clasped hands with each man, meeting their eyes with silent reassurance before they disappeared into the black night.

In the distance, Tom watched as Dromdaire burned.

Finally, it was time. Tom hefted his pack over his shoulder and led his group of seven men west. Moving as quickly as the rugged terrain allowed, they wove between rocky outcroppings and stands of oak, the trees providing welcome concealment. Tom's resourcefulness shone through as he found alternate routes to avoid areas that may be heavily patrolled, leading them along forgotten deer trails and across hidden streams. His adaptability, honed by years of surviving in America during the Civil War, served him well in the face of this new challenge.

With each mile between them and the British pursuit, Tom felt the knot in his chest loosen slightly. They would make it to the safe house ahead, rest and regroup. The battle was far from over.

"Keep low, lads," he urged his men in a hushed whisper, his eyes never leaving the horizon. "We need to make it over that ridge before dawn."

The moon hung low like a spectral lantern across the forest floor as it peeked through the tangle of branches overhead. The night was alive with danger, every rustle of leaves or snap of twigs sending hearts pounding and breaths held. Tom could feel the dampness of the earth seeping into his boots, chilling him to the bone.

"Wait," Tom whispered suddenly, his hand shooting out in front of Sean's chest. The shadows around them seemed to twist and dance, as if conspiring with the enemy. He strained his ears, listening intently to the distant sounds of marching footsteps and faint murmurs of the Redcoats. His instincts told him they were close, too close.

"Down!" he hissed, pressing himself and his comrades against the cold forest floor. Their heartbeats thudded loudly, as if attempting to betray their hiding place. Tom watched through narrowed eyes as the Redcoats passed by, mere yards away from where they lay concealed. He held his breath, praying that none would stray from their path and discover them.

"By God's grace," Brendan McCarthy muttered as the last of the Redcoats disappeared from view. "That was a close one."

"Too close," Tom agreed, shaking his head with a

mixture of relief and frustration. "We can't afford any mistakes."

"Are we going to make it?" Brendan asked, his voice shaking with exhaustion.

"Have faith," Tom replied, his own fears buried deep within him as he pressed on. "We've come this far, and we're not giving up now."

***

Under a sky of inky blackness, Tom's breath was ragged, his lungs burning with each gulp of air as he led the weary band of Fenians through the night. The camaraderie that had once bound them together now strained to its breaking point, yet still they trudged on, driven by a desperate need for survival.

As they continued their desperate escape, the relentless pace began to take its toll on the men. Their once-straight backs now bent beneath the weight of exhaustion, the fire of determination in their eyes waning with each step. The constant fear and uncertainty gnawed at their spirits, causing tempers to flare and patience to wear thin.

"Tom," Brendan gasped, falling to his knees amid the ferns. "I can't... I can't go on."

"Get up, Brendan," Tom urged, his voice strained with worry. "We can't stop now."

"Leave him," Patrick Fitzgerald snapped, his eyes narrowing in frustration. "He's only slowing us down."

"Enough!" Tom barked, glaring at Patrick before

turning back to Brendan, offering him a hand. "We're all tired, but we have to keep going. We'll rest when it's safe."

"Safe?" Brendan questioned bitterly as he struggled to his feet. "Will we ever be safe again?"

"Only if we stay together and keep moving," Tom replied firmly, his gaze sweeping over the weary faces of his comrades.

With those words hanging heavy in the air, the men pressed on, their bodies aching and minds reeling from the constant strain of evading capture.

"Stay close, lads," Tom murmured, leading the way through the moonlit forest. "We'll find a place to rest soon, I promise."

As the night wore on, their every movement fuelled by a potent mix of fear and sheer willpower, the hunted Fenians continued their harrowing journey, haunted by the knowledge that the spectre of capture loomed ever closer.

Tom led his band of weary Fenians along the rugged western slopes of the Caher Mountains, moving as swiftly as their exhausted bodies allowed. Though the morning sun now shone high above, little of its warmth reached them in the shadow of the peaks. The lack of sleep and constant vigilance had taken its toll. Eyes were rimmed red, faces gaunt and footsteps heavy. Tempers ran short, and Tom often had to intervene when minor squabbles threatened to erupt.

"Steady, lads, we're nearly there," he encouraged, though in truth he couldn't be certain how much farther the safe house lay. He recognised none of the surrounding terrain.

By midday, clouds rolled in, and a penetrating rain began to fall. The group pulled their collars up and pressed on through muddy tracts now running like streams. The bone-chilling damp cut through their threadbare clothing, making the prospect of a fire and dry shelter all the more enticing.

Just when it seemed they could go no further, a small, ramshackle cottage came into view. With renewed vigour, Tom led the men toward it. They had found shelter, however humble and temporary, a refuge for the moment, but no guarantee of safety. The men collapsed on the cold stone floor, their bodies trembling with relief and exhaustion.

"Rest now," Tom told them, his eyes scanning the surrounding area for any sign of danger. "We'll move out again once night falls. Get the fire going, and we'll soon have some heat and dry clothes," Tom said, clapping one of the men on the shoulder. Weary smiles creased their bearded faces. The long trek was over for now. But tonight would bring new trials. Tom knew the respite would be brief. Soon they would need to be on the move again, staying one step ahead of the British patrols tirelessly hunting them. But for now, his band of men could recover their strength.

"Tom," Conal, a stout, middle-aged man, whispered. "We can't keep going like this. We're exhausted, and the Redcoats are getting closer. We need a plan."

Tom knew Conall was right. He needed to scout ahead to get a sense of the troop movements and vulnerabilities. He would not risk leading his men forward into unknown terrain and potentially leading them into hostile territory. He decided that he would scout ahead first.

"All right, men, listen up," he said, his voice low and steady. I'll scout ahead and see what we're up against. If I don't return by nightfall, assume the worst and carry on without me."

"Tom, no!" Conall said, "you can't go alone! They'll kill you!"

"Better me than all of us," Tom replied solemnly.

"Then, be careful, brother," Conal said, gripping Tom's arm tightly. "May the wind be at your back."

With a nod, Tom disappeared into the forest, his instincts guiding him as he navigated the wooded terrain.

The cold rain continued falling in sheets, masking his movements as he stalked silently from tree to tree. The forest was large but had little undergrowth to obscure potential threats. Cresting a rise, Tom peered down at a road slicing through the forest below. A company of red-coated soldiers marched along it, rifles glinting dully in the grey afternoon light. Tom's jaw clenched. The enemy were too close. Edging backwards, Tom turned and worked his way east through the woods parallel to the road. He needed to determine if the soldiers had set up checkpoints nearby. Pressing onwards, he remained vigilant, one hand resting on his rifle. The lives of his comrades depended on what he discovered out here alone.

Tom continued for hours moving stealthily through the woods, using the rain and foliage as cover. As he neared a bend in the road, he caught a glimpse of movement up ahead. Crouching low, he crept forward and saw a small platoon of British soldiers standing guard near a bridge spanning a rain-swollen river.

It was just as Tom had feared – they were setting up checkpoints along the main roads to try and catch any fleeing rebels. He studied the scene, counting the number of soldiers and scanning for any hidden snipers that might be concealed nearby. By his estimate, there were perhaps a dozen men. Enough to pose a serious threat, but few enough that he could potentially deal with them if necessary.

Tom withdrew into the trees once more. He needed to loop back and find another route across the river for the others. Time was running short; the light would soon begin fading. Moving as swiftly as he dared, Tom retraced his steps. The rain pattered against the leaves in a constant susurrus. In the distance, he heard the occasional crack of gunfire as the British troops fired on anything that moved.

Heart pounding, Tom realised just how alone he was out here. Cut off from his comrades, hunted by a vicious enemy. But he swallowed down his fear. The others were relying on him, he couldn't let them down.

Spotting a large elm tree spanning the creek, Tom clambered atop the slick, moss-covered trunk. Balancing carefully, rifle held aloft, he worked his way across. The makeshift bridge creaked and swayed beneath his weight but held firm. With a quiet sigh of relief, Tom dropped back to solid ground on the far side. Now to find the others before night fell.

Tom moved swiftly through the forest, ducking beneath low-hanging branches and vaulting over fallen logs. The fading February light threw long shadows between the trees, making it difficult to spot possible threats. In the distance, he could hear the occasional shout or volley of gunshots as the British troops continued their search.

With utmost care, he crept forward. Peering through the underbrush, he spotted the small dwelling, smoke still billowing from the chimney. As he drew nearer to the cottage, a gnawing unease settled in his stomach. Tom paused to listen intently; the forest was too quiet. The usual sounds of the night seemed muted. An ominous silence hung in the air. Tom's pulse quickened. Something was wrong. He quickened his pace. The sight that met him when he stepped towards the cottage turned his blood to ice. Scattered packs and belongings lay strewn about the forest floor. Signs of a struggle were everywhere. Tom cautiously entered the cottage, his rifle aiming straight ahead.

The door hung ajar, swaying gently in the breeze. He crept closer, hand instinctively tightening around the grip of his gun. His breath was shallow, each exhale a silent prayer that his instincts were wrong. But as he crossed the threshold, the dim light from the dying embers of the hearth revealed a scene of horror. Tom's stomach dropped. His men lay scattered across the floor, their bodies twisted in grotesque final poses. Blood had pooled beneath them, dark and viscous, soaking into the wooden floorboards. His mind struggled to process the carnage. Seven men, good men, who had fought beside him and shared dreams of Irish freedom, now lay cold and lifeless.

Kneeling beside the nearest body, he recognised the face of Brendan McCarthy. His eyes were wide open, staring sightlessly at the ceiling, a bullet hole marking his forehead. Barry closed his eyes with a trembling hand, a silent act of respect. He moved from one body to the next, confirming each identity, each loss tearing at his soul.

How had the Redcoats found them? The cabin was supposed to be secure, hidden well off the beaten path. Tom's thoughts raced as he pieced together the tragic sequence of events. The enemy must have tracked them somehow, perhaps had a spy among the local populace. The thought filled him with a searing rage. Betrayal, he knew, was a dagger that cut deep. Grief and rage churned inside him, but he forced it down. Now was not the time. He exited the house and melted back into the forest. He was alone now, with no one to rely upon but himself. The British were closing in from all sides, bent on capturing the last of the rebel fighters. Tom's chances of escape grew slimmer by the hour. But he refused to give up. Gathering his courage, Tom vowed to keep fighting for his lost comrades, if nothing else. The future remained dangerously uncertain, but he would face it with iron determination. This wasn't over yet.

Suddenly, the snap of a twig shattered the silence, and Tom froze, his body tensing like a coiled spring. A group of four Redcoats emerged from the shadows, their bayonets glinting in the moonlight.

"*Oi*! Who goes there?" One of them barked, levelling his rifle at Tom.

"Your worst nightmare," Tom muttered under his

breath, adrenaline surging through his veins as he leaped into action. Gunfire erupted around him, and he ducked behind a tree, his heart pounding in his ears.

"Damn it, damn it, damn it..." he whispered, fumbling to reload his rifle. He knew he had mere seconds before they closed in on him as he prepared himself for the firefight to come.

Tom sprang out from behind the tree, his gun blazing as he took aim at the nearest Redcoat. The man crumpled to the ground, but another quickly took his place. Every muscle in Tom's body screamed with fear and tension, but he forced himself to focus, relying on the skills he'd honed in the Civil War. Rolling across the forest floor, finding cover tree by tree, rising to shoot and diving again. One by one, the Redcoats fell, their bodies littering the forest floor like broken dolls. But Tom knew he couldn't afford to linger. Trembling and covered in sweat, he sprinted as fast as he could, not knowing where he was going. Fearing that he could be running straight into a much larger Redcoat unit.

***

Tom stumbled on through the dark forest, exhaustion weighing down his every step. He had been on the move for what felt like days now, stopping only briefly to rest before pressing on again. The forest was still, save for the rapid pounding of Tom's heart. He crouched low behind a moss-covered log, his breath coming in short, panicked gasps as he strained to listen for any sounds of pursuit. His

249

vision blurred. I just need to rest, he told himself. Just for a minute. Hunger gnawed at his stomach, but he did not dare try to hunt or forage. Making a fire would draw the Redcoats right to him. When was the last time he'd eaten? Two, maybe three days ago? Tom shook his head, trying to clear the fog from his mind. But the gnawing emptiness in his belly made his head spin.

The thicket of trees and bracken enveloped Tom in darkness as the pale moonlight struggled to penetrate the dense forest canopy. Each ragged breath and frantic heartbeat thundered in his ears as he crept through the underbrush, wincing at the crackle of dry leaves under his boots. The dense foliage surrounded him on all sides, concealing him from view but also obstructing his vision. Eyes darting nervously, Tom scanned the shadowy trees, searching for even the slightest hint of movement.

His mind raced with escape plans, each more desperate than the last. He was no stranger to hardship, but this – being hunted like an animal – was more than he could bear. "Easy, lad," he cautioned himself, forcing his wild gaze to focus and his trembling hands to steady. A single misstep could mean capture, or far worse. Bile rose in his throat at the thought of it.

With great care, Tom shifted to peek between the leaves, risking detection for a better view of his surroundings. In the distance, he could just make out the faint glow of lanterns through the trees. His breath caught in his throat as he realised the search party was closer than he thought. With painstaking care, he threaded between the knotted trunks, ducking under gnarled branches that snatched at his coat. The lantern lights of his pursuers flickered in the distance. He could almost see the glint of rifles among the trees and hear the snapping jaws of dogs thirsty for rebel blood. Tom shuddered, wiping a grimy sleeve across his damp forehead as he crouched beneath an ancient oak tree, its gnarled limbs reaching outwards like the twisted fingers of fate. The distant howls of hounds pierced the air, accompanied by the rustling of leaves and the mournful whispers of the wind.

He sank down against a fallen log, every muscle in his body screaming for relief. Laying his head back, Tom let his eyes fall closed. He would get moving again in a moment, he just needed a short rest to gather his strength. Gripped by fear, Tom weighed his options. He could keep hiding and hope they passed him by. Or he could try to slip away under cover of darkness and continue his desperate bid for freedom.

"Was it worth it?" he murmured, momentarily forgetting the need for silence. His voice, barely a whisper, sounded foreign to his ears. He knew that the choices he had made, the lives he had touched, were like ripples in a pond, spreading outwards with unforeseen consequences. Regret and bitterness gnawed at him; a relentless beast that refused to be silenced. He thought of all the events that had led him to this moment, alone and hounded in the heart of the Irish wilderness. How many times had he looked death in the eye and walked away unscathed? And yet, here he was, the ghosts of his past nipping at his heels like a pack of ravenous wolves.

"No use dwelling on it now, keep it together, Tom,"

he whispered. There was no time for regret, no space for recriminations. Tom forced himself to focus on the present moment. He needed every ounce of cunning and willpower to elude the Redcoats, to survive long enough to see his comrades again, and to strike back at the iron fist that sought to smother the spirit of his people.

Tom's steps grew slower, more faltering. He staggered, crashing into a nearby trunk as despair threatened to crush his spirit. But he shook his head violently, banishing the dark thoughts. He had to keep going. With newfound resolve, he melted into the shadows once more, moving swift and silent as a spectre through the trees, blending into the darkness and becoming one with the night.

His chest heaving from exertion, he paused to catch his breath in the oppressive darkness of the forest. Fear coursed through him as adrenaline fuelled every heartbeat and each ragged breath. He had no choice but to flee or face capture. But as he forged ahead, a new sound cut through the silence, freezing him in his tracks like a beast caught in the hunter's sights. Footsteps, heavy and unyielding, grew closer with every heartbeat, pounding a relentless rhythm that echoed the terror surging through his veins.

"God help me." He breathed, pressing himself flat against the forest floor as his eyes scanned the shadows for any sign of his pursuers.

And then he saw them, their crimson uniforms materialising like devils in the darkness. Lanterns shone eerie pools of light on the ground, revealing a group of

Redcoats with rifles in hand, searching the area with grim determination. He counted at least a dozen soldiers. Too many to take on in a gun battle. Their voices carried through the night, low and menacing, a symphony of danger that sent shivers down Tom's spine.

Tom's heart hammered in his chest as he watched the soldiers fan out, prodding through bushes with their bayonets. inching ever closer to him. He knew that even the slightest movement could betray him, but the urge to run was almost unbearable, a primal instinct screaming for release.

Desperately, he scanned the darkness, searching for an escape route. Stay put, he told himself, swallowing his fear as he willed his body to remain still. Wait for the right moment, then make your move.

A narrow deer trail caught his eye, winding its way up a rocky slope. If he could reach it undetected, it might offer him a way out. But the soldiers were closing in fast, their voices carrying through the chill night air.

"Spread out." One of them barked. "He can't have gone far."

"Keep your eyes peeled, lads." Another added. "This one's a slippery bastard, I'll give him that."

Tom hesitated, paralysed by indecision. Making a break for the trail was risky, but remaining hidden was becoming impossible. As the enemy fanned out, encircling his position, he knew time was running out.

A bearded sergeant paused, holding his lantern aloft as he studied the forest floor. Tom shrank back, watching the man's boots edge ever closer to his hiding spot. This was it. He braced himself, ready to fight to his last breath. Fortunately, the sergeant turned and walked in the opposite direction.

Then a shrill whistle sounded in the distance. The sergeant straightened, bellowing for his men to regroup. Tom sagged against the tree as the Redcoats hurried away, their lights fading into the blackness between the trees. That had been too close. He let out a shaky breath, willing his hammering heart to slow.

Saying a silent prayer, Tom darted for the trail. Twigs snapped under his boots, each crack sounding as loud as a gunshot in the tense silence. Panting, he scrambled up the trail, the baying of hounds ringing out below as the hunt pressed on. He didn't dare look back. His fingers curled around the cold steel of the rifle at his side. The voices of his past echoed in his head, urging him to persevere, to survive. Refusing to let their memory of his family be forgotten like the ashes of a dying fire.

His breath came in ragged gasps as he pushed his aching body faster. Glancing over his shoulder, he saw no sign of his pursuers. The trail had bought him some time. But for how long? Slowing to a jog, thoughts turned to Cathleen. Her kind eyes and gentle spirit had stirred something in him long forgotten, hope. Hope for a future beyond this endless struggle. But such dreams felt impossibly distant now.

The trail emerged atop a rocky ridge. In the valley below, the lights of a distant village beckoned. If he could make it there undiscovered, he might find refuge for the night. With cautious optimism, Tom made his way down the far side of the ridge. Fortune had been on his side so far. Perhaps, against all odds, he could still find a way to freedom.

Tom crouched behind a moss-covered rock, his heart thundering in his chest like a wild stallion. He looked to his left and observed a mill wheel turning in a fast-flowing river. Tom's pulse quickened, and he retreated down the riverbank into the cold water and hid under a nearby bridge, his senses sharpened by adrenaline, his mind racing to devise a plan. Perhaps he could make his way into the village through the river channel, he pondered. From his hiding place, he could see a road. A checkpoint loomed ahead, manned by two armed soldiers who scrutinised each passerby with steely suspicion. He realised that the river was too deep, and he would never survive for too long in its fast flowing and freezing cold water. Should he chance his luck getting through the checkpoint. He listened to the soldiers as they chatted, their voices heavy with exhaustion.

"Another bloody night," one muttered. "And for what? They say Tom Ryan's long gone or dead."

"Orders are orders, mate," another replied with a resigned sigh. "We keep looking 'til they tell us otherwise."

"What does he look like anyway?"

"I haven't a clue, typical-looking Irish bloke I suppose, they all look the bloody same to me."

Tom held his breath, their words ignited a spark of hope within him, but he could not afford to be careless. He rubbed his clothes with handfuls of damp mud from the nearby riverbank., trying to hide any blood stains on them. He decided to leave his rifle behind. He had a pistol stuck inside his jacket pocket, if his plan failed. He climbed up the bank and onto the road, taking a large swallow as he approached the checkpoint.

"*Oi*, you there!" One of the soldiers called out, catching sight of the dishevelled man approaching them. "State your business."

"Jus' headin' home after work, sir." Tom replied, his voice shaking with nerves. "Mill's been runnin' us ragged these days. Working day and night."

"Workin' the mill, *eh*?" The soldier mused, eyeing the Tom sceptically, then nodded gruffly. "Go on, then. Be on your way."

With a curt nod, Tom walked on, his relief palpable. But he knew better than to let his guard down.

As he continued on his path, the anguished cries of a woman being dragged from her home by soldiers reached his ears.

"Stop!" the woman screamed, her voice raw and filled with pain. "My children, please! Let me say goodbye!"

"Enough of this!" a soldier barked, striking her across the face. "You're coming with us!"

Tom's blood boiled at the injustice before him, but he knew that intervening would only draw attention to himself. With a heavy heart, he forced himself to turn away, whispering a silent prayer for the woman and her family.

As he skirted past a tavern, raucous laughter spilled out into the night. His stomach gnawed with hunger, and his mouth watered at the scent of meat and ale. He wavered, tempted to slip inside in search of a scrap of food, but the risk was too great. Jaw clenched, he turned away and continued on. He would endure this discomfort as he had endured so much else. All that mattered was putting more distance between himself and his pursuers.

It was a small village, and within five minutes, its lights faded behind him, the night grew darker and colder. Tom's steps slowed, each one requiring more effort than the last. He scanned the moonlit fields for somewhere to rest his weary body. In the distance, he spotted a small barn. Hope flickered anew. Perhaps within those walls, he might find a few hours of safety and respite. With renewed vigour, Tom pressed on towards the solitary structure.

Gripping his rifle, Tom cautiously crept forward. The barn looked abandoned. The door creaked open with a groan, cobwebs clinging to Tom's face as he slipped inside. The musty scent of old hay filled his nostrils. He sagged against the wall, legs nearly buckling with relief at being out of the cold night air, every muscle in his body screaming out in agony. As good a place to rest as any, he decided. The silvery light of the moon filtered through the holes in the roof of the barn. Tom could hear his own heartbeat as he lay against the damp hay, the scent of decay and old earth permeating the air. He tried not to think of what vermin might be lurking in the darkness. Exhausted, he drifted off to sleep.

Tom wasn't sure how long he had slept, he was awoken by the chugging and hissing of a steam engine. He peeked out through a crack in the barn wall and realised that he was close to a railway station. He exited the barn, the station materialising before him in the dim light of dawn. His heart leapt at the sight of the freight train, idling on the tracks like a lifeline offered by fate herself.

"Get on it," he urged himself, scanning the area for any signs of danger. "If ye want to live, get on the bloody train."

A single lamp glowed dimly on the platform, but he saw no sign of movement. After scanning the area once more for any threats, he darted across the open ground and slipped into the shadows by the tracks.

Tom's pulse pounded as he approached the train. This was his chance. Moving as silently as possible, he pulled himself up into an empty freight car and hunkered down, making himself small among the boxes and bags. He held his breath, listening for any indication he had been spotted.

Mere minutes later, the sound of voices outside made Tom freeze. Through a gap in the wooden slats, he saw two Redcoat soldiers speaking with the train driver.

"Have you seen anyone climb aboard?" The gruff voice of a Redcoat outside jolted Tom back to reality, his breath catching in his throat. He strained his ears to hear the response.

"Not a soul, sir," replied the train driver, his voice betraying no hint of suspicion. "Just me an' me crew."

"Where's this train headed?" The Redcoat demanded, his tone tense with frustration.

"Cork docks, sir."

"Very well. Keep your eyes peeled. We are looking for a number of Fenian bastards on the run from

Dromdaire."

"Yes, sir," the driver said, and Tom could feel the anxiety radiating from him even through the walls of the carriage.

Tom exhaled softly in relief as the soldiers finally moved on.

Ten minutes later, as the train rumbled and lurched to life and began slowly rolling out of the station, he allowed himself a slight smile. He was on his way to Cork and to Cathleen.

Chapter 22: Harbour Lights
February 18th, Ballyduff Train Station

Tom, nestled uncomfortably among wooden crates and bags of grain, scanned his dim surroundings with wary eyes. His legs were curled up against his chest, knees digging into his ribs, and the musty scent of livestock from the adjoining freight cars filled his nostrils. The train rumbled beneath him, its shuddering movements jostling his makeshift hiding place, making it difficult for him to stay still.

His heart thundered in his chest each time the train screeched to a halt at a station, fearing discovery by the ever-watchful railway personnel. He heard their muffled voices outside the car, punctuated by the occasional harsh laugh.

"Keep it together, Tom," he whispered to himself, focusing on slow, controlled breaths. The need for food and water weighed heavily on his mind, but he knew drawing attention to himself could be disastrous. His life depended on remaining undetected.

As the train continued its journey, the Irish countryside sped past him, visible through slits in the wooden planks. Rolling hills, dotted with sheep and cattle, gave way to quaint villages where the smoke from peat fires wafted through the air.

Damn it, he thought, his stomach growling loudly. *I need to find something to eat, and soon.* The lack of sustenance was taking its toll on him, sapping his strength and dulling his senses.

How long had he been trapped in this infernal box? Twelve hours, at least. He licked his chapped lips, longing for a drop of water. Tom sighed, shifting to find a more comfortable position.

"Christ," he muttered under his breath. The ache in his body was relentless but paled in comparison to the gnawing hunger that plagued him.

A sliver of light pierced through the darkness as Tom carefully pried open a small gap between the wooden planks. Beads of sweat trickled down his brow, stinging his eyes as he surveyed the dimly lit interior of the train car. The space was filled with an assortment of cargo: large trunks, sacks of grain, and crates that bore the marks of their various destinations. "All right, let's see what we've got here," Tom said. He crawled on hands and knees, navigating the cramped confines. He eyed the bags of grain nearby, wondering if desperation would drive him to eat the rough animal feed. His hand brushed against something, a potato, tucked into the corner of a crate. He grasped it eagerly, devouring the shrivelled vegetable in three bites. The starch eased his hunger pangs, for now. But it wasn't enough. He needed water if he was going to make it to Cork. Just as he reached for another crate as he searched for water, a door slammed shut outside, causing Tom to flinch. Footsteps approached, heavy boots echoing on the platform.

"Check every corner, lads. We've got word there might be a stowaway," a gruff voice commanded. Panic seized Tom's chest as he scrambled for cover, slipping behind a stack of sacks piled precariously high.

"Stowaway, *eh*? I'll bet it's one of those damn rebels," another voice sneered.

The footsteps grew closer, and he held his breath, praying the shadows would conceal him. The sound of trunks being dragged across the floor filled the air, punctuated by the occasional curse or grunt of frustration.

"What's this sack doing open?" One of the men called out, drawing nearer to Tom's hiding place. His heart pounded furiously as he desperately weighed his options: fight or flee?

"Probably just poorly secured, or maybe rats got at it," another voice replied, sounding disinterested. "Let's move on. There is nobody in here."

"Fine," the first man grumbled, the footsteps retreating. Tom didn't dare breathe a sigh of relief until the heavy door had slammed shut once more, leaving him alone in the darkness.

Too close, he thought, feeling weak from both hunger and fear. Gritting his teeth, he resumed his search, tearing into a sack that contained salted meat.

"Thank you, God," he whispered, clutching the provisions tightly to his chest. As he chewed on the dry meat, a flash of light temporarily illuminated the freight car. In those brief seconds he read on the side of one of the crates, 'Powers Whisky'. He dropped the meat to the ground, and with his fingers aching, he pulled apart the crate and reached in a pulled out a bottle of whisky. He frantically pulled out the cork and took a large swallow, it tasted good, and he took another. Time moved a little quicker as he enjoyed the warm bite of the ginger liquid.

"Approaching Cork now," a voice called out, muffled by the wooden walls of the cargo hold. Tom's heart raced, his stomach knotting with anticipation. *This is it*, he whispered to himself, pressing his face closer to the slats for a better view. *Not much time left*. The train whistle blew as it slowed, approaching Cork station. Tom sat up, pulse quickening. He waited until the train came to a full stop, then crept to the cargo door and peered out. The station platform was crowded. He waited for the precise moment when a cluster of passengers obscured the view of the nearest railway worker before swinging open the door and leaping onto the platform. He stumbled slightly, his stiff legs protesting against the sudden movement, but he managed to maintain his balance.

Now to find clean clothes, he thought to himself. Tom scanned the platform, searching for an unattended bag or coat he could borrow. There, a trunk had spilled open, shirts and trousers tumbling out. Tom hurried over and grabbed a plain shirt and pants, then ducked behind a pile of cargo to change. He stripped off his bloodied uniform, soiled from his escape, and dressed in the borrowed clothes. They were tight on his large frame but would have to do. They weren't the finest garments, but anything would be better than the bloodstained, muddy rags he had been wearing. The simple act of donning fresh clothes felt like shedding the weight of his past, if only for a moment.

Emerging from behind the cargo, Tom melted into the throngs of people on the platform and made his way out of the station. With each step away from the train, he felt a mixture of relief and trepidation. The streets of Cork stretched before him. The city was both a sanctuary and a potential trap, and only time would tell which one it would become. Somewhere in this city, Cathleen was waiting alone and vulnerable. Vulnerable because of him.

Tom set off into the streets, nervously scanning every alley and courtyard for soldiers. The future was uncertain, but he knew one thing for sure, he wasn't leaving Cork without Cathleen by his side.

The sun hung low in the sky, painting the harbour with a warm, golden hue as Tom made his way along the quay. A cacophony of seabirds and the gentle creaking of moored vessels filled the air. It was a picturesque scene, but Tom's mind was too focused to appreciate it.

He approached the first hotel, a stout, red brick building with ivy climbing up its walls. Inside, a middle-aged woman stood behind the front desk, her greying hair coiled tightly in a bun atop her head. She looked up as Tom entered, a practiced smile spreading across her face.

"Good evening, sir," she said, "how may I help you?"

"Evening, ma'am." Tom felt sweat prickling at the base of his neck, but he kept his voice steady. "I'm looking for a friend, Cathleen Fitzgerald. I believe she may be staying here."

"Let me see," she replied, rifling through a stack of papers. After a moment, she shook her head. "I'm sorry, we have no guest by that name."

"Thank you," Tom said, trying to keep the disappointment from his voice. He left the hotel and continued down the line, the same sinking feeling accompanying each rejection.

As the sun dipped below the horizon, despair threatened to overtake him, anxiety gnawing at his gut with each dead end. What if she had already left Cork? Worse yet, what if something had happened to her? He refused to consider that possibility, not when he'd come so far.

But then, at the fifth hotel, a grand, limestone structure festooned with sculpted gargoyles, fortune finally smiled upon him.

"*Ah,* yes, Miss Fitzgerald," the young man behind the desk replied when Tom inquired. "Room 207, top of the stairs."

"Thank you." Tom breathed, relief washing over him like a wave as he hurried up the stairs.

He knocked softly on the door to Room 207, and it swung open almost immediately. There she was: Cathleen, her blonde hair cascading over her delicate shoulders, her eyes widening in shock and joy at the sight of him. For a moment they only stared at each other, green eyes meeting blue. Then Cathleen's face lit up with joy, "Tom! You came back to me."

Cathleen stepped forward, closing the distance between them, and wrapped her arms around Tom's waist, her body pressed against his.

"I promised you I would."

Cathleen drew back to gaze up at him, tears

glimmering in her eyes. "You kept your promise. I didn't think I'd ever see you again!"

She led him inside, closing the door behind them. The room was modest but comfortable, with a canopied bed and a small fireplace flickering against the encroaching darkness. Tom felt the weight of the day's exhaustion pressing down on him, but he fought against it, his desire for Cathleen burning even brighter.

"Tom," she whispered, her fingers tracing the contours of his face, her touch sending shivers down his spine. "I've missed you so much."

"I missed you too, Cathleen," he replied as he reached for her with trembling hands, his fingers brushing against her soft cheeks, still flushed from the intensity of the events that had unfolded. Their lips met in a passionate embrace that seemed to burn away all the fear and uncertainty of the past days.

"Thank God you're safe," he murmured, the words choked with emotion.

"Tom, I… I don't know what I would have done if you hadn't come," Cathleen whispered, her voice muffled by the fabric of his shirt.

As they made love, the world outside their door fading away, leaving only the two of them in this perfect moment. They clung to each other, their bodies entwined, hearts beating in unison. Time seemed to stand still as they held each other. The warmth of their embrace chased away the lingering chill that had settled deep in Tom's bones. He felt whole again, as if the missing part of his soul had been restored.

Cathleen ran her hands over his back, feeling the tension in his muscles slowly ease under her touch. The weight of everything they had endured seemed to melt away, leaving room for joy and laughter and light. As long as they were together, nothing else mattered.

Later, as they lay spent in each other's arms, Cathleen nestled her head against Tom's chest. Her breath came in shallow, even sighs, the rise and fall of her bosom timed with the rhythmic beat of his heart. The air around them seemed to *hum* with an energy that was both electric and serene, as if the universe itself had paused to bear witness to their reunion. She turned to find Tom watching her, a tender expression on his face. His eyes were the colour of the sky at dawn, hopeful and bright.

"What is it?" she asked.

He shook his head. "Nothing. You just look happy."

"I am, but… what do we do now?" she asked, her voice soft and vulnerable.

Tom pulled back to look at her, his eyes soft with affection. He brushed the hair back from her face, tucking a loose strand behind her ear. "What do you say we get out of here?" he asked, a hint of a smile curving his mouth.

"Where do you have in mind?" she asked, her voice steady despite the gravity of their situation.

"Anywhere but here," Tom replied, a determined glint in his eyes. "We'll find a way to put this all behind us, Cathleen, I promise you that. I was thinking we could head west to New York first and then maybe to San Francisco. Start over somewhere new. Build a life together, just the two of us," Tom whispered, kissing her forehead. "We'll find our freedom, and we'll never look back." He searched her face, looking for any sign of hesitation or doubt. "If you want to, that is."

Cathleen smiled, blinking back the tears pricking her eyes. A life together, a chance to begin anew.

"I'd like that," she said softly.

Tom lifted her hand to his lips, pressing a kiss to her knuckles. Cathleen leaned into his caress, covering his hand with her own. After all the pain and heartache, they had found their way home, to each other.

Chapter 23: Stars in the Dark Sky
February 19th, Cork Harbour

The next morning, Cathleen slipped out of bed and dressed quietly while Tom continued to sleep, his breaths slow and steady, oblivious to her departure. She paused at the door to glance back at him, a soft smile playing on her lips. The first light of dawn filtered through the thin curtains, casting a gentle glow over his sleeping form.

The narrow streets of Cork were just beginning to stir as Cathleen stepped outside, the cool morning air brushing against her cheeks. She wrapped her shawl tighter around her shoulders and made her way toward the pier, the cobblestones damp from the night's rain.

Down at the pier, the hustle of the early morning was already in full swing. Fishermen were preparing their boats, merchants were setting up their stalls, and dockworkers moved crates and barrels with practiced ease. Cathleen took a deep breath, the salty tang of the sea invigorating her senses. She approached the large, imposing building of the shipping company, its wooden sign creaking gently in the breeze. Inside, the office was busy but orderly. A few people milled about, discussing their travel plans with clerks behind a long counter. Cathleen waited patiently, when it was her turn, she stepped forward to speak with a middle-aged man with a kind face and spectacles perched on the bridge of his nose.

"Good morning," she began, her voice steady. "I'd like to inquire about departures for New York."

The clerk smiled warmly. "You're in luck, miss. We have a ship leaving this very afternoon. *The Ardent*. She's a fine vessel, and there are still tickets available."

Cathleen's heart leapt. "I'll take two tickets, please. For myself and my husband."

The clerk nodded and began the necessary paperwork. As he worked, Cathleen gazed around the room, taking in the maps of far-off lands and the posters advertising voyages to distant shores. Her mind raced with thoughts of the adventures that awaited them.

After what felt like an eternity, the clerk handed her two tickets, neatly printed with their names and the ship's details. Cathleen clutched them tightly, her fingers trembling slightly. She paid the clerk and hurried back toward the hotel, her steps light and quick.

The streets were beginning to fill with people as the morning wore on, but Cathleen hardly noticed. She was lost in her own world, imagining the look on Tom's face when she showed him the tickets. She could already see the joy and relief in his eyes, the way his smile would light up his entire face.

Back at the hotel, she climbed the stairs two at a time, her excitement barely contained. She paused outside their door, taking a moment to compose herself before quietly slipping back inside. Tom was still asleep, his arm draped over the pillow where she had lain.

Cathleen crossed the room and gently shook his

shoulder. "Tom," she whispered, her voice filled with excitement. "Wake up, love."

He stirred, blinking up at her with bleary eyes. "Cathleen? What is it?"

She could hardly keep from grinning as she held up the tickets. "We're going to America, Tom. This afternoon. I've got the tickets right here."

Tom sat up, rubbing the sleep from his eyes. When he saw the tickets in her hand, his expression shifted from confusion to disbelief, then to overwhelming joy. He reached out and pulled her into a tight embrace, burying his face in her hair. They held each other for a long moment, the enormity of what lay ahead sinking in.

***

Tom got up, washed and got dressed. He stared out the window at the bustling port, the ships bobbing on the water. "No more hiding or running. Just a life together, the way it was meant to be," Tom said as he held Cathleen.

"Yes, my love, now I must pack, and you need to buy some clothes." Cathleen smiled.

"I think I need some breakfast first; I haven't eaten a meal in days," Tom said as he rubbed his stomach.

After devouring a hearty breakfast in the hotel restaurant, Tom and Cathleen took a walk outside and headed towards the bank where Tom decided to withdraw what was left from his army savings. He made his way to the stately granite façade of a nearby bank. As he stepped inside, the cavernous marble interior echoed with the low *hum* of commerce. He was still nervous that he could be spotted by an RIC officer or soldier. His description had most likely been passed around to police stations across Munster at this point. He approached the teller, a stern-looking man with a bushy moustache who barely acknowledged his presence. "Here to make a withdrawal," Tom said, his voice steady despite the nerves coursing through him. The teller peered at him over his spectacles and nodded. Tom exchanged the necessary documentation. Then the teller meticulously counted out the crumpled notes. Tom stuffed them into his trouser pocket with a sweaty hand. This was it. The last of his savings from years of toil and hardship. Every cent he had left to his name. Tom contemplated as he stood outside on the pavement.

"Are you sure about this, Tom?" Cathleen whispered, her gentle voice breaking him from his reverie. She stood beside him, her green eyes shining like emeralds in the sunlight.

"Never been more certain," Tom replied, "this is our chance for a fresh start, Cathleen."

Cathleen smiled, her features softening. "Now, let's get you some new clothes for the journey," she said, taking Tom's hand and leading him towards a clothing store. The bell above the door jingled merrily as they entered, announcing their arrival to the shopkeeper.

"Good morning," the shop assistant greeted them with a warm smile.

"I need a full suit of clothes," Tom said awkwardly.

"I can certainly help you with that, sir, follow me," the

assistant said as he led Tom towards a long rail of suits.

Tom tried on several outfits, each one more dapper than the last, until finally settling on a dark green vest, a crisp white shirt and black trousers.

"Looking good," Cathleen said approvingly, her eyes sparkling with pride.

Tom paid for the clothes, and they returned to the busy street outside. "Okay, that's us ready to go, let's make our way to the ship."

"Tom, I need to send a telegram to my parents before we leave."

"Of course," he agreed, guiding her towards the telegraph office.

Once inside, Cathleen began to compose her message, nibbling her lip anxiously, her hands shaking slightly as she wrote. She wanted to break the news gently that she was leaving for America with Tom. She knew they would worry, but she prayed they would understand.

Dearest Mother and Father,

Tom and I are to travel to New York to start a new life together. Please do not worry for my safety. Tom will take good care of me. I know you will miss me, but I will write a proper letter as soon as I arrive in New York.

All my love,

Cathleen.

"Ready?" Tom asked, sensing her hesitation. He could tell she was torn between the excitement of a new beginning and the heartache of leaving her family behind.

"Ready," Cathleen confirmed, her voice wavering only slightly. She handed the telegram to the operator and watched as he tapped out the message, each click echoing her resolve.

***

Tom and Cathleen stood together at the pier, surrounded by the hundreds of passengers preparing to board the ocean liner that would take them to America. Families clutched their belongings and children; excited chatter was punctuated by the occasional sob of farewell. Clutching their tickets, Tom and Cathleen looked up in awe at the sheer enormity of the steamship looming above them. It loomed tall in its majesty, a titan built from steel and iron, crafted by human hands yet seemingly imbued with the spirit of the ocean itself. Rivulets of saltwater coursed down its hull, carving shimmering trails that sparkled like diamonds in the afternoon sun.

"Isn't she beautiful?" Cathleen murmured, her eyes wide with wonder as they traced the ship's towering outline. "I've never seen anything quite like her."

Tom's heart raced, his palms slick with sweat as he spotted a soldier checking passengers' tickets as they boarded.

Stay calm. He told himself, as they inched closer to the soldier. He pulled his hat down over his forehead.

"Tickets, please," the Redcoat demanded, extending a gloved hand towards Cathleen.

"Here you are, sir," she said, her voice steady despite

the fear that tightened her chest as she handed over their tickets.

The soldier scrutinised the tickets, his eyes narrowing suspiciously as he studied Tom's face. Each second seemed to stretch out into an eternity as Tom fought to keep his composure.

"Very well, all in order. Welcome aboard the Ardent," the soldier said, handing back their papers.

"Thank you, sir," Cathleen replied, her breath catching in her throat as she took Tom's arm and guided him onto the ship.

Cathleen let out a small sigh of relief, and Tom felt the tension leave his shoulders. This was it. The journey was beginning. They had made it this far, through trials and tribulations that would have broken lesser souls. As they walked up the gangplank, Cathleen glanced at Tom, her eyes reflecting the same mixture of excitement and apprehension that he felt. Tom set his jaw, refusing to let the doubts creep in. "We'll make it, Cathleen," he said firmly.

Cathleen managed a brave smile. "You're right," she said, "no looking back now."

Hand in hand, they took the first steps onto the deck. The die was cast, the future unwritten.

As they walked onto the main deck, the enormity of the steamship became apparent. Towering above them, the funnels scraped the sky as waves lapped rhythmically against the steel hull. The deck vibrated slightly under their feet with the thrum of the engines. Tom surveyed the activity around them. Stewards shouted orders, guiding passengers to their berths. Dockworkers loaded trunks and supplies into the cargo hold with pulleys and ropes.

Cathleen gripped Tom's hand tightly, intimidated by the sheer scale of their surroundings.

"Are you frightened?" Tom asked, his voice barely audible above the cacophony of sailors shouting commands and the creaking of ropes and pulleys.

"Of course, I am." She nodded, not taking her eyes off the horizon. "Just feeling a bit overwhelmed is all. So much is changing so quickly."

Tom pressed a kiss into her windswept hair.

"But I'm also excited for the life we'll build together in America. Mostly, I look forward to making a home with you. Starting our life without all the violence that plagued us in Ireland."

Tom turned to face her, his expression serious. "I know you're worried about what awaits us, but I swear to you I'll do everything in my power to make you happy, Cathleen."

As they stood, the rumble of the engines grew louder.

Cathleen met Tom's gaze. "This is really happening, isn't it?"

Tom nodded.

Just then, a shudder passed through the deck. The lines were being cast off. The ship let out a long, low whistle. They were moving! As the ship pulled away from the crowded harbour, Tom and Cathleen exchanged anxious glances with other passengers, each bearing the weight of their own dreams and fears. Among them were families seeking a fresh start, young men eager for adventure, and old souls hoping for one last chance at happiness.

Tom looked over to Cathleen, whose eyes were fixed on the shoreline, her blonde hair dancing in the ocean breeze as the ship picked up speed, slicing through the waves. The wind whipped at their clothes, the salt spray kissing their skin. Tom's thoughts turned to Dan, Liam and his family, the sacrifices they had made and the bonds that bound them together.

"Goodbye, Ireland," he muttered, the words catching in his throat as the coastline faded into a hazy blur.

"Hello, America," Cathleen added, her voice tinged with hope and resolve. "We're coming for you."

As the sun dipped below the horizon, the ship ploughed ahead, forging a path through the dark waters towards the promise of a brighter future. An hour later, the moon cast a silver glow over the restless waves. Tom and Cathleen, still standing side by side on the deck, gazed up at the starry night sky, lost in the vastness of the celestial expanse. The chill of the Atlantic breeze whispered across their faces, a gentle reminder of the great journey ahead of them.

"Look at the stars, Cathleen."

She nodded, her voice soft with quiet resolve. "*Aye,* Tom. They are the lights that guide us through the darkest nights. And just like those stars, we will shine brightly in the new world."

As the ship sailed onward through the moonlit sea, their gazes remained fixed on the heavens, drawing strength from the stars above.

Tom wrapped his arm around Cathleen's shoulders reassuringly. The conflicts of home were behind them now. The future was theirs to discover – a blank canvas waiting to be painted with all the colours of freedom.